SANCTUARY II

A FAN FICTION COLLECTION

NICKI NANCE   LINA ACEVEDO

SABRINA DIAZ   SHERI-LYNN MAREAN

COLE JACKSON   LEIGH BULLIS   ALICE SABLE

CECILIA AGETUN   TRINITY BLACIO

DAWN CHARTIER   EVA NELA

SARAH COMPTON   C STRIPES   HUNTER J SKYE

Foreword by
SHERRILYN KENYON

OLIVER-HEBER BOOKS

Cover Design: Dar Albert

Published by Oliver-Heber Books

0 9 8 7 6 5 4 3 2 1

FOREWORD

SHERRILYN KENYON

Come in peace. Or leave in pieces.

The Sanctuary motto that greets all visitors. Fans have often asked me where it comes from.

It was something my older brother used to quote to me when I was a kid in the 1970s. Since we grew up at Ft. Benning, I have a feeling it was probably something one of the soldiers imparted to him, or even our drill sergeant father.

I don't know for sure. I only know that it's something that left an impact on me as a young girl.

Just like the need for sanctuary. Being Catholic and with my love of all things medieval, I was always captivated by the concept of "holy" ground where no one was allowed to fight or spill blood.

A special haven for anyone.

Any fan of Dark-Hunters knows the legend of Sanctuary, as well as the Were-Hunters who frequent and populate it.

It's the cornerstone in the series that stands as a sentinel against outside ills.

A true sanctuary for anyone who needs it.

But why is it a bar and grill? The idea for that spun

out of the clubs and places I frequented as a teen and young woman.

The Dungeon, 688, Little Five Points Pub, Rock Fish Palace . . . Those were my refuge from the evil in my real life. So when I was building the Hunterverse, it was only natural that the very thing I relied on for relief in my real life would be brought into my fictional world.

I had no idea just how popular Sanctuary or the Dark-Hunters would become.

The idea behind Sanctuary was to be a meeting ground for people of all walks of life and from widely different backgrounds.

All accepted.

All equally loved.

Therefore, I could think of no better title for these series of anthologies as it represents the breadth and depth of Dark-Hunters fandom. A safe meeting place where the fans can let their own ideas flourish without fear.

I'm thrilled that so many fans turned out for the project and honored that so many have embraced my series for so long. We are now working on our third decade of readership.

It's so surreal.

And I have a special thank you to Carol who took time from her own writing schedule to spearhead this project, and read and edit all the entries.

Thank you all!

I hope you enjoy this foray into my universe as explored by the fans who have made it what it is.

And I will leave everyone with one small reminder: These are fan stories, written by fans. While I gave them the ability to write in my world, what they have done isn't necessarily Dark-Hunter canon and I haven't read any of the stories from any of the anthologies.

This book and the stories within exist outside of the timeline of the Dark-Hunters.

I hope all of you enjoy this little side adventure.

Hugs!

LOVE'S ABSOLUTION

NICKI NANCE

1

"I'll give him the message, but I'm not giving you his number," Dev Peltier growled. "I'm hanging up now." He ended the call, slid off the barstool, and ran a hand over his face.

"Trouble, Brother?" Dev jerked around to find his sister, Aimee, the owner of Sanctuary Bar and Grille, looking at him with arms akimbo and raised eyebrows.

Dev reached out and tugged on one of her blonde pigtails. "Don't worry, little boss lady.

I've got it."

"Exactly what is the it that you've got?" she persisted, not changing her stance.

Dev took a deep breath. "Noah Ridgely is looking for Shem. He says it's a family emergency."

"Well, *he's* up to something. He hasn't been around since you tossed him." She thought for a moment. "God, that was 12 years ago."

"The sad part of that story is how long I've been a bouncer. I really need to branch out."

"You're trying to distract me." She poked at his shoulder with her long, bright pink nail.

"Ow!" He pushed her hand off. "I think Shem's at

Magique. I'll tell him in person in case he needs some help."

"Still want to take care of him, huh?" She rubbed the spot where she had been poking him with her thumb.

"Nope. Just being a friend."

"He's come a long way from that waif of a kid Nick dropped on our doorstep." Aimee walked Dev out. "Take your time, I'll get Kyle to cover the door."

Dev walked the half block and rounded the corner to Magique, the shop Shem managed for his witchy psychotherapist girlfriend, Mar Greico. Dev didn't see anyone when he walked in, but Shem saw him.

"Hey, Dev," He called. "Are you in the market for some magic?"

"Not my thing." Dev looked around until he spotted Shem, strategically positioned to see the whole shop from the conference room. Dev strolled back and lowered his big body into a rolling chair. Shem was in a button-down shirt with his long hair tied at the nape of his neck. *Not a kid anymore.*

Shem sensed a problem coming his way. "You look worried, Dev. What's up?"

"Uh, yeah..." Dev took a breath. "Your brother called Sanctuary. He's looking for you."

"Well, he can keep on looking. I've got nothing for him," Shem snapped.

Dev put his hands up. "Don't kill the messenger." He hesitated. "He said there's a family emergency."

Shem scoffed. "As if I had a family." He looked down.

"Ouch."

"You know what I meant. You're the best brother I never had."

Dev scowled at him. "You *had* all of us, and you still do."

Shem met Dev's eyes. "Sorry, Dev. I didn't mean to —"

"We're good," Dev assured him to thwart an awkward apology. He extracted himself from the cramped chair and started for the door.

Shem walked him out and clapped him on the back. "Thanks for coming in to tell me. I couldn't ask for a better brother."

Dev smirked. "Me either, and I have a lot of choices."

Too shaken to work, Shem locked up the shop as soon as Dev left. His thoughts raced as he took the building's steps two at a time to Mar's second floor therapy office. He stopped at the open door and watched her clear her desk. The sight of her calmed him.

Mar felt Shem's turmoil in the pit of her stomach before she looked into his stormy eyes. "Are you alright, Sweetheart? You look lost."

"Noah is looking for me." He rubbed the back of his neck.

She got up and went to him. He took her into his arms and kissed her lips once, twice, three times and whispered, "I love you."

"I can never hear it enough. I love you, too."

He took her hand and pulled her to the couch. When he sat down, she perched on his lap with her hands on his shoulders. "Are you going to let Noah find you?"

He shrugged. "I don't know. He told Dev it was a family emergency."

She massaged his shoulders. "When was the last time you saw Noah?"

"When I graduated. I spotted his Howdy Doody hair in the crowd and went out the back door... Brave, huh?" He looked into her honey-colored eyes. "What do you think I should do, Babe?"

"I don't know. When I have two equally awful choices, I try to choose the one that can most easily be undone."

He stared off as he considered her words. "That helps. If I see him and it sucks, I can always leave. I have to think about it. He's a bully and a con." Shem shook the thought of his brother out of his head then pulled Mar closer. "Let's go home. I'm cooking for you tonight."

THE NEXT DAY, Dev stopped Shem and Mar at Sanctuary's door. "Your brother is inside."

Shem huffed out a breath. "He doesn't get to decide whether I see him."

"Do you want me to send him on his way?" Dev offered.

Shem answered decisively. "Could you tell him to settle up his tab and come out here? We'll be right across the street in front of the vacant shop."

"Done." Dev went into Sanctuary and emerged a few minutes later with Noah, whose face was as red as his hair. Dev pointed Noah to Shem and nudged him off. As Noah crossed the street, he kept his gaze on Shem. When he noticed Mar, he stopped. "Your lady?"

Shem glared at him. "What do you want, Noah?"

Noah cringed at Shem's aggressive tone. "Mom is in hospice. She's asking for you."

Shem's heart sank, but he held his ground. "OK. Got the message. Don't come back." When Noah opened his mouth to protest, Shem snapped at him. "I got it!"

Noah winced, then he looked back at Mar. "Can we do this privately?"

"I haven't said we can do *this* at all, so don't try to negotiate rules of engagement." Shem felt Mar's comforting hand on his back.

Noah put his hands up. "OK, not negotiating. Can I have a few minutes of your time?"

"Five minutes." He crossed his arms over his chest and glared.

"I need to make things right with you. I'm not who I used to be, Brother. I haven't been for a long time. I hate myself for how I treated you, for what I did."

Shem scowled at Noah. "Did you do something to Nick?"

"What? No! Is that what you think?" He looked into Shem's angry eyes. "I know I made his life miserable, but I would never have hurt him. Why would you even think that?"

"Because you hated him? For what? What did he ever do to you?"

Noah raked a hand through his wiry hair. "Nothing. He didn't *do* anything. He *had* everything. Everything I didn't have. Looks, brains, a mother who adored him. When he took you, I—"

"Took me?" Shem shouted. "You say that as if anyone wanted me." He paced back and forth and stopped in front of Noah. His fists were balled. "Nick didn't take me. He saved me. From you, Noah. He was afraid you'd kill me."

Noah looked at the sidewalk. "I'm so sorry, Shem." His voice was shaky. "When Mom left, she told me to take care of you. I didn't know how." He rubbed his face. "Dad went out of control when you started talking. You creeped him out."

"When I was three," Shem scoffed. "This just gets better and better."

"You knew things. You would tell Dad that Mom was in trouble before the ER or the cops called. When Dad heard you talking to people we couldn't see, he started slapping you around. He said you belonged with Mom's 'Freak Show Devereaux' family. I—"

"Stop!" Shem shouted. He paced back and forth. "Stop. Please. I've reached my capacity for this shit."

Noah sighed. "I understand." Defeated, he turned to leave but looked back. "What should I tell Mom?" He was searching Shem's eyes, and Shem was searching for an answer. When Shem finally shrugged and shook his head, Noah broke the silence.

"Listen, if you want to see her, call me so I can clear Dad out for you. Dev has my number." Noah walked away with his head down and his hands in his pockets.

Shem took a few deep breaths. Mar was suddenly beside him. He put his arm around her, kissed her temple, and walked her back to Sanctuary.

Dev palmed Shem's shoulder. "You good, Buddy?"

Shem considered that question. It was a lot to process. His mother was terminally ill. His brother was sorry. He creeped his father out. Dev and Mar were right there for him. He grinned at Dev. "Oddly, I am."

Shem and Mar sat across from each other in their usual booth. He took her hand off the table and kissed her knuckles. "You haven't said a word."

"You were amazing. You had charge of that whole exchange." She smiled at him. "Very sexy."

"It didn't feel sexy." He played with her fingers.

"My head was buzzing when I told him to stop." He sighed. "Mar, what was he saying? Was I psychic when I was little or was I a little psycho?"

"Psychic isn't much of a stretch. Your mother is a Devereaux." She took his hand in both of hers and looked in his eyes. "Those gifts are for a lifetime."

"They would come in handy right about now. Do I need an access code or something?"

She chuckled. "You might be blocking them. Probably because you associate them with being slapped around. I'll show you how to tease them out when you're ready."

"Yeah, that would not be now." He looked around. "Babe, I think I'm crashing from the adrenalin. Let's get these burgers to go."

At home, Shem headed straight for the bedroom. "I need a nap. Come with?"

"Right behind you."

EARLY THE NEXT morning Shem woke to Mar's honey-colored gaze. "Watching me sleep?"

"It's a beautiful sight," she teased. "I didn't want to wake you up early on a Friday."

"Friday? Shit. You have a reading tonight. Do you want me to reschedule it?"

She rolled on her back and stretched her arms over her head. "No, I feel great. We should go to bed at four in the afternoon more often."

"You should stretch like that more often." He crawled over her and nuzzled her neck. "The shop doesn't open until noon."

. . .

MAR'S READING RAN OVERTIME. Shem watched Mar walk the forty something well-dressed woman out and lock the door behind her. "You look exhausted, Babe. Rough one?"

She shrugged. "Not bad, just long."

He pulled her to him and kissed the top of her head. "I don't know how you do it for a whole session. As soon as I get a glimpse of someone else's thoughts, my own thoughts scatter."

Mar squeezed him. "Reading requires a deep connection. It takes a lot of effort – kind of like keeping an inflated balloon under water."

"Do you ever read my thoughts?"

"What? No." She looked up at him. "Why would I when I can simply ask you? Like now, for instance. What on earth made you ask me that?"

"You haven't seen my future?" He looked serious.

"No, never." She rubbed his arm. "If I did, I would have told you right away.

"Right." His tone was sarcastic.

"You're in a mood."

"I guess I am," he confirmed. "What should I do about Mom?"

She pulled him close. "Honey, that's up to you."

"Not helpful." He stiffened in her arms, so she pulled back.

"I don't know how to help. I do know if your mom is in hospice, you might not have a lot of time. Maybe you should ask Noah about—"

"Why the hell would I ask him anything?" He flung his hands open. "You think I should trust him because he had a moment?"

Mar struggled to keep her voice calm. "You don't have to trust him to find out how—"

"Back off, Mar. You don't understand anything about this."

Mar's shoulders dropped and her eyes welled with tears. Her voice was shaky. "You asked me what I thought. You can't invite me to the party then call me a crasher. I'm tired and I'm leaving. Go find somebody else to rail at."

Shem was as still as a statue as Mar unlocked the door and walked out. His heart sank when he saw their car pass Magique. He went through the motions of closing for the night and then walked to Sanctuary.

Dev cocked his head when he spotted Shem. "Didn't I just see you drive by?"

Shem shook his head. "That was Mar. She left without me." His voice broke. "God, Dev, I really fucked up. What the hell is wrong with me?"

"I'm not a doctor, but I think it's your species." Dev sat down against the wall and put his elbows on his knees in anticipation of a long talk.

Shem glared down at him. "What?"

Dev pointed at him. "You, my friend, are human. Mistakes come with the territory. Hence the term 'human error.'"

Shem paced a small circle, then sat next to Dev. "I don't know how to fix this, Dev. I don't know if she'll let me."

Dev turned his head to look at Shem. "What the hell did you do?"

Shem raked his hair. "I went off on her." She asked me about Noah, and I told her—no, I shouted at her—to back off. God, I'm such an idiot."

"You aren't an idiot. He was a prick to you." Dev chose his next words carefully. "Listen, Noah tried to talk to me." Shem looked up at him. "I pretended to ignore him, but for what it's worth, I thought he was on the level." He looked directly at Shem. "You know, you aren't who you were 12 years ago. Maybe he isn't who he was either."

Shem nodded after some private thought. Then he looked to Dev. "You have his number?"

When Dev stood up to retrieve his phone from his back pocket and scrolled through the numbers, Shem huffed out a breath. "Shit. I left my phone at the shop." He stood up and took a few steps.

"Hey," Dev clapped a huge hand on Shem's shoulder. "Use mine."

Shem took the phone, hit 'send' and fought off the impulse to hang up when he heard Noah's voice.

"Dev?"

"No, it's me. Can I see her Sunday?"

Noah said "yes" emphatically, then reeled in his enthusiasm. "Sure, Sunday's good."

"Around eleven? Which hospice?"

"The one on Dublin. Eleven is good. I'll try to have Dad out of there."

"You don't have to." He paused. "Thanks for offering, though."

Noah cleared his throat, twice. "I'm glad you called." He hung up.

Shem looked at the phone. *Is my brother crying?* He pushed the phone at Dev as though getting rid of it would perish that thought. At Dev's suggestion, he went inside to get food for Mar. The shot of bourbon was his own idea. He lifted the glass. *Here's to being an idiot.*

Acheron's voice seemed to come from 20 feet

above him. "I didn't think you drank." Shem jumped and the bourbon splashed onto the bar.

"Doesn't look like I'll be starting tonight." He reached across the bar for a cloth and wiped the puddle of bourbon. "Rough night," he nervously explained to Acheron, who surprised him by sitting on the next stool. "I hurt Mar's feelings...over my asshole brother." He continued to polish the bar, though the bourbon was long gone. "She thinks I should... Shit. I don't even know what she thinks...thought she was pushing Noah on me... can't go there." He didn't know if Ash was even listening. *God, I'm babbling to Acheron.*

"If you really want to do some damage to the guy, forgive him."

Shem stopped polishing the bar to look at Acheron. "Huh? I don't get it."

"Being forgiven when you haven't forgiven yourself is gut wrenching. It's like having a dislocated shoulder yanked back into place. The pain is intense, the relief is short lived, and the lingering dull ache is...well...unforgiving."

Shem nodded. "Nick told me you have the answers to questions that haven't been asked yet."

"I don't have all the answers. I have a brother, though." He stood and picked up his guitar case. As Shem was paying for his order, Acheron said, "Go home, Shem. Let her gut you with her forgiveness." Shem turned to answer, but Ash was gone.

"Hey, Bud, need a ride?" Shem was surprised to see Dev catching up with him on the sidewalk.

"Nah...I need to clear my head."

"A conversation with Ash will do that to you. My bike is right here. Let me get you out of the Quarter.

You can clear your head closer to home." Shem climbed behind Dev on the iron monster. The roar of the engine and Dev's broad back in front of him blocked most sights and sounds. By the time Dev stopped for gas a few blocks short of his neighborhood, Shem's confusion was lifting.

Dev clapped him on the back. "Go take care of your girl." Shem climbed off the bike. At a loss for words, he gave Dev a quick shoulder-to-shoulder man hug and walked off. On the way home, he replayed his conversation with Noah. The call was his peace offering to Mar, but he did feel like visiting his mother was the right thing to do.

"She's home." Shem breathed a sigh of relief to see their car in the driveway. He clumsily unlocked the door, stuffed the smashed take-out bag into the fridge, and went to the bedroom. Mar was still in her clothes, curled up on the edge of the bed with her back to him. His throat tightened and he rubbed at a pain in his chest. He knelt at the side of the bed and put his arm over her. His hand found hers. He kissed her cheek and whispered, "Baby, I'm so sorry."

"I'm awake. You don't have to whisper." Her voice sounded cold.

He straightened. "Can I lay with you?"

She scooted over without looking at him. "Come on."

He curled around her and put his head on her pillow. The feel of her against him brought tears to his eyes. *Don't lose it.* He took deep, quiet breaths to settle himself. In minutes they were both asleep.

Mar was trapped under Shem's arm when she woke up. *I need to get this guy a teddy bear.* He stirred when she slid out of his hold. "Baby?"

"I'm going to make coffee and take a shower. Then we can talk."

It was still early when he joined her on the glider. The porch was Mar's masterpiece, with artfully arranged hanging flowerpots, crystals, windchimes, and the aroma of potted herbs. Mar was a vision in her favorite denim dress. When she turned to face him, his stomach fluttered. *She's breaking up with me.* His heart pounded. He frantically searched her eyes.

She tilted her head. "Why do you look terrified?"

"I'm afraid of what you're going to say." He looked down. His hair curtained his glistening eyes.

"It isn't goodbye, if that's what you're worried about."

He swiped a rogue tear and sighed. "I worry about it all the time," he confessed.

It saddened Mar. "You've been left more than once by people you loved." He nodded.

She placed her hand over his. "Sweetheart, I'm not them."

Finally, he looked at her. "I'm so sorry, Mar. You're everything to me. I never want to see you cry. I never thought I would be the one who would make you cry."

"Ironically, you are probably the only one who can. You're everything to me, too."

Those words brought a small sob and more tears. This time he let the emotions run their course. *Acheron had this right—gutted with forgiveness.*

"Don't beat yourself up. You're on overload. Your mother is dying. Noah is around. Anyone would be edgy." She pushed his hair back and kissed his cheek. "I'm sorry, too. I should have stayed and argued it out with you. I won't leave you like that again. I promise." Shem lifted his shoulder to wipe the last tear with his sleeve. He pulled Mar into his lap and let the slow rocking of the glider lend its comfort to their kisses and caresses.

SHEM FIXED lunch from what was in the smashed take-out bag. Mar helped him make a salad. As they cleaned up together, Shem told Mar about the visit with his mother. "Can you come with?"

"Of course." She pulled him into a hug.

Shem kissed her temple. "Sorry I'm so needy."

"Are you kidding? You never ask for anything."

"Because you give me everything before I ask." He nuzzled her hair. "I wish I knew how to make this up to you."

"Make it up to me in bed."

She felt him smile before he scooped her up and carried her to their bed. He crawled over her to kiss her eyes, her lips, her neck. She pushed him back. "Let me take care of you. Roll us over."

Obediently, he rolled with her in his arms. Mar lay on top of him kissing his chest and neck. She unzipped his jeans and yanked them from his hips, then pulled her dress off. When she tugged his t-shirt with her teeth, he whipped it off. They devoured each other in a kiss. He was hard and panting. She licked and nipped her way to his shaft, then ran her tongue up and down the length, teasing and licking, stopping, and starting.

"Baby, please..." She sat up and lowered herself onto him, laced her fingers with his, then took his length over and over. The sight of his shaft going in and out of her undid him. The feel of it undid her. She collapsed beside him with her arm across his chest and her leg over his. When their heavy breathing eased, he pulled her closer. "That was amazing."

"Oh, I'm not done with you." She moved off him and sat back on her heels. "Roll over." He complied without question. Mar straddled him and slowly massaged his neck and shoulders. She kissed her way down his spine and rubbed her face on his butt. When she spread his cheeks and blew her warm breath into the crack, he shivered.

"Baby..." he moaned. "What are you doing to me?"

"Having my way." She slowly kissed and nibbled down one leg and up the other. She squeezed his butt cheek, stroked and licked the underside. Then she bit him. Hard.

"Ow...That hurts!" He bucked and reached back to protect himself.

She pushed his hand away, licked the deep bite mark, and kissed it tenderly. When he relaxed, she gave his other cheek the same treatment. He twisted around. "Ow. Ow, Ow! Are you punishing me?"

She gave his cheek a squeeze. Then she slid up his body, put her arm over his shoulders, and put her face next to his ear. "Probably. Does that make you hard?"

He moaned. "Painfully hard."

She rolled onto her back and pulled his head to her breast. "Show me."

Shem's sensual apology was slow, sweet, and thorough.

NOAH MET them on the steps of hospice. "Dad is with her. I'll get him out."

Shem thought for a moment. "Let's go in together and see how it goes."

Noah showed them to the cozy room. Their father was sitting on the bed holding his wife's hand. When he saw them, he scowled. "Well, if it isn't Stupid Shit and Freak Show."

"Abe, don't." Shel yanked her hand away. She was frail, but beautiful. Her voice was strong. Abe kissed her forehead, then glared at his sons and left.

Shel looked at her visitors and sighed. "Noah, honey, help me into the chair." Noah lifted his mother easily, carefully lowered her to the chair, and put a pillow behind her. She kissed his cheek. "Make sure Daddy isn't getting into trouble." Noah looked at Shem, who nodded.

Shel smiled at Shem. "Come closer so I can look at you. I haven't seen you since you graduated. You aren't that boy anymore."

He didn't move. "You were at my graduation?"

"I was." Shel patted the bed. "Sit with me, Shem. Who is this pretty girl?"

"My girlfriend." His terse answer hung in the air.

Mar stepped forward, crouched in front of Shel, and took her hand. "Hi, Shel. I'm Mar Greico. I see where Shem got his beautiful brown eyes."

Shel smiled. "Yes, he certainly is more Devereaux than Ridgley." She held onto Mar's hand. "I feel magic." Mar smiled and Shel chatted on. "Shem has it, too. He was born *en caul*. It was beautiful. Abe thought the drugs caused it. I never told him otherwise."

Shel looked at Shem. "Are you stuck, honey?"

He looked down at himself. "I guess I am. I'm not sure what to say."

"Come closer. Let me touch you while I still can." When Shem sat on the edge of the bed and took Shel's hand, she laughed. "You are full of magic!"

Shem smiled. "So I'm told. What does *en caul* mean?"

"You were born in a pretty bubble. It's a sign of

having magical gifts." She paused. "Baby, I'm so sorry for not being there to teach you."

Noah returned with coffee for everyone. Shel smiled. "You're right on time, honey. I'm fading."

"Let's get you back in bed." Shem and Mar sipped coffee and watched while Noah skillfully straightened the bed and made Shel comfortable.

Mar went to the bedside and took Shel's hand again. "We'll let you rest."

"Thank you for loving my son. Be everything I wasn't for him." Mar moved away. Shel's eyelids were fluttering.

Shem stepped to the bed and kissed Shel's cheek. "I'll come back tomorrow."

She smiled as her eyes closed. "I'll be waiting."

Noah walked them out. Shem turned to him before they left. "How long have you been taking care of her?"

"A little over a year." Noah's face was flushed.

Shem patted Noah's shoulder. "Sorry I didn't check with you. Can we come tomorrow?"

"Come any time." He teared up. "The doctor says she has a month at most."

THREE WEEKS LATER, Abe, Noah, Shem, and Mar were the only ones remaining at Shel's grave. Abe was struggling. "I talked more to her in the last month than in the last 20 years. She opened my eyes before she left this earth." He took a deep breath and blurted, "I know I wasn't a good father. I can't take it back." He looked down. "There isn't a damn thing wrong with either of you. You're good men in spite of me."

Mar whispered in Shem's ear. He nodded. She took Abe's arm. "Sanctuary is serving lunch for everyone who was at the service. Abe, Noah, will you join us?"

AT SANCTUARY, the Devereaux women caught up with Mar, fussed over Shem, and told stories about Shel. Noah sat by a subdued Abe, occasionally patting him on the back.

Shem was quiet. When people started leaving, he leaned into Mar. "I'm on overload."

"Why don't you go hang with Dev? I'll be right behind you. I have to settle up with Aimee." He kissed her cheek and headed for the door.

When Mar walked out, Dev and Shem were watching the last of the guests leave. Noah walked toward Shem with a shopping bag in his hand. "I almost forgot. Mom wanted me to give you this." He handed the bag over.

Shem thanked him. "You've been taking care of Mom and Dad all this time. What will you do now?"

He shrugged. "Go back to work and try to get normal."

Shem nodded. "I never even asked you what you do for a living."

Noah surprised Shem with a smile. "I'm an EMT."

Shem shook his head. "I really don't know you at all, do I?"

Noah pulled Shem into a tight hug. "Just know I'm your brother."

SHEM LOOKED through the bag that evening. On top was a scrapbook of his childhood with his kindergarten drawings, school photos and a lock of his hair. Shel wrote letters to him for every birthday. Next, he found a wooden box holding a candle snuffer, a tarnished silver cup, and velvet pouches that held jewelry and charms. Her grimoires were at the bottom of the bag with a note. "Share with your pretty girl." Shem knew where to find his pretty girl.

Mar sat in the grass with her arms around her knees and looked at the stars, she thought that whoever said "to forgive is divine" had it wrong. Forgiveness is a selfish act. It dispels helpless rage and resets relationships, but it is only one step in a long journey that can't be started until the wrongs have been fully felt, even if they can never be fully righted.

As he walked outside to join her, Shem grabbed Mar's sweater from the back of the kitchen chair. He draped the sweater over her shoulders, kissed her cheek and sat beside her. "Making a wish, Baby?"

"Casting intentions." She put her head on his shoulder. "Peace for Abe, purpose for Noah, healing—"

"Anything for me?" He teased.

"As a matter of fact, yes." She nudged him playfully and smiled. "I intend to share some magic with you in the bedroom."

Shem grinned as he pulled her into his arms. "Best intention ever."

MUSIC AND STORM

LINA ACEVEDO

1

Her thick, dark, long hair clung to her face as she danced in the rain, her headdress and hairstyle long gone. The robe of a rich and deep dark blue colour hugged her body, and he knew it must cost a fortune. If it had been a different colour, it would have been transparent long ago.

But that was not what caught his attention, it was her smiling face devoid of any makeup, although it would never be considered beautiful, made his heart ache. Her face was not as round or pale as the beauties of the city. Her skin was a shade of deep almond. Her dark eyes were too large, her nose was too wide, she was too tall and not curvy enough.

She was neither blonde nor red-haired, and everyone, including him, considered her most attractive feature to be her lips, full and fleshy. For him, she was perfection incarnate. After all, she was the woman to whom his heart belonged. And the sound of her laugher, for Baal's sake, squeezed his heart in the best way.

At that moment, he opened his eyes and cursed under his breath.

He looked around him not recognizing where he

was. After a couple of seconds, he remembered. He was in America. New Orleans, to be exact. He looked at the clock on his bedside table. He still had some time before he had to go, but he knew he wasn't going to sleep no matter how hard he tried. He got up, turned on the lights, took out his pencils, and began to draw the lady of his dreams.

For as long as he could remember the woman had populated his dreams. He had never seen her and yet she haunted him more than anything else in the world. For a time, he had thought that an Oneiroi had caused them. But he had been told that this was unlikely. The ghostly appearance of the sleep gods did not match her. Perhaps a Skotos, but he didn't think that was it either, since he'd be dead or insane if that had been so, he supposed.

So, he decided to believe that she was true. That this lady had existed at some point and that for some reason he could dream of her. With the help of hunters, he managed to locate in a very vague way that she could be from Tunisia or the vicinity. That she'd have lived two or three thousand years ago. Apparently, there were not many hunters who had lived in that place during that millennium so they couldn't be of much help. Besides that, the memories of them overlapped with each other, which helped him even less.

That was why he had wanted to be a squire. To be able to delve deeper into the vast world of hunters and all the records that existed. To his surprise, he had not been deemed worthy of being appointed a squire. Acheron himself had prevented his appointment.

That had happened a year ago and it still hurt. He didn't understand why, except for his overwhelming yet secret obsession with her. He had been an exemplary squire. He had learned everything that was expected of him. He had obtained the best grades. In fact, he had been considered the best candidate of his generation in all of Greece. But it hadn't been enough. He planned to know why. That's why he'd travelled to the USA, specifically New Orleans, to ask Acheron in person.

And looking at his watch, he saw that there were only a couple of hours before their meeting, so he went to exercise and get ready.

❧

ACROSS TOWN, she opened her eyes and saw a woman staring at her. She had no idea what was going on, who the woman was or even who she was herself. She blinked and a whirlwind of words cut through her thoughts. *Cold. Stewardess. Boy. Air control. Afraid. Storm. Blue. Family. Disgust. Food.* She clenched her jaw at how overwhelming and confusing it all was. She looked down at her arm, at the tattoo that adorned it. Four phrases written in elegant calligraphy took her back in time and helped her connect her ideas a bit.

I'm Eliša.

She was Eliša, that was her name and she had never changed it.

I'm a dark hunter.

She remembered the smell of death and smoke, the taste of blood in her mouth, the corpse of her Nizar, whom she had cradled in her arms while she felt life seeping from her through the fire. Her shriek of pain and fury. Her heart crying out for vengeance for what had been taken from her.

I am the beloved daughter of Himilce and Aderbal.

The burning sun of her beloved Qart-ḥadašt, the

graceful dance of her mother in the gardens, the strong arms of her father that carried her with pride in the parades.

Music and storm.

The unique shade of Nizar's eyes when he smiled, a colour that, after two thousand years, she had discovered was called Prussian blue. His scent of sandalwood and tangerine that she hadn't found in anyone else, the almond tone of his skin that turned peach when he blushed, his hair so thick that was impossible to tame even though she tried to comb it for hours. The warmth of his voice, accentuated as he hummed songs by sharpening weapons, causing her broken mind to focus on the present. The sensation of her body next to his when they escaped to dance in the rain, the smell of the rain, their feet buried in mud, the sound of thunder, their laughter and their hearts racing like a song. A kiss that she had wanted and had never happened.

In that moment, she remembered. The woman was a flight attendant and she had asked if Eliša could buckle up as they were landing. She nodded and fastened it then looked out the window for New Orleans before she lost track of her thoughts again.

She wondered why Acheron had called her to New Orleans. Ever since she had been assigned to the Carpathians 2,500 years ago, a century or two up or down, she rarely left her home, not even for emergencies.

There was a good reason for it: She was flawed.

Probably no one had seriously considered how conflictive it could be to create Dark Hunters, born of revenge and betrayal, with an origin story so tragic that it made them choose to sell their souls and become soldiers in an endless war. How difficult it would be to live a life immortal and full of solitude to obtain a little peace in their hearts. Not only that, but to give them powers that many coveted.

She had confused memories of her human life. She remembered that she knew things that no one else knew because she heard the voices of the gods in her head. However, at the hand of Artemis when she became a dark hunter, Eliša's ability was reinforced, and her mind couldn't bear so much strain, thus she was broken. Her mind was nothing more than a wild whirlwind full of splinters; it was impossible to follow a thread of thought. She knew so many things because the voices in her head told her, but they had no order or context. Instead of clarifying things, they anchored her in the present, making reality increasingly difficult. Which made her useless. She couldn't even fight Daimons most of the time because she ended up engulfed in thoughts or forgot who she was and what she was doing there.

As her squire took her by the hand and led her from the plane, the usual voices in her head increased in noise and intensity. *Demons. War. Apostolos. Truce. Prophecy. Acheron. Family. Gods.* For Baal's sake, why did they never shut up? When she returned to reality again, they were arriving at a bar. It was large and guarded by a Katagaria, who kindly let them pass. She entered and was overwhelmed by the amount of people talking and laughing in the place. It was not difficult to notice Acheron's dark hair, so she headed there.

All the voices in her head were suddenly silenced and she was paralyzed seeing Nizar sitting there.

THE SANCTUARY, a bear-run bar in New Orleans, was such a well-known place that it was a cultural landmark for everything supernatural there. Everyone could enter regardless of their species—humans, demons, Katagarians, Arcadians, Dark-hunters, Apollites or even Daimons, and there was only one rule: *Come in peace or leave in pieces.*

Basil walked in and, although at first glance he felt he was out of place with his immaculate charcoal three-piece suit, upon noticing the disparate styles of those there, he decided he was not so striking. He glanced around the bar, and it was impossible to miss the seven-foot man, goth, with sunglasses and black hair. He sighed to gather his courage and stepped closer.

Acheron, or Ash, as he had heard some refer to him, was a strange dichotomy a part of him seemed like someone who could gut one without breaking a sweat, while another part seemed friendly, approachable.

"Basilius Nizar, you are the son of Demetrius, right? A great squire."

Bas nodded and since on a personal level he didn't like beating around the bush, he got to the point and made his case. Acheron didn't seem surprised and didn't interrupt him at all.

"I know you want an explanation and it's a fair demand, but I can't give it to you." Before Bas could cut him off indignantly, Acheron continued. "However, I can withdraw my request to deny your appointment on one condition."

"Which?"

"It is very simple. In the span of a week, you will help a Dark-Hunter on a mission that I am going to assign to you. If at the end of the seven days you wish to be a squire, you will be named as one."

Bas nodded without even thinking. Acheron raised his hand and pointed at him, then Bas realized he was pointing to someone behind him and turned around.

"She is the hunter you will have to help. Her name is Eliša."

His heart skipped a beat.

The woman of his dreams, the one he had sought all his life with an obsessive passion was standing there staring at him in a daze.

AFTER THE TWO of them looked at each other for a moment that felt eternal, Eliša walked over and sat stiffly in the remaining chair. The voices that had inhabited her head were so silent that it was easy to ignore them. She, who generally only wanted silence, was not interested in all the information that she did not understand and was being bombarded with. She asked them who he was. Their almost whispering responses confused her. *Of yours. Of yours. Of yours.*

"What kind of cruel joke is this, Acheron?" She hissed at him in Punic.

The man next to her, the Nizar´s copy, frowned for a moment and then added, "I agree with her, what kind of game is this?" He spoke in English.

She blinked, wondering how he had understood it. Almost no one spoke Punic, few hunters spoke it, and in the modern world it was a dead language. She left her musings when Acheron answered.

"It's not a joke, or a game. The only thing I can tell you is that there is a mission that the two of you must carry out together. What you discover or not, during it, does not concern me."

She would let this go for now. Acheron must have been too desperate to send for her, and then when that was over, she could question him with more calm. If he didn't answer her for good, she would have to use some of the secrets she knew about him. She wasn't very amused, but no one played so cruelly with her without repercussions. She glanced at the man next to her. He was so tense that it seemed at any moment he would jump on the table and punch Acheron. She knew that the odds were in favour of the Atlantean, but she was sure that he would not let himself be intimidated, like her Nizar, who had never backed down no matter that the odds were not in his favour. She smiled.

"What kind of mission?" Nizar—Basil— relented and accepted his role.

"You have a couple of very dangerous Daimons to hunt... In a graveyard. Eliša is one of the few hunters who can enter the cemeteries. However, she cannot go alone, so Basil, you will go with her." After that, he gave them a few details about the type of Daimons that were there and what they should expect.

They both nodded once he was done. Before either of them could do anything else, Acheron got up and to her surprise, disappeared into the crowd as if he had never been there in the first place. That had its merit since he was taller than most people and it was hard to miss a Goth, but they were in a Limani, and the Limani had their own peculiarities.

She turned to Basil and he was already looking at her with an intensity that surprised her. She was nothing more than a shadow on the periphery and she was used to going unnoticed. Her heart twisted as she remembered that the only person who had looked at her like this before was her Nizar.

A fractured mind like hers saw things differently and focused on details that most people ignored and ignored details that everyone could see. So instead of focusing on the logical thing— the mission—she asked another question.

"You speak Punic?"

{⚓}

BAS HAD HAD CRAZY NIGHTS, yes, but this was the most surreal of his life. Not only had he met the legendary Acheron Parthenopaeus, but he had also met the lady who had populated his dreams for as long as he could remember. And apparently now he could understand Punic. Which, if someone asked him, was mundane compared to the rest. *Eliša, Eliša, Eliša.* Her name was beautiful and elegant, it matched perfectly with the graceful and ravishingly beautiful woman he had fallen in love with, in his dreams.

"I'd tell you that you don't have to sound so surprised, my lady, but since I just found out myself too, we can both admire together." He was sure that if his father heard him speak to a Dark Hunter that way, he would beat him up and buy a whip just to rip his back apart with it.

He saw her purse her lips for a moment and when he was already giving up his possibility of being a squire, she laughed. The sound of her laughter was identical to that of his dream's persona, and he felt his heart squeeze.

"As fascinating as this is, I'm afraid we should focus on the mission, then we can discuss this..."

She frowned, as if she were searching for the right

word. "Curious situation. By the way, I am not your mistress, nor are you my servant, call me Eliša."

He nodded and they both got up, left a generous tip, and headed for the cemetery.

&.

THE TRUTH WAS he didn't know what to expect if a Dark-hunter other than Acheron entered a cemetery. He knew that they could do so, physically they could, that they would be possessed was something very different. A part of him imagined that they would burst into flames or something similar if they did. Luckily, Eliša entered calmly and made a solemn gesture with her hands. He looked at her carefully, fearing that at any moment she would pounce on top of him and try to kill him. She didn't seem affected at all.

"Why can you come in?"

She kept walking as if she was unaware of his presence. After a couple of minutes, she responded. "No spirit can long resist the madness that dwells in my head. One or two of them try for a couple of minutes, but when they can't, they spread the word and the others usually leave me alone for the rest of my stay in the cemetery. Not that I spend too much time in them, I should clarify."

Madness? He remembered a child version of the Eliša from his dreams covering her ears with her hands so that the voices of the gods would be silenced. How they were killing her, reducing her from her vibrant and magnificent Eliša to small moments of lucidity amid madness. Such had been his despair that he had made a single wish for his father. Bas shook his head, that didn't make any sense. They both continued touring the cemetery deep in thought.

After an hour, maybe two, Eliša spoke again. "Are you okay? You seem thoughtful."

"I know you're not going to believe me, but..." How the hell did someone just say these sorts of things? He doubted that a *hey, you've been in my dreams for as long as I can remember, and I think I'm half in love with you* will work.

"I've seen you before, and although it sounds very cliché and like a bad pickup line, you've been in my dreams. I see you dancing wearing dresses of a vivid blue, wearing a veil that covers you completely while you run through a market in a place with a huge wall." She froze and looked at him horrified, he kept talking. "I see you playing or even eating. I even saw you hug a sword so tightly that your forearm ble—"

He cut off his sentence when he saw a flash of blond after an annoyed Eliša. He pounced on the Daimon before he touched Eliša. He'd love to say that it was all very heroic on his part, but... No. While he managed to tackle the Daimon before he got close to Eliša, he was wounded himself with a dagger that the Daimon carried before it pushed him so hard against the wall of a mausoleum that the vision of him danced black. It was likely that he had a concussion because he only remembered flashes of Eliša's fight against that Daimon. She fought the two others that had appeared later.

Even though Eliša could be very distracted, however, she knew how to defend herself well when she was able to pay attention to something. Compared to the Daimons, she was small, but she was more graceful than them, so she used it to her advantage.

He saw her use a kind of judo kick to immobilize and stake one. He saw her pounce on another one and she disappeared from his sight. He tried to get up to try to help her or call Acheron, but though he struggled to gain his footing, the dizziness sent him back to the ground.

An eternity later Eliša appeared with a few scrapes but no serious injuries. She walked over to him and knelt in front of him. Taking a mobile phone from her jacket pocket, she called someone then spoke in a low voice. He couldn't hear the conversation through the ringing in his ears. She held the phone with one hand and used the other to gently check him for wounds. He felt her stop at a thin, pale mark that rose from the left side of his neck. It extended from the bottom of his neck to his jaw, the mark with which he had been born and that looked like a scar.

After she hung up, she took off the jacket she was wearing. He made out a scar of thirteen inches that ran down her right forearm, followed by three sentences written in an alphabet that he could not read. It was this scar that he had seen in his dreams. He had a vision of him bleeding or, more precisely, bleeding while he was thrown onto a pyre. An injured Eliša jumped onto the pyre and hugged him while they both died together. In the vision, he prayed that they had a chance to be together on the other side despite belonging to different castes.

"Nizar?"

"Mhhh?" He replied, almost falling asleep.

She gave him a smile so bright it was painful to watch as she used the padded part of her jacket as a makeshift pillow for him.

"I think I already know why you can remember me."

"I think, so do I, Liss. I think I do too."

IT HAD BEEN EXACTLY seven days since Acheron had assigned them that mission. Bas couldn't be happier. It was a bit strange to know that past lives existed and that one had had an epic love story that you see once in a lifetime.

Luckily, the hit and stab had been superficial, so while it hurt him because he wasn't super-human or a Dark hunter, he could do things that didn't require much effort. The first days had been spent talking about everything that had happened. Eliša had told him about historical events such as the fall of Carthage, and had clarified things that were still blurry for him. He, in turn, told her things about his life and tried to immerse her in the modern wonders that she had previously lost to the voices in her head.

As for the infamous voices, Eliša said that she could still hear them, yet they had been silenced until it was very easy to ignore them, like the sound of appliances.

The last three days, they had explored the city, had eaten many local foods, and had taken sightseeing tours that a shocked and amused Eliša denied or confirmed with her cryptic comments. He would bet the fortune of his family that she did it on purpose to exasperate him. Though the sound of her laughter healed him in ways he hadn't thought were injured, she listened to the crazy conclusions he drew based on what she said.

By this time, they were back where it all began, waiting for Acheron. The mythical Sanctuary. Eliša leaned against him as she drank a milkshake, into which she periodically dunked her French fries, much to his horror. Bas saw him enter and he saw everyone around them subtly move away.

Acheron sat across from them. Eliša gave him a

smile and continued eating. There was quiet at the table for a moment. She dunked another salty fry into the rich chocolate treat and popped it into her mouth.

"And? Do you want to be a squire?"

"As tempting as the offer is, you're right, I don't want to be a squire anymore." Bas could swear that Acheron raised an eyebrow. Acheron hadn't removed his glasses so he couldn't be sure. "Well, to be honest, I want to be, I was raised for it, but if I have to choose between spending the next four decades being a squire or with the woman I love, I think the answer is obvious."

"Good choice, Basilius, good choice," Acheron said, not looking or sounding the least bit surprised.

"My lady, Acheron knew that didn't he?"

She dropped her shake and looked at him solemnly. "Acheron knows many things."

"Liss!" Acheron scolded her.

Eliša just laughed and gave him a condescending look, but in the end she added. "Acheron knew it from the start."

"You could have asked me, you know," Acheron said.

"Most hunters and squires can unanimously say that an apocalypse is more likely to occur than you dropping a pledge."

Acheron chuckled.

Bas smiled and leaned down, almost bowing. His parents would like to know that his manners weren't so lost. "Then I owe you a big thank you," Bas said, feeling every word. After all, thanks to Acheron, he hadn't become a squire. He had reunited with Eliša and now they could be together until he died.

Acheron nodded with something akin to solemnity.

"Although, you know, it wouldn't have hurt if you had brought us together so much earlier." He felt Eliša nudge him. "I'm just saying."

Acheron gave her the same sly smile Eliša was so well known for. "There are things that have to happen at a certain time... and in a certain place."

≉

ACHERON SAW Bas and Eliša laugh as they went up to one of the upper floors of the Sanctuary. Apparently Eliša wanted to learn to play pool and Bas was trying to get her to tell him why Valerius wanted to eat a pasta that was sold in a sex shop.

For a moment, he wondered when one of them would ask for Eliša's soul and how much he would have to give Artemis for it. He tried to see their future and to his surprise, he did not see them grow old or die. He considered the possibilities when he sensed a presence behind him that he had not seen in over two thousand years—Baal, a god whose cult existed and was extinguished in Carthage long ago.

Tall, dark, with a lion's mane of hair and eyes a brilliant Prussian blue, he wore modern clothes and was not making any display of power. He simply looked like another human. As Acheron returned his gaze, Baal nodded and sat down in the position that Basil had held not long ago.

"For two thousand five hundred years my son has been looking for his beloved. And two thousand five hundred years later she was lost until he found her."

Basil was the son of Baal? No, he remembered, but Eliša's Nizar had been.

"They have already met again, and they will be able to have a life together." At that moment, Acheron noticed the jewel that Baal had in one of his rings. A jewel that contained a soul.

Seeing where Acheron's gaze was directed, Baal added. "Artemis and I had a conversation a couple of days ago. A week if you want to be more exact."

Acheron felt a wave of nausea. He, better than anyone else, knew the cost and desperation it took to make a deal with her. "Why would you go to deal with her?"

The look Baal gave him reminded him that although he was older than Baal, being older did not imply that he had lived and lost more. There were many things that he, until Tory had appeared in his life, had not been able to experience, some good, such as love, others bad, such as the pain of loss.

"To all my mortal children I have granted them a single wish. They have asked for fame, glory, and power in all its forms. Nizar..." He shrugged. "He was a beggar condemned to a life of suffering and deprivation. Instead of asking for something like that as his brothers, or even being able to be with the woman he loved, he only asked that she could have a chance and be free from the madness." He fell silent and his gaze dropped to the ring. "It requires a great level of sacrifice to give up what you most want in the world, so that someone else has a chance." He gave Acheron a wicked smile. "And for that, even though I did grant it to him, she would have to be with him to be safe from hearing the ether. She would never leave him that way. Not that any of them know or care."

"Love is the only form of loyalty that puts the interest of the loved one above the lover."

Baal nodded.

"And so, I'm not going to allow that after two and a half millennia of suffering they only have a few decades before either of them dies. You would do any-thing for your children, Acheron, and I will do the same for mine." Baal said as he toyed with the jewel that contained Eliša's soul.

"Why are you telling me?"

"Lest you waste your time playing Artemis' games, she can be very devious when she proposes," Baal replied with a sly smile before flashing away.

THE END

FOLLOW THE THREAD

SABRINA DIAZ

A *Titan.*

A Titan sat across from Nyssa Barnes. It took every bit of her self-control not to panic and run out of Sanctuary. The headache and nosebleed the Titan had given her when he entered the bar and grill left her disoriented enough to know she needed time to recover.

Nyssa had what she called the Sight—the ability to see through the magic of the supernatural world. She saw someone's true identity despite their appearance. What she imagined shades looked like in the Underworld would appear next to the person, a ghost-like figure showing what someone was under their mortal looks. For a shapeshifter, she saw their animal form.

It was a power she'd always had, yet she didn't understand it until she was much older. Nyssa found Sanctuary when she kept getting headaches walking down Ursulines. She noticed that the man guarding the door had a bear shade. Determined to get answers, she wandered in. Immediately, she was overloaded by the number of supernaturals hanging out in the bar.

Lucky for Nyssa, the harsh reactions only occurred

for first-time encounters. Afterwards, she would only see the shades that trailed next to someone.

Spending time at Sanctuary had helped because it forced Nyssa to learn control and manage the pain. Else the power currently radiating off the Titan would have knocked her out. Her eyes focused on the Titan's shade. He was on his knees with his arms raised above his head, as if he was holding something very heavy on his shoulders.

The myths she'd spent so much time reading to better understand this new world flashed through her mind as she tried to identify him. Based on her research and her experiences in Sanctuary, she realized who she was talking to.

Atlas.

She felt a mix of relief and dread. While it was encouraging to know who she encountered, she never knew whether they were good or bad. Gods were unpredictable. At least being in Sanctuary meant she was protected not only by the rules, but by those powerful beings she called friends.

Clearing her throat, she placed the bloody napkin on the table. "Why are you looking for me?"

Atlas smiled. She couldn't help but shiver at the intensity in his sky-blue eyes. His white-blond hair fell to his well-muscled shoulders. Even without her Sight, it was clear he wasn't mortal.

"I believe you can help me." Atlas glanced around before placing a golden rope on the table.

The power coming off the rope danced across her skin, leaving a tingling sensation in its wake. An instinct deep inside wanted to reach for it, but common sense took over. Magical items could be dangerous.

"Are you familiar with Ariadne's thread?"

Startled, she tore her gaze away from the rope. "Of

course. The myth says Ariadne bestowed it to Theseus so he could navigate the Labyrinth." She sat back, realizing she had subconsciously leaned closer to the enticing power.

He nodded. "What the myths don't say is that the thread could lead one to powerful magical objects." Atlas brushed his fingers across the rope. "But the thread has to choose its wielder. One with Sight and of a powerful bloodline."

Was it possible he knew about her abilities? But how? She didn't advertise it and only those she trusted in Sanctuary knew.

Nyssa cleared her throat and focused on the other question. "Are you saying that this is the thread from the myths?" Magic radiated off the rope, but that didn't necessarily mean it was Ariadne's thread.

"I am."

"Why do you need me?"

"I believe you can wield it. You can see things, can you not Nyssa Barnes? See things for what they truly are." He shifted closer to her. "The supernatural world cannot hide from you."

"What are you looking for?"

"A golden apple from the Garden of Hesperides."

An apple from that Garden was one of immortality. "Why would you need that? Last I checked, Titans were immortal." Then a thought occurred to her. "Wait, if you're Atlas, shouldn't you be holding the sky?"

His lips curled as he leaned back and brushed a hand through his hair. "Let's just say I have a few days reprieve."

Noting he avoided her first question she was about to ask how when she noticed something branded on his wrist. Apollo's sun symbol.

Atlas glanced at his exposed wrist and sighed. "I guess you know who liberated me."

"I'm not helping you," she croaked. She spent enough time with the Peltiers to know the dangers of Apollo. Everyone in Sanctuary could be in danger.

"I guess we have to do this the hard way."

Not waiting to find out what that was, she tried to run. She didn't make it far.

Atlas shoved the table so hard it hit the wall and broke into pieces. His fingers brushed her wrist before she was jerked away. She found herself behind a wall of Fang and Dev.

"Whatcha think you're doing, buddy?" growled Dev.

"Looks like he missed the sign," replied Fang. "Come in peace or leave in pieces. In case you wondered. Plus destroying our property *and* trying to put your hands on a woman without her permission? Well, let's just say you're no longer welcome here. Lucky for you, I'm letting you pick how you want to leave."

Atlas opened his mouth then closed it. Nyssa realized the bar had gone quiet. Even the Howlers had stopped playing. She followed Atlas's gaze and saw Urian, along with Aimee's family, had moved closer. Atlas was outnumbered.

There was a promise of retribution in the Titan's eyes when she met his gaze. "This isn't over." Before anyone could blink, he disappeared.

Something touched her shoulder and she jumped. Hand to her chest she relaxed when she turned and saw it was Aimee. The bearswan gave her a reassuring smile. "Are you okay?"

Nyssa cleared her throat. "Yes. Sorry about the table."

Aimee waved a hand. "Not your fault. Why don't you sit down and tell us what happened?"

Before Nyssa could answer, Fang signaled to the band to keep playing. Moments later, the bar filled with chatter and music. Part of her wasn't surprised. The regulars had seen worse over the years. Aimee led her to an empty table in the back where they sat down. Fang, Dev, and Sam joined them. Urian stood nearby keeping guard.

"Who was that?" asked Dev.

"Atlas," said Nyssa.

"The Titan?" Fang asked. "Damn, what did he want?"

"He had Ariadne's thread and he said he needed someone with the power of Sight to wield it," she explained. "Oh, and that person had to have a powerful bloodline. I'm not sure why he thought that could be me."

"You'd be surprised how many people have a magical bloodline in them," said Urian. "Our friend Jo is a long descendant from Zeus. For all you know there's some Greek deity in there."

"Zeus would be my guess based on all his past relationships," said Sam, her gloved fingers tapping on the table. "Either way, having a Greek divinity in your bloodline would explain your ability."

Nyssa realized she never considered the ability being hereditary. Though in her defense she grew up without a family.

"Why did he want you to wield the thread?" asked Aimee, pulling Nyssa from her thoughts. "Did he say what he was looking for?"

"An apple of immortality from the Garden of Hesperides."

"There isn't much he could do with that as he's a Titan." Dev echoed Nyssa's earlier thoughts.

"He did have Apollo's sun branded on his wrist. Perhaps he was the errand boy in exchange for his freedom," suggested Nyssa.

Urian scowled. "If he's working for Apollo, that can't mean anything good. Is it possible for him to find an apple?"

Sam shook her head. "I don't think so. From what I know, the Garden was destroyed after Herakles took one and killed the dragon that guarded it."

"Not exactly."

They turned to the new voice. A tall, beautiful red-headed woman stood next to Urian. He grinned before wrapping his arm around her waist. He drew her close and gave her a kiss. When she pulled away, her green eyes danced with mischief and love.

Xyn, Nyssa realized as her head pounded and nose started to bleed. She reached for a napkin as a shade formed behind Xyn. A very large dragon stared back at her.

"Are you okay?" Xyn watched Nyssa wipe the blood from her nose.

She gave Xyn a nod. "What do you mean, not exactly?"

"The dragon who guarded the Garden survived." Nyssa heard the protectiveness in Xyn's voice. "If anyone knows about the survival of an apple it's Ladon."

Urian's brow creased. "Are you sure bothering him is a good idea?"

"He's been isolating himself for too long," replied Xyn. "It's time he leaves his cave."

❦

LADON FELT her before he saw her.

Xyn.

He sighed. If his sister was here, she was trying to get him back into the world.

He may have been glad to see her alive after thinking for centuries she was dead, but that didn't mean he wanted a lecture. He was a perfectly happy dragon that stayed away from, well, everyone.

"Ladon," Xyn called.

Surprised that she was speaking out loud, he opened his eyes. She stood before him in human form.

He reached out to her mind. *No.*

Xyn threw her hands in the air. "You don't know what I was going to say."

He gave her a droll look.

She rolled her eyes and stepped close enough to scratch his nose. Despite his annoyance, he appreciated the contact. After losing so many siblings... He needed the reminder.

"It's time, little brother," she said, softly.

He pulled away from her. *No.*

She put her hands on her hips. "Yes. It's time you get your ass out of this cave and back into the world. Don't make me get Falcyn."

He scowled. *Falcyn let me live here, he won't take it away.*

She sighed. "I need your help, Ladon."

Whatever it is, I'm sure you can handle it.

"Atlas is free," she stated. "He's searching for an apple from the Garden. He believes one is still out there."

Ladon's body locked up. A chill ran through him. Memories surged to the surface of his mind. Betrayals by those he thought he could trust. A fight that brought him to the brink of death. The fire that burned down his one purpose. His breathing changed and his head spun. Black spots appeared in his vision.

"Ladon. Ladon! I'm sorry. Breathe. I'm here." She ran her hands over his snout in soothing motions.

Shoving his memories aside, he focused on controlling his breathing. *That's impossible.*

"Apollo freed him. They're after the apple and want to use a mortal woman to find it. We need your help. Please." She stepped closer to him. "Don't let him win, Ladon. Don't let him imprison you any longer."

❧

NYSSA WAS AN IDIOT.

She had no clue why she thought it was a good idea to step outside of Sanctuary while Xyn teleported away. Her excuse was that she needed a moment. *Stupid.*

Of course, Atlas was waiting for her.

"I'll give you one more chance. Help me, or I'll make you."

"No. You're working for Apollo. All around bad guy."

He smiled coldly as Ariadne's thread hung from his fingertips. "Fine."

Before Nyssa could run, he snapped it at her. The moment the rope touched her skin it came alive. It coiled like a snake up her arm, becoming tighter and tighter. The beams of golden light that came from it shone brightly. She cried out as the painful burn brought her to her knees. She tried to rip the thread off, but it refused to budge. Nyssa's stomach roiled with nausea and her vision blurred. She squeezed her eyes tight praying for the pain to pass.

She opened her eyes. Her vision was filled with golden threads that led in different directions.

Nyssa heard Atlas's triumphant laugh. "Find the golden apple of immortality."

Her mind latched onto the words and wove through the golden threads in her vision, discarding the ones that were wrong. Then, she felt a strong tug. The string demanded to be followed.

Nyssa felt a blast of heat next to her. She saw Atlas dodge the blast of fire before he disappeared.

Exhaustion claimed her, tipping her body over. When she thought she would kiss the pavement, she was pulled into a set of strong arms.

Nyssa looked up and a pair of blue eyes met her own. A scream built in her throat until she realized the blue was darker than Atlas's. Dark, mysterious, with a sadness that lingered deep within. Yet, there was something else...

The darkness claimed her.

🐉

THE MORTAL WOMAN had been sleeping for hours. His dragon rubbed against his skin in apprehension.

Ladon wasn't sure why he was feeling this way about her. He didn't even know her. The instant he caught her gaze... He never felt this pull toward someone before.

He wanted to see her eyes again. Brown with specks of shades of gold that shone so bright. He touched a lock of her soft, long, brown hair that had streaks of gold, too. There was a splash of freckles on her face that absolutely fascinated his dragon with its unique patterns.

Ladon's attention snagged to her left arm where the golden thread rested. The magic had gone quiet when she passed out.

Atlas.

His anger resurfaced at the thought of the Titan. *He* did this to her, and he would pay.

"Any changes?"

Ladon turned to see Aimee. Worry etched on her face, but she didn't come closer.

"No."

"Nyssa is tough. Tougher than anyone gives her credit for. She'll be okay."

Nyssa. He liked the sound of her name.

"Let me know if there is anything I can do." Aimee shut the door behind her.

Ladon looked at Nyssa in time to see her eyelids flutter open. She sucked in a breath.

"How are you feeling?" He passed her a glass of water.

She blinked and her gaze went to something next to him. Her expression turned to confusion, but she sat up and took the water from his hand and drained the glass before handing it back.

"I-I'm okay."

A sense of relief washed through him as the sound of her voice soothed his dragon. The tension left his shoulders. It startled him to realize how concerned he had been. An instinct deep within was slowly treading to the surface—

"It's the first time we've met, right?" Nyssa asked, pulling from his thoughts.

He nodded.

Her gaze switched from him to next to him and back again.

"May I ask what you find so fascinating behind me?"

She blushed. "It's...it's just that when I meet new supernaturals I tend to get a headache and a nosebleed."

His lips twitched as he fought a smile. "That doesn't sound like a compliment."

"No, I didn't mean it like that. It's just you're a dragon. A powerful one. That power should overwhelm me, and it should hurt. For once, I'm not in pain meeting someone new. It's...nice." She smiled.

Understanding flashed through him. "You can see us for what we truly are." An ability that was rare. It was no wonder Atlas was after her.

"Yes, I see a shade appear next to someone who isn't human. For you, I see a dragon, yet I know you aren't a were-hunter."

"I'm not," he confirmed. "I'm a drakomai, and my name is Ladon."

"Nyssa." She held out her hand. He saw the moment she realized the golden rope was on her arm. Her eyes widened and she brushed her fingers carefully across it, as if she was afraid of the reaction.

"Does it hurt?" He remembered her cries of pain from the alley, but he hoped that it faded.

"No, not anymore."

"We'll find a way to get it off you," he promised.

Nyssa's resigned gaze met his. "No, we won't."

ૐ

DEEP DOWN, Nyssa knew that Ariadne's thread was stuck to her for good. It would take a lot of power to destroy it. The magic was quiet now, but it was only a thought away.

They needed to find the apple before Atlas did. He would be back, she knew it. She looked at Ladon. He was the most beautiful man she had ever seen. His blue eyes were even more intense in the light. His blond hair was cropped short in a way that suited his face. She noticed that he had burn scars on his face and arms. But that only made him more attractive to her. The scars proved he was a survivor. Nyssa couldn't explain her attraction. Was it because for the first time living in this supernatural world, she looked at someone and it didn't hurt? Her powers were quiet even though she could see his dragon and feel the power that radiated off him.

"We need to find the apple."

Nyssa saw his slight flinch, but he nodded, nonetheless. "We do. Does the string work?"

"I saw threads of gold when it latched onto me. I'm guessing those threads lead to powerful objects. When Atlas commanded me to find the apple, my mind automatically grabbed onto that, and the other threads fell away."

"Do you think you can do it again?"

Nyssa took a deep breath and focused on the thread, willing the magic to life. This time the magic flowed through her eagerly and gently. There was no pain. It felt like the most natural thing in the world, like an ability she was always supposed to have. Golden threads filled her vision.

"I see them. Some are...brighter than others."

Knowing she needed to narrow them down, she focused her thoughts on the golden apple. The rest of the threads faded away. Nyssa reached out as if to touch the one thread. She jumped when she felt its warmth. She grasped the thread and gave it a tug. The power filled her body and grew hotter, giving her the feeling that whatever was at the end of this string was close.

"I've got it."

Ladon's piercing gaze was like a spark of electricity shooting through her veins. "Let's go find it."

NYSSA'S EYES glowed gold and they were focused on something Ladon couldn't see. Her lack of awareness worried him, as he had to keep her from walking into a door or falling down the stairs. She didn't seem to notice. They entered the bar and he heard his siblings before he saw them.

"I told you to leave Ladon alone, Xyn."

Ladon smiled. He liked Falcyn. His surly attitude rivaled his own. Plus, his brother understood his need for isolation. His life was protecting the Garden of Hesperides until it was destroyed under his care. He was near death before Falcyn healed him and after that he wanted to be left alone. Falcyn gave him that.

"Ladon." Falcyn stomped over to them, Xyn and Urian on his heels.

Ladon grabbed Nyssa around the waist and pulled her to him before she could walk out the door. She startled and looked up at him before taking in his siblings.

"Xyn filled me in on what's going on," said Falcyn. "Let me fry that pathetic Titan's ass."

Ladon shook his head. He appreciated his brother's offer. Despite Falcyn's attitude, he cared deeply for all his siblings and would do anything for them. But this was one fight Ladon needed to do himself. Xyn was right. He couldn't keep hiding. The Garden was his responsibility. A task he was born to do. Memories of agonizing screams and burning flesh threatened to crush him, but Nyssa's touch on his arm soothed him. He took a deep breath and let her scent ground him, the memories drifted away. He focused on Falcyn. "I failed to guard the apples in the past, I won't do that again."

Falcyn growled. "Fine. But the second you need us, call."

"We'll protect it," Nyssa said, her face set with determination. "Together."

NYSSA'S FOCUS on the thread led them to the streets of New Orleans. She fought to concentrate on her surroundings and not fall prey to the magic of the thread. Nyssa glanced at Ladon and wondered if he was okay. Earlier she sensed his fear and did her best to soothe him.

Her heart clenched though when she realized that wouldn't happen. Ladon would leave soon after finding the apple. The thought of never seeing him again... This wasn't the time to think about it.

Nyssa soon realized where they were heading. "It's leading us to Karma's."

"Who's Karma?"

"A friend. She tends to keep interesting magical objects in her house. It doesn't surprise me that the apple is hidden there."

"Will she hand it over?"

Nyssa sighed. "I don't know. We may have to convince her that we can protect it."

Ladon tensed beside her.

"What happened to the Garden?" She had heard bits and pieces from everyone, but she wanted to know his story.

"My life was dedicated to protecting the Garden of Hesperides. But I failed. Herakles came. The nymphs I had sworn to protect drugged me and my dragonstone was destroyed. Atlas wanted freedom in exchange for giving Herakles the advantage to kill me and retrieve an apple. He succeeded, but burned down the Garden as he did so, killing everyone who lived there. I was dying and with one last burst of strength I released a *Bane-Cry*. Xyn and Falcyn came. He healed me but I wasn't the same. I learned later that Atlas was only free a few days before he was sucked back to the Garden to hold the sky. He betrayed me and sacrificed his children for *nothing*."

Heart breaking for Ladon, she wrapped her arms around him. "I'm sorry. It wasn't your fault. You didn't deserve what happened to you. To be betrayed by those you trusted..."

Ladon stiffened, but after a moment he returned her hug.

Nyssa looked up and caught in the blue intensity of Ladon's eyes, let it consume all of her. Before she could overthink, she stood on her tiptoes and brushed her mouth against his. His surprise lasted a moment before his hand cupped her face and held her there. His kiss was all consuming and nothing like she'd experienced before. She met him kiss for kiss and only pulled back when the need for air became necessary. She saw the smile on Ladon's face and returned it. He opened his mouth but closed it and looked behind Nyssa.

"We have to go," he said. "I can sense Atlas. He isn't far."

They made it to Karma's front door in no time. "Karma!" she called. "Let us in!"

Karma Devereaux's face filled the doorway. "Nyssa? What are you—?"

"A Titan is after something in this house," she warned. "I need to get it before he does."

"He's here," stated Ladon. "Find the apple. I'll hold him off." Before she could protest, he gave her a quick kiss. "Go." His blue eyes flashed to gold and suddenly there was a large gold dragon in Karma's front yard.

"Come on," urged Karma, tugging her arm. "Go find what you're looking for."

Pulling her gaze away from Ladon she said, "Call Sanctuary and get to safety."

Karma took off. More gold threads filled Nyssa's vision. Karma's house was full of treasures, and it threatened to overload her senses. Focusing on the task, she brushed the other threads away and held tight to the Apple of Immortality. The thread led her upstairs. On the second floor, she darted down the hallway, passing door after door. A roar came from outside.

Fighting the need to run back to Ladon, she opened the door the thread had gone through. There was artwork on the walls and vases displayed. But Nyssa knew these were no ordinary pieces. She focused and carefully walked through the room. She faced a painting. It was *The Son of Man* by Edward Burne-Jones. It depicted a man in an overcoat and bowler hat standing in front of a cloudy sky and sea. An apple obscured his face.

"This can't be it," she murmured. She studied the painting. The apple in the original was supposed to be green, but here it was gold. She reached for the canvas. Her hand brushed against the apple. She gasped.

It went through the illusionary painting. She grasped the other end and pulled.

Her eyes widened as she stared at the apple in her hand. Nyssa noticed it was now missing from the painting. She'd found it. The last Apple of Immortality. The hum of power filled her hand.

The house shook. Nyssa started running, she had to help Ladon. She burst through the front door and saw that Ladon was no longer in his dragon form. He was bleeding but was still fighting Atlas. The good news was that Atlas didn't look much better.

A sharp pain in her head, a trickle of blood from her nose, and—

"I'll be taking that."

Nyssa whipped around. In front of her stood a beautiful woman with long jet-black hair dressed in a black peplos, a knife twirled between her fingers. A goddess.

The shade that appeared next to her held an apple in her hand. Nyssa locked eyes with the shade and could only see chaos swirling within. The shade winked and at that moment, Nyssa knew.

"Eris," she breathed.

The goddess of strife and discord smiled, a predator claiming its prey. She pointed her knife at Nyssa. "Very good. Now hand over the apple, mortal."

"No," said Nyssa. She held it closer to her chest. "You want to create another apple of discord for Apollo." It made sense now. That apple was one of the factors that eventually led to the Trojan War. In Apollo's hand, he could pit his enemies against one another. She couldn't let that happen.

"Fine, we'll do this the hard way," said Eris, throwing a blast of power at Nyssa.

❧

"MOVE ASIDE, DRAGON," Atlas gasped. His breathing was labored, and blood ran from a cut on his cheek. "Give up the apple and I won't punish your mortal."

Ladon growled. Atlas didn't understand what dragons would do to protect what was theirs. Nyssa was his to protect. He wiped the blood from his mouth.

"You're not looking so good, old man," said Ladon. "tell me, how long did Apollo give you to retrieve the apple? The way your form keeps flickering, I imagine not long."

Atlas's jaw clenched. Ladon knew he was right. The magic would pull Atlas back again, he only had to stall. Atlas advanced, throwing a punch at Ladon. Anticipating the move, he dodged and used Atlas's momentum against him. He threw Atlas across the yard and closed in when a shout of pain grabbed his attention.

He whipped around and saw Eris standing over Nyssa as she ripped a knife out of Nyssa's chest.

The dragon within raged. Ladon sent a blast of fire at Eris who had raised her blade once more. Fear flashed in Eris's eyes before she teleported away.

Ladon slid to Nyssa's side and placed his hands on her bloodied chest. The blood stained his hands. Nyssa's face was pale. The gold in her eyes had dimmed and her breathing was shallow.

"Nyssa," he croaked.

Nyssa's gaze found his. "Ladon. I got the apple," she whispered. She held it in front of him. His breath caught. "You didn't fail. You can still protect it," she rasped. She started coughing and blood dripped from her lips.

An idea formed in his mind. There was only one way he could save her *and* protect the apple.

❦

NYSSA WOKE for the second time in Sanctuary, except this time Ladon held her. His eyes were closed, and his hair was disheveled, he looked so peaceful and vulnerable. Memories came flooding back and her hands scrambled to her chest. Her shirt was torn and bloody, but no wound remained.

"You're healed." Ladon stared intently at her.

"How?" she asked.

"The apple."

Her eyes widened. "You fed me the apple?"

His arms tightened around her. "It was the only way to save you."

She leaned her head against his chest. "Atlas?"

"Gone. With the apple consumed, the magic that bound him to hold the sky pulled him back."

She sighed in relief. "Eris?"

His eyes flashed to gold. "She ran off after she stabbed you. If she ever shows her face again it will be the last thing she does."

"Not if I get there first," she murmured.

Ladon chuckled and placed a kiss on her head. It was the first time she heard him laugh. She wanted to hear it more.

Nyssa lifted her head. "So, I'm immortal?"

He sat up and took her with him, so that she straddled him. His hands rested on her hips and their faces were now only inches apart. "You are."

"I'm not sure how to process that. Will you... Are you going home?" She wasn't ready to say goodbye to him.

He smiled. "Looking to get rid of me?"

"Well, you did decide to make me immortal. I think that means I'm kind of your responsibility," she teased. "Plus, I think this will need to be protected." She raised her arm where Ariadne's thread rested, but she gasped when she noticed that it had seeped into her skin. It looked like a tattoo.

"It is a dragon's responsibility to protect its treasure."

He watched her. Nyssa's heart melted before Ladon closed the distance between them. Immortality wouldn't be so bad if she had her dragon by her side.

WE ALL GOTS BEASTS

SHERI-LYNN MAREAN

1

Genna's stomach rumbled as she placed the last of the peeled hot dogs on the ground in front of the small, stone, Garden gnome. She watched the little bearded male with the largest spade. His expression was fierce and like the others he wore a red hat, though his eyes seemed to stare right through her. But Genna knew different—there was life in there.

Only, as she waited, nothing happened.

"Figures!" She grabbed the empty box, stood, and shoved her long black hair out of her face. Then she gazed through the dark over at the other five gnomes spread around the yard. "I not know if I believes you 'bouts this." She spoke in a low voice, just enough to carry to anyone close by, but not loud enough to wake the humans inside their home.

She'd been feeding the gnomes for a while now, so why did they still refuse to talk to her—to show themselves? Only one had, and he'd been a grump for sure. Maybe 'cause he only had a thin pickax? He'd also claimed that the rest of them didn't like the skins. Of course, that was after she caught him stealing the others' hot dogs.

Maybe she needed to install a hidden camera. She

had told her YouTube fans that the gnomes came to life at night. Genna would really love to show them it was true.

Except, the stone creatures would probably know if she recorded them. Then they'd never show their real live selves and Genna wanted to talk to them. Find out where they came from and where they went when they became stone, cause surely, they didn't just stay frozen but aware. Did they? Kinda seemed like a boring and silly life if they did. She also wanted to know what their purpose truly was here.

Though she was twenty years old, most of Genna's learning until now had been from the internet during her years as an Ilyium captive. That was, until her magics grew up and got too strong for them to hold her. Now Genna could teleport anywhere, and it seemed that everything caught her curiosity. Besides, the internet suggested two different theories about gnomes. One was that they came to life to Garden, while the other claimed the little bearded men guarded buried treasure.

Genna loved treasure.

"C'mon Peanut," she whispered, then smiled when the small tabby cat darted out of the bushes and over to her. He'd been the reason she'd found out gnomes came to life in the first place. Genna picked up the little cat and rubbed her face against his fur. "You're so soft," she said as he started to purr. If Peanut hadn't escaped the house a couple weeks ago, setting everyone in a frenzy looking for him, Genna would never have come here. She'd also never have seen one of the gnomes move.

Finding Peanut that night had been a long shot. This little farm was a half mile down the road from where she lived with a bunch of other supes. But something made Genna head this way, and here he'd been. Whether the cat had gotten here himself, or something else had brought him she didn't know. Though after discovering that the gnomes were more than simple stone, Genna wondered if they had something to do with it.

Peanut was just a cat, but he was important to everyone, especially to Thaniel, the were-leopard living with them. Genna inhaled the crisp spring air and shifted half-way into her dragon form. Black scales appeared on her upper arms, but it was the freedom of letting her midnight wings out that made her sigh with pleasure. She was about to take off and fly when her phone dinged with a text. She pulled her phone out and looked at the message. It was from Simi, one of her biggest fans who'd quickly become a friend.

Genna shifted back into human form, replied to Simi, then teleported home. She gazed around the kitchen. Normally someone would be in here cooking up a storm, but tonight the room was empty. "Who be making supper tonight?" she asked Peanut. They generally all took turns, well, except Genna—no one liked her cooking, which was fine with her. Of course, she had different tastes, but no one was thrilled when she brought home live snails to eat.

She was about to put Peanut down and teleport to Simi when the sounds of Sami and Jax in the next room stopped her. She was wicked amazing in a fight, but maybe bringing help would be a good idea. "Jax and Sami be very bad-ass in battle," she murmured to Peanut, rubbing his soft head.

Genna hurried into the great room and set Peanut on the couch where Jax and Sami sat playing a video game "Hey, I gots an idea, how about I take you both to New Orleans and we get us some supper at Sanctuary?"

"What's Sanctuary?" Sami, a large, good-hearted male with scruffy dark-blond hair and kind emerald eyes, asked. He always reminded Genna of a teddy bear she once had.

"It be a sanctuary for supes, and a bar," Genna added. "My friend Simi tells me they gots the bestest Cajun food and I never ate any before."

"I don't know. I thought maybe we'd just order a pizza tonight." Jax, who sported short black hair and the same blue eyes as Genna replied. "Plus, our mates will be home from baby-shopping soon."

"Yes, but they'll eat before coming home," Sami said.

"True ..." Jax narrowed his gaze on Genna. "What's going on, why do you want to go all the way down to Louisiana for supper?"

"My tummy hungry." Genna rubbed her belly.

"I could eat as well," Sami shrugged. "We've never been to New Orleans before. It might be fun."

"Maybe," Jax said, though doubt rang in his voice.

"You gots money?" Genna asked.

"Yeah," Jax replied.

Sami patted his pocket and nodded.

"Good." Genna grabbed their arms. "Also, there may be something bad happening." Then she teleported them into Sanctuary.

"I knew it," Jax snapped as she let him go. "I knew there was another motive for bringing us here."

"Genna?" Sami inquired as a large male with long curly blond hair, and who smelled of bear, approached their suddenly materialized trio.

Genna turned to Sami and Jax. "I bring you as backup. My friend Simi say it be emergency."

Jax groaned.

"Who are you and why are you here?" The bear blocked them.

"I be Genna, Simi text me to come."

The guy relaxed. "Simi's down the hall, third door on the left."

Genna waved Jax and Sami to follow.

At the door Genna knocked. It immediately swung open to reveal a young woman with long black hair and horns on top of her head.

2

Simi squealed at the sight of her and Genna wondered where she got her clothes—they were so cool. "Your text say emergency, so I bring backup." Genna indicated Jax and Sami.

"Oh, it's not that kind of emergency." Simi drew Genna into the room, revealing a dracones male going through his awakening.

❧

WHEN SHE FINALLY EMERGED WITH Simi from the room a little later, satisfied that the male would survive his awakening with his mate's help—now that Genna had shown her what to do—she found Jax and Sami sitting on the floor with their backs against the wall not looking impressed. They stood up.

"What's going on Genna?" Jax asked Genna, then shook his head. "Never mind, I probably don't want to know. I think you should just take us home."

"I not know that I not be needing your help when I bring you here. I heard emergency and you are both good fighters. But I take you home now if you be wanting to go, or we go eat." Genna shrugged, leaving it up to them, though she really wanted food.

Sami looked at Jax. "We are here...?"

"Fine, I am hungry. But as soon as we're done Genna takes us home."

Genna refrained from shouting in happiness and instead turned to Simi. "You gots your barbeque sauce?"

"Always. Follow me." Simi led everyone down to the main floor and over to a table. "You have to meet my Akri, he'll be here soon." Simi waved at someone across the room. "Sit down and I will be right back, I have to go talk to someone."

Aimee, who Genna met in the room upstairs came down and handed them menus.

"I already be smelling the food." Genna looked at the various items with no clue what any of it was. But it didn't matter, her tummy was grumbling. She set her menu down. "Aimee, where be the Ladies room?"

"Over there." Aimee pointed.

Genna left Sami and Jax at the table, but when she emerged from the restroom a few minutes later, a disturbance in Sanctuary's protections made her pause. Then she saw Aimee at the bottom of the stairs with another exceptionally large, blond-haired guy. He had a frown on his face. "What's going on, Aimee?" He looked just like the bear Genna met earlier, but his mental signature and scent was a little different.

"Is it that Sawyer character? I knew he'd be trouble."

"Nothing for you to worry about, Dev," Aimee told him and nodded at Genna. "But he could use your help."

As Dev left with a grumble, Genna followed Aimee back upstairs. "What happened?"

"Sawyer needs you to track his mate and teleport him to wherever she is," Aimee said.

"I can do that."

Genna was back in no time.

"Everything all right?" Sami asked when she took her seat at the table.

"You were gone a while," Jax added.

"All good," Genna said, surveying the menu. "You know what you're getting?"

"Yes," Jax and Sami both answered, then Simi joined them with a tall male who had long black hair and dark sunglasses covering his eyes.

"This is my Akri—Acheron." Simi introduced him as they sat down.

Acheron appeared about twenty-one, though Genna felt in her bones that he was much older. But it was his stare—it didn't matter that she couldn't see his eyes, Genna could feel the power he emanated as he regarded them.

"Akri, this is my friend Genna. I texted her to help the new guy," Simi said. "And ..." She licked her lips as she eyed Jax and Sami. "Genna, your friends look super yummy."

"Ick, that be my family you ogling. Simi, you gots to promise me you not eat them, okay?" Genna said. "If you don't, then their mates be real pissy with me."

"Fine. I promise, but they still look delish."

Genna indicated Jax who was scowling. "This be my brother Jax. We gots the same father, only he gots a mother too. I mean, he did. But I don't cause I be born of magic. And this guy—" Genna nodded at Sami. "He be my brother's brother Sami. They gots, I mean had the same mother."

"Who's this new guy?" Acheron said.

"Sawyer. He's a dracones." Simi thumbed up at the ceiling.

Beside Genna, Jax and Sami tensed.

"I know what a dracones is, but what's wrong with him?" Acheron asked.

"He's going through his awakening," Simi said.

"Awakening?" Acheron raised an eyebrow.

Simi gasped. "How do you not know what an awakening is? Akri! I can hardly believe what my hornies just heard. You know everything about ... well, everything."

"Apparently not today," Acheron said wryly.

At the mention of dracones and awakening, Jax and Sami looked at Genna.

"That's what you were doing, helping someone through their awakening?" Sami's voice wavered.

"Yes." Genna patted his arm. "But you nots worry, he be fine now."

"Yes, now meal time," Simi smacked her lips.

"He has a mate?" Jax asked skeptically.

"She be Ilyium." Genna wished she could take back her words when their expressions turned dark. "She a good witch, she loves Sawyer."

"She does," Simi smiled dreamily.

Genna took pity on her brother. He might act all tough and growly, but inside he cared about everyone. "I know your awakening be bad Jax, but Sawyer be fine now. Promise."

"And no one has answered my question yet," Acheron said. "What is an awakening?"

"It's what a dracones goes through so their dragon can come out," Simi said. "Which sounds pretty silly if you ask me. None of us have to wait to let our beasties out." Then her eyes grew wide. "Can you fix that Akri? It so does not seem fair."

"Sorry, not within my scope of things," Acheron said.

"Pooh! Oh, Akri, I'm ravenous, I could eat a cow!"

"Simi, Acheron, how do you know about dracones?" Jax inquired after Aimee took their food order.

"Akri knows because he knows everything. Well, almost, and I know because Genna told me," Simi said.

Jax and Sami shared a look before pinning their gaze on Genna.

"Simi, you know Genna how?" Infinite patience laced Acheron's tone.

"I follow her YouTube channel," Simi grinned. "I gave her a tip on something and then we became friends."

Genna squirmed under Jax and Sami's stare and realized bringing them here maybe wasn't a good idea.

"What do you post on this YouTube channel?" Jax asked, voice low and slightly menacing.

Genna looked around, hoping the food would come quick and save her from having to answer.

"She posts about being a dracones, about the mean Ilyium, her wings. All kinds of things." Simi shrugged.

Genna tried to ignore Jax's glare. "When the food coming? My belly starved."

"Genna even posted a video of the fight with the demon angel." Simi waved her hand, oblivious to Jax and Sami's horror over her words. "It was amazing!"

"Genna, why are you telling everyone what we are?" Jax ground out.

Sami blinked. "You took the video."

Genna bit her lip. "I not tell everyone, and humans not believe anyway. And I not record the video, I just take it from the girl who did. I was gonna give it to you Sami, but figured it not hurt to post on my channel first. I only had ten followers, and they think I be nuts."

"Dang Genna." Sami swiped a hand through his hair.

"It was a good video," Simi added. "It got Genna lots of new followers."

Jax groaned.

Sami sighed. "Do you any idea how much time I spent cleaning up that mess, wiping those videos and discrediting it all?"

A bad feeling pinched Genna's gut. "I not know it go viral, and when I see you upset, I take it down. Only it kinda be too late."

Before Sami could reply, Aimee arrived with their food.

Genna inhaled the spicy aroma and tried to ignore the guilt as she decided what to eat first.

"Aimee, you joining us?" Simi asked as she doused her plate in barbeque sauce.

"No, I have work to do."

"Thank you," Sami replied. "This smells and looks amazing."

"You're welcome." Aimee smiled at everyone. "Enjoy, and ya'll let me know if there's anything else I can get you."

"So did the avocados work?" Simi asked Genna.

Genna nodded, closing her eyes as she took her first bite of gumbo. Flavor exploded in her mouth. "Yes," she said between bites. "They make my wings real soft."

"That's why you bought crates of avocados?" Jax paused with his fork halfway to his mouth.

"I not know they go bad so fast." Genna pouted.

"What about your Garden gnome problem?" Simi enquired between mouthfuls.

"Garden gnome problem?" Jax said, puzzled. "We don't have any Garden gnomes."

"Shhhh." Genna tried to kick at Simi under the table, but it was too late.

"Genna says they come to life at night," Simi told Jax. "Said she gonna put hot dogs out, cause they gotta be hungry sitting as stone all day." Simi turned to Acheron. "Did you know they come to life and not tell me? They might be real good eating."

"That's what you've been doing each night?" Jax asked Genna. "Why didn't you tell me?"

"I not want you think I crazy," Genna admitted, though she hated feeling vulnerable.

Jax opened his mouth as if to say something, then closed it and looked at Sami.

"We know you're not crazy." Sami paused. "You're just very ... unique."

"What he said," Jax added, looking relieved.

Genna grinned at them. "I am, aren't I?"

"What makes you think these Garden gnomes come to life, anyway?" Sami asked before taking another bite of jambalaya.

"Because I saw one move in the neighbor's yard the night I found Peanut," Genna explained. "My hot dog plan worked. Only, one gnome stole all the hot dogs. He say they not like peoples. I tell him I not be peoples and show him my wings, claws, and glowy eyes. But the grump say it not matter." Genna tore off a piece of bread. "Then he spit and say the skins be disgusting. Say gnomes not like skins. So, I peel the weenies now, though I not sure I believe Grumpy. He gots bad teeth, and the rest not show me their live selves."

As everyone stared at her, Genna wiped her plate with the bread and popped it into her mouth, chewed and swallowed. "Simi, you not lie, this be the best food ever." She looked at Jax. "You think Thaniel can make this for us at home?"

"I can certainly ask." Jax set his fork down on his empty plate. "Why is seeing these gnomes come to life so important?"

"I gots to know. Do they take care of the roses, or..." Genna glanced around the table. "Maybe they protecting treasure."

"I love me some sparkly pretties," Simi said.

"Me too." Genna grinned at her.

Simi's eyes went wide. "Maybe your gnomes don't like hot dogs. Maybe you need some good ol' Cajun food. I bet Aimee give you leftovers from the kitchen if you ask."

Genna thought about it. "It be worth a try. I gots to take Jax and Sami home or their mates yell at me for stealing them. You want to come with, then we go stakeout the gnome Garden?"

"Definitely!" Simi turned to Acheron. "Akri, I can go?"

"Yes, and I'll take Jax and Sami home." The fatherly look Acheron gave Simi made Genna think of Caden. He used to care for her, but she pushed away. Then Acheron waved Aimee back over.

"You want the bill?" Aimee asked.

Acheron nodded.

"I got this," Jax said and pulled out his wallet. He handed Aimee a bunch of bills. "Thank you, keep the change. The meal was fantastic. We'll be back."

"Glad to hear it, and we'll be happy to feed you again," Aimee smiled.

Jax faced Acheron again, studying him as if trying to figure out who or what he was. "How do you plan to get us home? You teleport as well?"

Simi snorted. "Course, Akri can do anything."

"We're north of Spokane, in Washington State," Sami added as they all stood up.

"I know," Acheron responded drolly.

"He read your mind." Genna smirked at the puzzled looks on Jax and Sami's face, aware how much that would bother them.

Acheron's gaze landed on Genna.

She shrugged. She'd felt the sweeping touch of Acheron's mind trying to read her from the moment he joined them. She'd also noted his surprise when he failed. However, his brooding darkness—pain from his past—hurt her heart bad. Kind of like Jax and Sami did before she learned to tune them out. "You not read my mind cause I gots a super strong shield. I had lots of time to weave it good and tight."

Acheron stilled. "You're in my head?"

"Welcome to our life," Jax said with a wry grin.

"Sorry, we keep telling her it's not right to invade other's minds," Sami apologized.

"I try and stay out of your heads, but some things you can't unsee." Genna turned to Simi. "You not eat me now, okay, we gots gnomes to feed, remember?"

"You're my friend, why would I eat you?" Simi asked.

"Cause I gots to do this." Genna went and hugged Acheron, laying her head on his chest. "You not worry, you got good shields too. And you be—are—a good male. We all gots beasts inside us, Simi's Akri. But your beast, he have a real good heart no matter what you think in your head."

As Acheron stood frozen, Sami chuckled. "Genna's an acquired taste."

With a dazed look, Acheron left with Jax and Sami.

Simi gazed at Genna. "I don't know if you're crazy after all. No one touches my Akri." Then she smiled. "Let's go see Aimee for gnome food."

3

Genna teleported her and Simi back to the Garden where the hot dogs lay like forlorn fingers in the moonlight. Not a single one had been eaten, not even Grumpy's. Disappointment swamped her.

"This must be a very pretty Garden in summer." Simi surveyed the yard. "You really think they guard treasure?"

"It is, and maybe. At least I hope so," Genna said.

"A girl can't have enough sparklies."

"Exactly," Genna replied as they began to distribute the food in front of the small statues. Then they sat down to wait.

"Maybe you should sing," Simi suggested.

"I don't gots any songs," Genna said.

"I do." Simi began to pelt out a pop song, and a wave of magic shimmered in the air.

Genna jumped to her feet as the gnomes came to life. "It worked!"

"Enough, please!" A gnome with a large spade dropped it and clapped his hands over his ears.

"Is that supposed to be music?" Grumpy glared at them.

As Simi stopped singing and stood, Genna grinned. "You gots the best ideas."

"I know, right?" Simi glanced up at the sky. "Someone's coming."

"It be Jax." Genna felt him since his dragon form was cloaked from sight.

Jax landed, shifted into his human body, and became visible. "Have I missed the excitement?"

"No." Genna watched the gnomes devour the food she and Simi set out for them.

When they were done, the gnomes wiped their mouths on their sleeves and smacked their lips. "About time you offered us something more than those stinking fake-meat sticks," said the one who demanded Simi stop singing. He reached down and picked his spade back up.

"That's why you not show yourselves before?" Genna asked.

Spade Gnome shook his head. "No, we just didn't want to talk to you."

"Why?" Genna frowned. "I be nice, I bring food."

Spade sighed. "Because we know you want the treasure we guard."

"I knew it!" Simi pumped her fist into the air.

Spade glared at her.

Simi cocked her head. "You guard it, but does the treasure belong to you?"

Spade hesitated. "No."

"Who then?" Genna asked.

The gnomes shared a glance. "No one anymore. The king we guarded it for died long ago, we been hauling it around to each new Garden."

"If it not belong to anyone no more, why you still guarding it?" Genna asked, curious.

"Because it's what we do." Spade puffed up his tiny

chest. "And we'll fight you if you try to take it from us. We may be small, but we're fierce."

"Bet we can take them!" Simi said excitedly.

Genna agreed, but the gnomes were just doing their job. Well, maybe. "So, all you gnomes take care of the Garden and guard treasure, and that be all?"

"What else you think we do?" Spade gnome snapped.

"Do you eat small critters who come around?"

A chorus of *Ew! No*, and *Disgusting* rang out as the gnomes spit at their feet.

"So, you not lure small animals here to harm them?" Genna's gut felt queasy as she waited for a reply.

"What? No!" Spade Gnome scrunched up his nose. "We don't want stinky critters desecrating our work. We take great pride in our gardens."

Relief filled Genna. "Good. But where do you go when you not be alive here?"

"Home," Spade Gnome said, as if that answered everything.

"Where's that?" Genna asked.

Spade Gnome scowled. "Why you so nosey?"

"Just curious," Genna said.

"Our homes are in Fairie," he replied. "You satisfied now?"

"Yes." Genna grinned at Jax, then turned to Simi. "Thank you for coming with me tonight. I better take you home to your Akri now."

"I'll see you at home." Jax moved away, shifted, and took to the night sky.

"That's one pretty dragon," Simi said before Jax cloaked himself.

"Simi, that be my brother, and he gots a mate." Genna shuddered.

"I know, but I can still look." Simi smiled.

"I guess. You ready?" Genna asked.

"Ready," Simi said.

But before Genna could teleport them away, Spade Gnome cleared his throat.

Genna looked back at him. "I not bother you again."

"We wouldn't mind if you bring us more of that Cajun food once in a while," he said.

The others nodded eagerly.

"I'll see," Genna replied, her mind already on to other things.

"Maybe we give you some treasure if you do," a shy gnome with his hands behind his back piped up.

Spade glared at him, then sighed and faced Genna. "He's right, it wouldn't hurt to trade some of it with you. But you have to bring good food, none of those warm skinless dogs."

"I'll see what I can do." Genna waved at them, grabbed Simi's arm and teleported back to Sanctuary.

"That stakeout was fun, thanks for taking me," Simi said.

"It was fun, and I'm glad you came with me." Genna gazed around, loving the atmosphere of Sanctuary. "This is a great place Simi. Maybe I come back and visit you again."

"Yes, then we can go shopping."

"Yes." Genna hugged Simi, then teleported back home.

4

As Genna entered the kitchen, she found her family gathered around, talking, laughing, and showing off baby items. There was going to be a few babies born here soon. Genna didn't know how she felt about that. It wasn't that she didn't like babies, but they couldn't fight or defend themselves. Though she supposed there were enough here who could protect them from any enemies. At least she hoped so.

"I hear you took Jax and Sami for supper," Tierney, Jax's mate said as she came over to Genna. "They've been telling us about their wonderful meal. Thank you for thinking of them while I was out shopping."

Genna blinked. Sometimes she didn't feel like she fit in, but other times she loved her new family so much it hurt. It also scared her—having someone to care for was a big responsibility, one that Genna hoped she didn't screw up like she had with Caden. Genna didn't know how she felt about him, but he was always on her mind. He'd also been magicless and defenseless, so she'd made him leave. Only, now she missed him. Maybe tomorrow she'd go see what he was doing.

As something rubbed against her leg, Genna looked down. Peanut meowed as she picked him up.

She cuddled him, savoring the softness of the small ball of fur. But as she felt eyes upon her, Genna looked up. A male with blue eyes and long white-blond hair, a good portion of it hiding half of his face, stared at her. Genna went over to him. "Hi, Thaniel." She handed Peanut to him. "You had a good supper at Clan Home?"

"Yes. I brought desert back with me and saved you some." Thaniel slid a plate with Genna written on the plastic covering across the counter to her.

"Thank you Thaniel, you're a nice kitty."

As red filled his face, Genna patted his arm. Then she scooped up one of the cherry-filled strudels and took a bite. It was the prefect desert after a good night.

Genna finished the confection as she went outside and shifted into her half-form. She inhaled a deep breath of fresh mountain air, then took to the sky.

But as she began to fly, a familiar male voice filled her head. *Can I join you?*

Jax wanted to fly with her? Yes, she said and waited for the large midnight blue dragon to catch up.

Thank you, Jax said.

For what? Genna asked.

For what you did tonight, he said. *You weren't wanting the treasure, you wanted to make sure Peanut was safe.*

I ... Genna suddenly realized that she really hadn't cared about the treasure after all, she only though she did. *I didn't want them to eat Peanut, or take him,* she said slowly, though why she was so concerned with a cat she didn't understand. Sure, Peanut was soft and cute, but he was just a cat.

You knew it would hurt Thaniel if he lost Peanut. Jax hit the matter dead in her heart.

Yeah, Genna responded, startled to realize it was the truth.

Come on, Jax said. *Let's have some fun. Then he dove down and skimmed the lake, his wake creating a spray of water that shot high in the air.*

Cool droplets pelted her as Genna flew alongside him and did the same.

A laugh burst from Genna's mouth.

Startled, Jax craned his neck around, but the eyes that regarded her were happy.

Then they flew straight up toward the moon before leveling off and gliding under the millions of twinkling stars.

The beast in Genna lightened as all her worries dropped away and she let herself enjoy being one with the night.

The End.

SAVED BY STONE

COLE JACKSON

1

The bitter tang of ill intent was a familiar taste on the back of his tongue. It danced through the energy of the night. Yet, the streets buzzed with expectation. Mardi Gras, the holiday that made this place famous, was only days away. It was the easiest time to hide among the masses. No one paid mind to the man who had a Victorian flare to his outfit and stone-grey eyes.

A cacophony of street musicians and the smell of Cajun seafood bombarded his senses. It was not always this easy to hide and habitually his gaze tracked over myriad faces. He took a moment to drag his feet on the freshly laid cobblestone. He let a soft chuckle of amusement escape. If only the masons of old could see this now.

There was a chiseled definition to his form that made it hard to determine his age. His hair was pulled back into a low pony. It was the only way to control the length of blond and pale grey that trailed down to the small of his back. He was tall with broad shoulders. His stride made the ankle-length overcoat billow behind him. It was more for show than necessary these days, like the familiarity of the walking stick in his left hand.

Quite suddenly he was brought out of his thoughts. His gaze narrowed to determine the source of the ill intention, the concentration of acid. It radiated from the line of the club nearby. There was very dark magic afoot. It was difficult to track and eradicate these days. Practitioners of the darker arts used to hide in the shadows. Now, it seemed as though they were frequenting high energy night clubs.

Assessing the line, he eyed each person. He nearly skipped over her. Hair pulled back into a mass of bouncing curls, her skirt and crop top outfit balanced sexy and modest in a high dollar form. The man behind the woman in line seemed a bit too focused... A bit too close.

Garin watched her shift weight from one heeled foot to the other. She was uncomfortable in them but probably felt them essential. It made sense. Without those heels she may have reached an inch over five foot. She was young enough to get carded for a drink and old enough to be served it. A girl her age would rarely come out alone at night and those that did would know to keep an eye over their shoulder. He watched her a moment more and realized that she wasn't from around here.

His brain told him to leave it alone, but his feet melted into the cobblestones. He stood there so long she glanced over at him, and their gazes met in a soft dance. Her eyes! He inhaled an audible breath and couldn't bear to pull away. Her eyes caught the light and he saw they were a striking mix of purple as soft as spring lilacs and as true as summer irises.

"Walk away, Garin," he told himself. "Just walk away. Don't do this to yourself. She isn't your Naomi."

But he couldn't leave well enough alone. He approached the woman. "Excuse me, miss, you must not be from around here. While this place is popular, there are a few other places in the city that you may find more appealing." His only hope was to stop whatever may be happening.

"And why should I go with you? I've been waiting long enough here that it should be worth something." Those violet eyes narrowed at him. The familiarity nearly drove him to his knees. "Besides, I don't even know your name."

He sensed her discomfort and nodded. "My name is Garin. May I have yours?" He was ever the gentleman. "And, if I may be honest with you, the character behind you is what brought me here. I only ask that you find a different place to be that's safer."

Frankie snapped around and eyed the man behind her. She caught him sneer at her new savior. "Frankie. And these are public streets in a city. I'm not sure any place is safer." She straightened and stood a bit taller but only for a moment before once again succumbing to the pain of the shoes.

Though her words were intelligent and spirited, he searched those familiar eyes and saw that underneath her bold and beautiful façade she was as lost and confused as she could be. He wondered why she would take an individual journey to a place like this. Surely there were more wonders in the world that would be far more interesting—and safer—to traverse. His mind attempted to reason with his heart that nothing good could come of this. Giving her one last soft look, he nodded.

So many distant feelings had once again reignited with her look. He struggled to choke back the feeling that she would not be safe. She might not even make it through the night. His heart felt like lead. He couldn't save the last human he truly cared about. Why should he try to save this one? But he couldn't walk away.

One last try. If she wouldn't listen, he would leave and allow the whole thing fade into the past. He looked up again with an offered hand. "I wish I could promise you that you'll be safe alone. Alas, New Orleans after dark is a treacherous place."

Garin waited as patiently as possible with his arm unwaveringly outreached towards her. He watched the conflict roll over her. The quick shift in her gaze, the soft bite at her lip, the strum of her fingertips against her leg were all tells.

The impatient man behind Frankie made a clear decision for all of them. Out of his jacket he drew an ornate, serpentine blade. It was a mere flash of metal before it was buried in her back between shoulder blade and spine. In an equally quick second, he pulled out the blade, thick with blood captured by channels in the steel. Then the stranger was off and running.

Garin automatically stepped forward. That same outstretched arm caught her as she began to crumple. His attention narrowed on her, keenly reading how to handle her best. He watched the emotions roll through her eyes—shock, then pain, then anger, before settling back into pain. Holding her petite form with a strong arm, he shrugged off the long coat and wrapped it around her before lifting her into his arms.

The motion caused a yelp, followed by the telling sound of teeth chattering. Soon after her body softened, and she surrendered to the dark.

Now he was on a mission. His heart ached that he couldn't immediately punish the perpetrator. There was a time where he would have left her in the care of a nearby person and pursued. Times were different now and no one was safe. Now, he had to get her to the safest possible place before he could worry about the stranger.

He looked around. No one noticed the stabbing. Those that might have turned a blind eye lest they get caught up. He took a moment to weigh his options. There was something compelling about her. Something familiar and yet new. Either way, she needed help. Shifting her body in his arms, it became evident she was bleeding through the coat.

Cradling her a bit tighter, he closed his eyes and took a focused breath. Yes—there was the familiar tang of dark magic. No human medical center would be trained to deal with this. Thankfully, there was another option. It had been many years since he stepped foot in the Sanctuary. He could only hope that bygones would be bygones and she could get the help she needed.

There was no telling who the man was or what the blood would be used for. That was out of his specialty. Fighting the man, that he could have handled. But this side of the dark arts was beyond his ability.

There was no way that he would make it there on foot in time. A quick sprint brought him to a dead-end alley known to only cats and rats. Checking behind him, he pulled his shoulders forward and stretched out great grey wings. The bones were light and supple and between them the skin pulled so tight it was translucent. They were meant for soaring, not for taking off in dark alleys. But this wouldn't be the first time he kicked off hard from the earth, his face tight in concentration, arms tight around Frankie.

His eyes glimmered icy grey, accented anew by the

wings that beat furiously around them both. She
stirred in his arms, and he realized he squeezed a bit
too tight. He loosened his arms and at the same time
lost a few feet of altitude. It had been quite some time
since he had dared spread his wings in the city, let
alone supporting another person. He closed his eyes
and focused back to the task at hand: Get the girl to
the Sanctuary.

🐾

"WHAT IN THE hell are you doing bringing a bleeding
hum—" Dev leaned into the sight in front of him. His
nostrils flared for a moment, gaze going sharp towards
Garin. "... a bleeding, cursed, unbedded human?"

Ah hell! That would complicate the situation. The
rest of Dev's protests fell on deaf ears as Garin pushed
his way into the bar.

"They never listen to me anyway, damn stone
beasts," Dev grumbled. He turned into the door and
hollered, "Someone get Carson!"

Garin moved towards the bar and was waved away
by Cherif, "Don't you get blood on my bar. Take her to
the house." As Cherif spoke, he walked towards a door
and ushered the two behind the bar. He keyed in the
code blindly and pushed the door open.

Cherif sneered, unamused, "If history serves me
right, you know the way."

Yes, he knew the way. Once upon a time ago he
went a bit mad and found himself in a Saturday night
cage fight. Very few individuals make it out alive and
those that do, well, they get a t-shirt. Partly disfigured,
he had been led down this same hall to a safe space to
recover. He hadn't been back since. Many unkind
words were exchanged that night.

Right, right, left, right and into the surgical room. Garin lowered the woman onto the table. Even though he was stronger than the average human, he began to feel the toll of flying with her.

Moments later the door swung open, and Carson appeared with a few others. "Why the hell didn't you take her to the med center? It's just down the road." His foot slammed the pedal down on the scrub station in the corner. Two minutes later he had donned gloves and assessed the situation. "We don't treat many humans here. They don't heal as fast and take more work to keep alive." His words were a protest, but he had removed the rest of her top and flipped her on her stomach.

Taking sentry close to the door, Garin allowed a quick roll of his shoulders. They were stiff after the workout they received. Normally he'd find a place to stretch out but there was limited space in the room. Instead, he channeled the energy into figuring out if he had made more a mess than helped.

While he knew this was neither the time nor the place, Garin couldn't help but look. Beneath the wash of blood was an expanse of creamy soft skin. Her hair was tousled to one side exposing her face. Eyes closed and lips parted, far enough into anesthesia that she could feel nothing. His gaze trailed across her shoulders and down the soft indent of her spine until it disappeared into the skirt left on for modesty. So strong and yet so pure.

An hour later and the energy in the room quieted. The woman was alive, but that's all Garin knew from the steady beep of the machine. At some point, Carson had murmured, "The wound was made by a kris knife, probably ceremonial. The curved blade made it especially nasty to stop the bleeding." He wiped his hands on crumpled towels. "It's up to her will to stay this side of the living. She has a few hours here before she'll have to be moved. This much human blood would be too tempting for some."

That meant he had few hours for him to try and figure out what to do. She couldn't stay here. She couldn't be left alone. He didn't have any other clues to her identity. For a moment he allowed himself to slump. His elbows braced on his legs and his head rested in his hands. There wasn't anyone in the city he trusted with her.

Someone obviously wanted her blood and didn't care what price it cost.

Garin took a deep breath and studied her. He stood up and arched his back in a deep stretch. Restless, he stepped closer to her. The wound was covered with a pile of bandages that made a hump under the thin white blanket they had laid over her. He frowned with concern. Even with the blood transfusion and fluids, she seemed paler.

The beeping of the monitor was steady enough that it faded into the background. He watched her, unsure of how long before she'd open her eyes. He reached out and allowed himself to brush a stray hair out of her face. There was a jump to the steady beeps. Her eyes moved behind her eyelids and her mouth tightened. Worried that his presence upset her, he stepped back and dug his hands into his pockets.

Was she coming to? Back on high alert, he looked around the room. True to form, there was a big red button on the wall right behind him labeled "emergency call".

Thump. Her leg kicked against the table. She took a deep, shuddered, raspy breath. It brought his attention back to her. On instinct, he reached up and hit the button as she let out a shrill shriek that filled the room. Garin winced. Two huge strides took him back to her side.

Her lithe form twisted and writhed on the table. The monitor screeched with her in rapid alert. He knew if she kept at it, she would rip open the wound. Garin threw a knee up on the bed and straddled her thighs. Leaning over her, he grabbed her arms and pinned them as gently as he could to the bed at her sides. "Shhh... You're safe." He spoke softly into her ear. "I won't let anyone hurt you."

She continued to thrash, irrationally pressing against him. So weak, so fragile she was that he worried he hurt more than helped. He was sore, tired, and wished that someone would come through the door to help. He continued to speak to her, hoping something would get through. "Someone's going to come help us. You must stay with me for another minute."

He closed his eyes for a moment remembering the last time he felt this helpless.

ﯾ

HE SAW Frankie's face shift to Naomi's—the woman who completed his soul. Centuries ago, he dug her grave by night on a hillside in what was now France. Cradling her body, he wove his one form of magic around her and turned her to stone.

Wracked by grief, he tore through the enemy. Night turned to day. Fighting in sunlight was much harder for his species. When he realized he could take no more, he crawled his way back to the place he had left his love. There he let the metamorphosis overtake him. He held her stone form and planted his feet in the earth. He crouched down and cradled her close and forced his wings out. His face twisted in agony and his skin hardened and turned grey.

There he stood sentinel with his love. For a century his body healed but his mind descended to chaos. Locked into his form he punished himself for ever allowing her to love him. She had been human. She had been fragile. She had been strong willed and a valiant warrior but, in the end, she was only mortal.

❧

"YOU CAN GET DOWN NOW." Carson's stoic voice snapped Garin back to reality. He disposed of an empty syringe.

Garin presumed it to be another dose of sedation. Ungracefully, he climbed off the bed. "I want your honesty. Will she be okay?" Garin looked to Carson for any glimmer of hope.

"I wish I could tell you," Carson sighed. Frankie was as white as the blanket he pulled back to expose the bandages. The tiniest stain had reached the top layer. Pulling the gauze back, Carson grabbed a stack of gauze layers from the cart behind him. He pressed them hard into the wound and brought his attention back up to Garin.

"It's not looking good. This is deep but it shouldn't continue to bleed. She fought to come up out of the anesthesia before she was ready. All signs point to dark magic here. Unless the source is stopped..."

Garin looked down at Frankie. There was no denying that something connected her to him. If nothing else, he must resolve it. To resolve it, she needed to stay alive. For her to stay alive, he had to go to work. "Keep her alive," Garin demanded before he exited the room.

HE SOARED ABOVE THE STREETS. The memory of that bitter tang in his mind. It was one of many skills gargoyles possessed. Deep in the swamps he coasted through Spanish moss. Garin slowed and landed on his feet with a soft thud, his wings furled to his spine. The boardwalk he trod had seen better days. He paid no mind to the wildlife that eyed him as he stormed up the wooden planks. The tiny house was in shambles, held up out of the water by eight tall poles.

A thin curtain over the doorway kept persistent bugs out. He entered to find four teenagers sitting in a circle. Around them were chalk drawings, a mix of runes and glyphs. Candles clustered in the corners for light along with a few colored candles in the center. In front of each of the children sat the skull of a small animal. In the center was a bowl. The kris rested there.

There was a hum to the shack, an energy that pulled at the senses and made him feel like he walked in mud. One of these kids knew what they were doing. He took a step closer to the circle. Two kids immediately got up and fled. The energy persisted—they were power sources.

That left a male and female.

The boy was dressed in black. A band's t-shirt draped over wide-legged pants. Accented with green they were adorned with chains. Fishnet gloves brought attention to his chipped black nail polish. He whipped his head to swoop the hair out of his eyes. He studied Garin with interest.

The female wore torn jeans and a college hoodie.

Nothing extraordinary, she looked as if she belonged in a library. Glaring over her glasses at Garin, she radiated power.

Garin returned the gaze. A spark of energy hit him, and his body tightened. It wasn't painful, but it did catch him off-guard.

Garin turned his gaze to the boy. "Go." The command hit the silence of the room like an anvil. It was a one-time offer. The boy considered it for a moment before looking to the girl.

Garin opened his wings and strode forward. The air became thick and heavy. When he proved that he could step into the circle uneasiness washed over the girl's face. She stood up, but just as quick Garin grabbed her by the shoulders and pushed her out of the protective circle. Closing his eyes, he let out a roar that shook the walls and rippled the water. Where his hands touched her shoulders, her skin turned grey and hardened. She shrieked, cursed, spit, and hissed at him but to no avail. He held her until silence filled the room.

"Blow the candles out and break the circle. If I ever see you again, you will join her." He didn't dare glance at the boy least he end him the same way. Instead, Garin reached down and picked up the kris. Holding the blade bare and bloodstained, he turned and left.

The wind burned his eyes. A release of emotion washed over him. His wingbeats slow, his muscles were unable to keep his flight steady. He hated ending a life, but he wouldn't stand by as she took more. The metal in his hand was a cold and constant reminder. Most of him hoped he'd saved her, yet there was a part that realized it would be simpler if he hadn't.

It was a clear night. The moon was high and full in

the sky. Shrugging off the chill, he focused back on his destination. Sanctuary.

~~~~~~

THERE WAS a squeak as he opened the door that he didn't remember from before. A soft glow outlined her sleeping form. She seemed to be resting peacefully and he crept closer to ensure she breathed. To his wonderment, the only blood he scented was older and drying. He moved closer and inhaled deeper. Did any whisper of the bitterness linger? Not even a hint.

The reality of her survival rushed to the surface. He had seen enough war and sickness to last a lifetime yet would never be immune to suffering. Easing himself into the chair he sat in earlier, he allowed himself to close his eyes and relax for a moment.

He opened his eyes and leaned back. Now here he was with a woman that could have been kin to the one he loved. There was an untapped strength in her. A perplexing paradox of innocence and untapped potential.

"This is not the same stone beast that came here looking to die."

Garin startled. His dreams had been wrapped up between his lost love and the wounded woman. He hadn't realized Aimee entered the room. He glanced at the at the monitor that just added a beep. Turning his gaze to Aimee, "I'll see to it that she lives, but that's all." His voice barely louder than a whisper. Looking back at Frankie he continued, "She's human."

"Aye, that she is," Aimee nodded. "And right now, I don't know of anyone else suited to ensuring that she doesn't fall prey to more of the same."

There was an intimation in Aimee's voice that

Garin caught. Something she was saying and not saying. Something...

"No! You know what would happen to her." The thought, even the hint of the thought, brought a rage through his bones that he never thought possible.

"I'm simply reminding you that it would solve your problems. The choice is yours." Aimee headed for the door. "Dawn is approaching. It may be easier to move her in the shadow of night. This is a lot of blood for some of our younger members to smell."

THE LAST EMBRACE of inky blackness of night filled up every crevice of the room. The dark cradled him with a familiarity that the day couldn't bring. The night had always been the security blanket that stood the test of time. The sun would reawaken the reality that he'd seen far too much and been too many places. His gypsy soul was old. Never in one place for too long, the modern convenience of an RV was exceptional. A bed, a coffee pot, and a door that locked. He didn't need anything else.

Except for tonight.

He was not about to rifle through her things to figure out where he should deposit her. His conscience sat too heavy to not ensure her safety. It was bad enough she'd wake up in a strange bed in a strange place with a wound that would take time to heal. He would not have her waking up beside a strange man as well. He laid her down in the only bed and pulled the thick blanket up around her.

Slipping out the door, he paced. Leaves crumpled underfoot, his hands tightened into fists until he lost feeling and tension caused his forearms to cramp in lightning bolts of pain. He forced himself to relax. Yet the cycle would begin again. He couldn't believe what Aimee had insinuated.

Perhaps she didn't know.

Walking towards one of the trees that surrounded the camper, he leaned against it and slumped to the ground. He kept replaying the past hours over in his head. How quick she'd become an addiction that he couldn't shake. He struggled to replace memories from earlier.

He wanted to erase how frail Frankie had felt under his hands and replace that with how strong he saw her in the club line. He could see her lips perfectly shaped with a prominent cupid's bow and her expressive eyes framed with lush lashes. The pure determination she had shown to live through the events of earlier. Maybe...

Aimee must have known. There was no way that she helped run that house full of every other beast under the sun and moon and didn't know. Females of his kind weren't born, they were made. They were made exactly how she alluded. If he should... It would take her mortality. It would... damn her to mirror his existence.

Rising to his feet, the pacing began once more. Worried about the noise, he sat down at the picnic table. In rage, his balled fist came down and splintered the wood. Then he heard the scream from within. Enraged with his own fury, he tore up the stairs and into the RV.

He hit a switch and soft lighting filled the room. She didn't seem to be awake but restless in the fevered sleep that comes with healing. She had rolled to her back, no wonder she screamed. Crawling into the cramped bedspace he grabbed a pillow. Garin eased her onto her side and placed the pillow at her lower back.

At his touch, she calmed. He stroked her face, pushing a stray lock of hair out of her face. He eased himself out of the bed. At once, she became restless, a low moan broke from her lips.

He raised an eyebrow and put a hand on her exposed arm. It didn't take but a moment for her to relax. It was settled. He kept contact with her as he unbuttoned his shirt. With another body in the space, it would heat up quick. He lifted each foot and removed his boots and socks. That left only his pants and those would stay.

He took his place behind her. He removed the pillow and pressed the front of his body against her back. There was no modest place to put his hand—either it was going to end up on her hips or across her breasts. Hips seemed less invasive. Exhaustion claimed him and within moments his eyelids dropped.

THE SUN CAME STREAMING through the windows and he stirred. He must have allowed himself some rest. He marshalled his strength and eased himself away from her. He needed coffee. He padded a few feet over and began to make a cup. He kept quiet to allow her to sleep.

THE ACTIVITY STIRRED her for the first time in hours. Frankie's eyelids fluttered and she stretched. She sat up and gasped at the pain. She looked down at a bandage wrapped around her ribs. She grabbed the blanket and pulled them tight to her upper body. Her panicked gaze found Garin only a few feet away. "I... what..." She shook her head trying to shake the fog away. "I remember the line at the club and then I wake up here?"

He cradled the coffee cup as if it were a magical elixir. He wanted so much to embrace her but dared not spook her. He opened his mouth to speak yet realized that he didn't have the words. "Would you like a cup of coffee?"

Frankie's nod was immediate. "Yeah, that sounds good."

With deft moves, Garin dropped in another pod. The filtered morning light filled the RV and soon the smell of dark, rich coffee filled the camper. "Milk, sugar?"

"Milk would be nice." She inhaled. Even in this weird predicament, she found he put her at ease.

One knee on the mattress, he handed her the coffee. After seeing her fumble with the blanket, he straightened, reached into an overhead storage cabinet, and produced a folded black t-shirt. He took a moment to shake it out before handing it to Frankie.

Elbows holding the blanket, she glanced around for a place to put the coffee cup. She saw Garin had turned his back in modest fashion. The shirt was so soft she took a moment to hug it. She eased both arms into the sleeves and lifted them to ease it over her head. A terrible whimper of pain broke free.

Garin whirled around, his eyes trying to find hers. Moving to the side of the bed, he reached to assist her slide the shirt over her head. He pulled back and took a deep steadying breath. "I will tell you everything that happened tonight, if you'll have it."

Frankie composed herself as best she could. She cradled the cup of coffee into her lap and turned gingerly toward him. They locked gazes in the moment before she nodded.

He took a sip of his coffee. Frankie took a moment to look at the shirt he had presented her. In white letters it clearly stated, *The Sanctuary*.

WENDIGO WEEKEND

HUNTER J SKYE

1

The fight broke out so fast I barely had time to duck. A flight attendant even smaller than I am rushed toward the row of seats behind me as two sweaty men threw awkward punches at each other's heads.

I'd thought a long weekend in New Orleans would give me a break from the nightly brawls and parking lot scuffles that broke out periodically where I worked at *Custer's Bar and Grill*. It was expected in Hell's Canyon, South Dakota. There wasn't much else to entertain. But twenty thousand feet in the air was entirely the wrong place for a dust-up.

"So, what brings you to New Orleans?" The giant bear of a man in the seat next to me rumbled. His calm conversational tone showed not the slightest hint of stress over the raging fist fight behind him. I grabbed my naked wrist where my anxiety bracelet usually hung. My grandmother had strung the "worry beads" together for me and crafted a sturdy metal clasp.

When I was a child, I'd fiddle with it whenever I felt stressed. Now that I was older, all I needed was to touch the beads and I'd instantly feel better. But I had been sure I'd leave the bracelet in a storage bin at the airport security station, so I'd decided to leave the precious jewelry behind. Now, I felt exposed and vulnerable without it.

"Um," I stammered, searching for an appropriate answer to the handsome man's question. I couldn't look into those simmering blue eyes and tell the truth. *I met a cute guy, Simon, on the internet and like any red-blooded, sex-starved, twenty-three-year-old woman, I cyber-stalked him. Now, I'm on a plane concocting a way to casually bump into him at his favorite bar in the French Quarter.*

Ari, you're an idiot, I reminded myself.

"Just needed a long weekend." I tried to sound casual. "Somewhere fun." I smiled, looking down so that my chocolate brown lashes swept over my hazel eyes. Oh, God. I'm flirting. I tore my gaze from the golden-haired mountain of muscles to see several flight attendants taping the two fighters to their seats. Applause filled the cabin.

"We don't want any trouble." My seatmate shifted his weight and gave me a penetrating look. "Make it a quick one."

I tilted my head in confusion. His ice blue gaze slid up and down my body for one slow, heart-pounding moment, then he turned away. What was that supposed to mean? Maybe it was my first taste of Cajun sarcasm. I looked down at my outfit. My floral blouse, skinny-cut jeans and strappy sandals were as sexy as my wardrobe got. I guess I needed to spice it up a little before I hit the locals bar where Simon's favorite band, the Howlers, would be performing. I wanted to look good for my six-foot, green-eyed computer guy who loves rock music and restoring antique cars.

There were no men in Hell's Canyon except for

sunburned tourists and whiskey-soured old men. If Simon looked even remotely like the Creole dream he made himself out to be on social media, he was about to get really lucky. This shy prairie girl hadn't had a date in two years. It was time to end my dry spell.

Ding. The buckle seatbelts sign glowed to life above me. It felt like an omen for the whole weekend.

BUTTERFLIES SET OUT lawn chairs in my stomach, lit fireworks, and proceeded to throw a block party. I couldn't even eat I was so nervous. The band would be starting in a half hour. Simon might already be at Sanctuary. I paced outside my hotel's restaurant going over my opening line.

On the other side of the plate glass windows, refined customers sipped wine and sampled delicacies I'd never heard of. I hadn't meant to select such an upscale hotel, but they'd had a cancellation and I was a lunatic with a credit card.

What am I doing here? Turn around, get your things, and go home, my inner voice chided. You can't meet a stranger. It's too dangerous. I reached for my missing bracelet and my fingers came up empty.

Something thudded against the glass next to me. I turned to see a woman gripping a steak so rare a chef would call it blue in her hands. She gnawed at the red meat with pearly teeth. Pink juice dripped down her chin as she shook her head from side to side in an attempt to rip a large chunk of fat loose.

"Good Lord." I stared in shock.

Passersby slowed as they took in the carnal sight. A waiter approached the couple's table and leaned in to speak to them. The well-dressed man at the table spoke to the woman and then the waiter. The woman lunged at the waiter and was now straddling him on the floor with meat still dangling from her mouth. A collective gasp rose on the street as the small group of pedestrians stepped back from the window.

I hesitated for a moment, not sure what to do. When a police officer showed up, the spell that held us in place lifted and we numbly walked away. I knew the Big Easy was an eccentric town, but that was something out of a zombie movie.

I checked my phone. There was just enough time to walk to the bar and order a drink before the band took the stage.

"Hi. Hey. Um, hey there. You look familiar. Is your name Simon?" I practiced as I walked. No one heard me over the bouncing music and jabbering street vendors. The buttery sweet scent of beignets drifted on the evening air. I took in the laughter and colors and sizzling smiles. On the corner ahead of me, three men threw dice and slapped each other in an animated way. On the other side of the intersection a cluster of motorcycles lined the corner bar. Sanctuary!

I'd just about reached the dice game when the slaps turned to punches and out of nowhere, a shiny gun appeared in one of the men's hands. Shouts lifted over the din of music and voices. People turned and ran in every direction. I froze for a second, gaze locked on the gun. A mesmerizing moment later a tall blond man dressed in biker leather and built like a monument to some gorgeous god stepped out of the shadows and grabbed the gun.

"You're done for the night. Split the money evenly and go home."

"But—" the man still holding the dice started to

complain. The giant turned his glacial gaze on him, and any arguments faded to silence.

"And you—" The second he turned away from the trio, they ran. The big man pocketed the gun and looked to be walking straight toward me. The tiny possibility that there was another seven-foot tall, excruciatingly handsome guy with laser blue eyes in New Orleans shrank to nothing as he pointed a thick finger at me. He was the man from the airplane.

"I thought I told you we didn't want any trouble."

"W—what?" My voice was a whisper as the man came to a stop in front of me.

"You think you can wreak havoc in our city for your own twisted pleasure then bail without so much as an apology?" He towered over me, muscles tensing for a fight. I blinked up at him. Shock and fear arm-wrestled in my brain. Fear won and I took a nervous step backward. My dressy but extremely impractical high-heeled sandal turned sideways taking my ankle with it. I yelped.

The big man's head tilted, and his shapely brow furrowed in thought.

"Apology? I—I'm sorry. Whatever I did, I'm sorry." I tripped over my words. My heart pounded against my ribs, and I took another step back.

"Jace," the man boomed and someone across the street answered. "Come here and bring your nose." I heard booted feet walk up behind me. "Smell this," the man jabbed his thick finger at me again.

"What Papa Bear wants Papa Bear gets." I turned in time to see another grinning, sex-on-a-stick blond with piercing blue eyes and rope upon rope of hard muscles on display beneath his tight-fitting T-shirt.

I kicked off my heels and turned to run in the direction everyone else had fled when two solid hands locked me in place. First, this person sniffed my hair, then my clothes.

"What do you think?" Papa Bear asked him.

"I gotta admit I didn't believe you when you said you sat next to a Wendigo on the plane, but there's no mistaking that scent."

"A Wendi—what?"

Two pairs of eyes fixed on me.

"You don't know what you are?"

"I'm, I'm a woman who's late for a date and if I don't show, he'll call the police." I tried to sound assertive. I wasn't a good liar.

"We can't leave her here to wreck the city."

"No." The bulky behemoth named Papa Bear glared at me.

"We could kill her."

"No, no. No, no, no. Listen, you want me to leave? I'll leave. I'm on the next flight out. Trust me, I'm happy to go. This town is nuts. I've never seen so many psychos in one place."

They exchanged a look between themselves and then a shrug.

"And you don't know why you've seen so many psychos?"

"What?" My voice was high enough for dogs to hear a mile away.

"Maybe Carson can explain this," the sharp-eyed man beside me offered. Papa Bear seemed to agree. He locked a big hand on my thin shoulder and steered me across the street. "You're coming with us."

WHEN WE PASSED through the door, I noticed a marquis with the words "Come in peace, or leave in pieces." I wondered at the sort of clientele that would require such a warning. The inside of Sanctuary was hot and loud. Someone ran through a collection of repetitive, ear-piercing notes as they tuned an electric guitar on stage.

We wound past the bar and skirted the edge of the boisterous crowd. A woman turned to me, and her eyes lit with a fiery glow. I watched in wonder as she grabbed the nearest guy and stuck her tongue down his throat. The man didn't seem to care, but the woman he was with turned a livid red.

"Knock it off!" A hand shoved my back so hard I stumbled forward. Someone caught me before I hit the floor. I clung to the strong hands that helped me. I straightened and looked into a pair of pale green eyes. Simon's eyes.

"You okay?" His smile. His dimples. His dark, curly hair.

"It's you," was all I could say before I was rushed away. The last thing I saw was Simon's delicious, shapely eyebrow quirk in bewilderment and then the crowd swallowed him.

THEY TOOK me up one floor to what looked like a miniature hospital or maybe a vet's office. Downstairs, the first song started, but we were far enough from the bar to easily hear over the music. We crowded into an examination room and the music thinned again.

"What have we here?" The man they referred to as Carson tucked his stunning, jet-black hair behind his ear. He had a powerful build and dark brown eyes as sharp as a hawk's. His Indigenous American features were filled with calm, contemplative curiosity.

I wanted to sob to him that I'd been abducted by these two gargantuan psychopaths, but something told me I was looking at psychopath number three.

"She's a shifter, but her scent is corrupted." The gruff blond who went by the name Jace gripped me by my arms and shoved me toward the man with the stethoscope hanging out of his pocket. "Smell."

The dark-haired man did more than sniff my hair. After a moment of consideration, he closed his eyes and raised his hands. Carson didn't touch me. His hands hovered a few inches from my body as if groping my aura.

"Cannibal Curse." The words fell from his mouth like rotten meat.

I'd heard those words before as a child but couldn't recall their meaning. I pushed away from him and watched his expression sour. Jace's hold weakened and allowed my move.

"I met a few up north near the Canadian border. Not a good crowd." Carson spoke to the men but looked at me. Why did I feel insulted when I didn't even comprehend what they were going on about? It didn't matter—this conversation was headed to a dark place. I needed to return to the land of the sane. I scanned the room for another exit.

"Can someone—" Jace waved a hand at me, "—be a Wendigo and not know it?"

"No." Carson answered without thinking. "That's impossible. The hunger for human flesh, the obsessive thoughts devour them if they deny their nature. Even if she didn't know, the evil can't be overlooked." The dark-haired man leaned in so close it felt like he was going to kiss me. "There's simply no way."

I shook with terror and my eyes began to flood

with tears. My inner voice was having a field day with the "I told you, SOS".

"I, I have some money saved up. You can have it. All of it. I want to go back to my hotel, pack my bag, and you'll never see me again." I tried to sound calm and nonchalant. The quaver in every word gave me away. "No more Wendigos." The truth was I would gladly write off my bag and go straight to the airport.

The three men exchanged another one of those wordless glances.

"Go get Lo," Papa Bear instructed gently. He pulled a chair over and gestured for me to sit. Jace nodded and disappeared through the door we'd entered from.

A few minutes later, Jace returned with a beautiful blonde woman. Her warm blue eyes scanned me thoroughly, then she turned her scrutiny on the collection of men. Her sturdy glare settled on Papa Bear.

"What have you dragged into my bar?" She whipped an apron off her muscular curves and sauntered over to the giant man.

I started to stand but a hefty hand clapped my shoulder and pressed down.

"This is—?" Papa Bear gave me a questioning look.

"Ari. My name is Ari," I rushed to answer.

"This is Ari. She's the one I told you about from the airplane."

"Hmm. I see what you mean. What's wrong with her scent?"

"That sweet smell overlaying the rot, but with no signs of decomposition? It's similar to a real Wendigo, but it's actually a hereditary Wendigo," Carson explained, circling me like a bird of prey.

"Hereditary?" the men and I all asked at once.

What the hell are they saying?

"You didn't know the Wendigo nature could be passed from generation to generation?"

"No," the big blond sounded genuinely surprised.

If the conversation didn't involve me, maybe I didn't need to be there at all. I leaned forward and made it a few inches out of my chair before I was pushed back down again.

"Yeah. Somewhere in that gorgeous little thing's ancestry was a desperate, possibly deranged fucker who, for whatever reason, feasted on human flesh. It happened more than you'd think back in the harder centuries. That act of cannibalism turned her ancestor into a Wendigo." He peered at me. "Somehow the creature still managed to reproduce."

We all stared dumbly at the handsome doctor-slash-shaman...guy.

"So, you're saying I'm a cannibal?" I found my voice.

"No. I'm saying someone in your family line was and you carry the curse he or she earned."

"Whoa. Talk about family drama," Jace piped up in a less than helpful way.

"Be careful though. She can still induce obsessive thoughts in others. The mantle of the Wendigo eventually leads to insanity. Either hers or someone else's. It's inevitable."

What in the name of all that's holy? I'm just a waitress from the Black Hills of South Dakota. I come from a line of miners and schoolteachers.

"I hate to contradict you, but there are no monsters in my family tree."

"She's shaking. Hand me that blanket." The woman they'd called Lo took a soft woven throw from Jace and wrapped it around my shoulders. Even though she barely looked a year or two older than me, she had a motherly energy that made me want to seek shelter in her arms.

"Something must be inhibiting the curse." Carson squinted at the space around me.

"I followed her from the airport. She seems unaware of the effect she has on others."

My mind yanked me back to the brawl on the airplane right behind me. Oh God, the woman in the restaurant. An image of her bleached white teeth trying desperately to rip her steak apart. And then, the men playing dice on the corner outside. The rage, the trembling, the gun.

"No." I spoke to no one. "No, no." All eyes settled on me. "That, ha-ha, that can't be. What are you even talking about?" My head swam. I shrugged out of the blanket as the room heated.

"Have you shifted yet?"

"Have I *what*? No."

"You smell like you're close." Jace growled and I could have sworn his eyes started to glow with a cerulean light.

Close? Close to what? A bunch of wackos? A nervous breakdown? Being turned into a skin suit? All the above? I needed a glass of water.

"How has she survived this long without going insane or killing people?" Lo asked with a look of genuine concern.

"Killing people?" I gaped.

"Have you killed people?" Jace questioned.

"NO!" I stood. Papa Bear tried to push me down again, but I knocked his hand away. Everyone's jaw dropped and they quickly stepped away from the huge man. Sweat beaded on my skin. "Why is it so hot in here?"

"Papa Bear, let's try and manage this situation,"

The woman soothed as the grizzly bear of a man clenched his hands into fists. "Carson, is there anything we can do to stop her from shifting?"

The tension level in the room climbed with every thundering beat of my heart.

"There's one thing." Carson jabbed a finger in the air. "The Anasazi Indians had a big problem with Wendigos during a certain time in their tribe's history. Their medicine men designed symbols to drive away the monsters. They painted them on boulders, houses, and stones. They even wore beads with the signs etched into them."

My hand went to my wrist and four pairs of eyes followed the movement.

"My bracelet." I started to hyperventilate. Anxiety washed over me. "My bracelet has symbols etched into the worry beads." I heard myself talking but didn't recognize my voice. The lower notes rang hollow like the wind as it cut through the canyon back home.

"Where is it?"

"I left it at home."

"Where's home?"

"South Dakota."

Jace shook his head gravely. "Well, shit."

This was all too much. My life flashed before my eyes as I pieced together every bit of crazed behavior I'd ever witnessed. Could I have been the common denominator for every fight at the bar? Every lecherous grope or desperate gamble? How many times had I watched a tourist overeat at *Custer's* Saturday night buffet to the point of vomiting? Could those incidents have been avoided if I'd simply worn my bracelet? Why hadn't my grandmother told me about the curse? Fresh fear crept over me. What else has Grandma not told me?

Several things happened at once. The light dimmed in the room, and it felt as though I was rising out of my body. I looked down to see that I wasn't rising so much as stretching. My leg muscles burned as my thighs lengthened. My joints screamed as they rearranged themselves under my burning skin.

"Can you remember what the symbols look like?" Lo dug through a drawer in a small desk. She took out a notepad and a pencil. "Hold her down." She ordered and the men launched at me. I hit the floor under a pile of straining muscle. "Free her hand." Papa Bear let go of my lower arm.

"Listen to Nicolette," Jace's voice strained. I focused past him to the woman they'd now referred to as Nicolette. Lo must be her nickname. The stray thought distracted me, calmed me for a second.

"It's going to be okay. Take this and draw the symbols on the beads."

I fought for a view of the notepad on the floor. Nicolette pushed the pencil into my hand. I tried twice to grasp it, but my fingers seemed to be expanding. My nails thickened, scraping the floor. I got the pencil in my hand and did my best to scribble the first symbol. She turned the page, and I drew the second sign. The third glyph was harder to draw. It had smaller intersecting lines with a circle above it.

"Let me help." Nicolette took the pencil from me and drew the rest of the symbols exactly as I described. She finished as a wave of insatiable hunger washed over me. When was the last time I'd eaten? I couldn't remember. All I knew was that I was unbelievably starved. Hungry enough to eat a horse. Hungry enough to eat... Oh, God.

I struggled against the men piled on top of me. A deep, guttural growl tore from my throat. Below us the music changed tempo and the crowd howled. I roared and voices below us screamed together as one raging beast.

Papa Bear's hand fastened on my throat, or maybe it was Jace's. I couldn't tell. I was blinded by my need, my craving, my thirst.

"Help me!" I managed to cry.

Nicolette dug in the desk and came back with a black marker. "Give me her wrist."

The next few moments were a blur of pressing bodies and howling need. Each wave of hunger felt darker, more corrupted. My mind drifted to places I could never have imagined. Visions came and went. One moment I was lying on the floor in the strange little hospital. The next, I was loping over the empty grasslands baying at the cold moon and searching for living flesh.

Something sharp and long stabbed at my head and the men readjusted their grip. I caught a glimpse of movement in the corner of a mirror hanging on the opposite wall. Red, roaring pain sliced through my head as something pointed and grooved pushed from my skull.

Antlers.

The cool tip of the marker dragged across my skin, drawing tingling lines on my wrist. The tingling turned to burning. Before I knew it, my wrist burned with white hot fire. All twelve of the etchings my grandmother had carved for my bracelet stretched across my skin.

Cool air washed over me and suddenly the weight on top of me was crushing.

"I. Can't. Breathe!"

Slowly, and with wary glances, the men eased off me. With a burning blush across my cheeks, I tugged my little black skirt back in place. One of the spaghetti straps on my top had torn so I stuffed it out of sight. Every move was a process as my muscles jerked and spasmed as my limbs returned to their original proportions. Everyone stared down at me as the quivering finally stopped. My hand drifted to my head. The only trace of the antlers was two tender spots on my scalp.

"What happened?" I asked weakly.

"You started to shift."

"I—I'm sorry." I sat up and the room tipped a little.

"Nice work," Papa Bear wrapped his giant arms around Nicolette.

Someone handed me a shot of tequila and then offered a hand up. What kind of doctor's office had liquor in it? The kind located over a bar, I guessed. I swallowed the golden liquid before I could think better of it and gaped at the ancient language scrawled around my wrist. Had Nicolette not thought to recreate my bracelet, what would have happened to me? Would they have been forced to rip my throat out? What was I going to do now that I knew I had an evil curse swimming through my veins?

"My grandmother has some explaining to do."

"I'd say so," Nicolette offered a comforting smile.

"Why did you help me? You could have just killed me."

"We call this place Sanctuary for a reason." Nicolette's soft words held a world of meaning.

"If we couldn't have stopped your shift, you'd be dead now." Carson explained. "Wendigos are creatures of chaos, and no one really knows the limits of their powers."

"What am I supposed to do now?" The words felt small and hopeless.

"Learn all you can from your family," Papa Bear answered.

"Educate yourself on the Anasazi and their particular brand of magic," Carson added.

"Breathe," Nicolette advised and opened her arms. I gladly walked into the hug.

"And have another one of these," Jace poured a second shot and handed it to me.

"Thanks for not killing me."

"You bet." Papa Bear clapped me roughly on the back.

"You know that Wendigo is pretty strong, little girl." A stunning smile spread across Jace's face. "I bet you could take Papa Bear in the ring."

"Ha," Papa Bear's chuckle sounded like a growl. Nicolette laughed and Carson seemed to be sizing me up.

Somewhere on the first floor a cute guy was listening to his favorite band and having a beer with friends. Simon was the reason I was here. The reason I'd discovered my family's curse.

"There's a guy downstairs. I was supposed to meet him. I—" My eyes burned with a new swell of tears. If what they were saying was true, how could I be anywhere near Simon? How can I be near anyone?

"How long will the marker symbols last?" Papa Bear asked.

"If she doesn't wash her arm, the charm should last long enough for her to make it back home."

"What would we do without you?" The blond giant kissed her on the head.

Nicolette gave him a contented smile. "Let's explain a few things to Ari and let her have a little fun downstairs. Then we'll move her flight and get her home before the symbols begin to fade."

"Agreed."

❧

BODIES THRASHED and hair whipped as the drums hammered and the guitars rang. The lead singer's voice pulsed through me, commanding me to surrender to the moment. Or maybe it was the tequila. I swam through the jostling crowd, bouncing and gyrating with the bodies around me.

"Hey!" Someone shouted in my ear. I turned to see sparkling seafoam green eyes surrounded by thick dark lashes. "Don't I know you?" Simon's lips bumped against me as he yelled into my ear. I savored the sensation as it spread warmth through my entire body. I leaned close to answer him. Close enough that my breasts pressed into his sweaty T-shirt. His arm came up in response and fastened around my waist.

"Yeah, you're Simon, right?"

"Yeah." He gave me an excited look.

"I'm Ari. We're friends online. I meant to tell you I was coming to town." I lowered my lashes and gave him a seductive look. "I remembered you mentioning how good the Howlers were, so I thought I'd catch a show." His wide mouth spread into a gorgeous smile. I felt the sudden compulsion to lick his thick bottom lip and suck it into my mouth. Oh, God. Was that the Wendigo talking? I looked down at the circle of symbols drawn around my wrist like a bracelet. Had they stopped working?

I glanced nervously at the crowd to see if my ancestral curse was leaking out of me again. Dancers swayed and nodded to the crashing beat of the drums. A few customers howled, while others sang along with the lyrics. No one behaved unusually. It was a normal

Saturday night at the best bar in town. Drinks were flowing and everyone was happy.

Besides, after everything Papa Bear and Nicolette had shared with me, I knew there were plenty of individuals in the crowd who were ready to rip me out of this situation if things went south. I was safe for the moment and so was Simon.

"I'm glad you came." His other arm came up and pulled me into a hug.

"Me too." I smiled. "You're even cuter in person." This time I let my lips brush his ear. He shuddered against me.

The first set ended, and the crowd shoved its way to the bar. Someone bumped into me from behind and I staggered into Simon. He pulled me close and anchored us in place as bodies shoved around us.

"How long are you here for?"

"Just tonight."

Disappointment washed over his face, then something deliciously devious replaced it.

"Well then, we better make the best of the time we have."

I met his desirous gaze with an invitation. I tipped my chin, and he lowered his mouth to mine. I melted into him as his hot, moist lips devoured mine. We both came away from the kiss breathless.

He lifted my hand to those luscious lips and laid a warm kiss on my palm. "Cool tattoo. What is it?"

I looked at the temporary markings. I had so many questions, so much to learn. "A piece of my heritage."

He gave me an approving smile and kissed me again.

BAYOU HONEYMOON

LEIGH BULLIS

1

———

Rafe drove too fast for the conditions. The snow was coming down heavily. The roads were getting slicker by the minute. It might be a few months late, but he was taking his wife on a real honeymoon.

The truck skidded to a stop in front of the ranch house. Rafe ran up the front porch steps and stomped the snow from his boots. "Jamie. Jamie, I got the tickets!"

Jamison appeared at the end of the hall. "What tickets?"

"Our tickets." He started to walk down the hall when she held up her hand and pointed to his wet boots.

"Devon is waiting on me. I have to go back out." Rafe held out the tickets to her.

When she got close, Rafe snaked an arm around her waist, pulled her close, and kissed her. When he lifted his head, his breath caught in his throat. Her shimmering emerald eyes told him how much she loved him. He forgot the tickets. "Mmm," he whispered against her lips before he sealed them with his own again. It took everything he had to step back. He turned and reached for the door, realized he still had the tickets, turned quick, winked, and handed them to her. Jamison shivered in the blast of cold as the door opened and closed.

Jamison looked at the plane tickets as she walked back to the kitchen. "Well Ty, I guess we are going on a honeymoon."

❧

DEVON PULLED the truck up the curb. "Rafe, get one of those carts to get the bags out of the back. Don't let her lift anything. You do, you got to answer to me."

"I promise, I won't let anything happen to anyone." Rafe went to get a luggage cart.

Devon turned to Jamison in the back seat. "You okay, little momma? You're looking a little green."

Jamison swallowed, "Yes, I'm fine."

Rafe opened the back door and held out a hand. Jamison stepped out onto the sidewalk in front of the terminal. Rafe shook hands with Devon. "We'll call when we head back."

Devon nodded. "Have a good time."

Rafe closed the door and waved Devon off. He turned and put his arm around Jameson's shoulders and pulled her close. "I love you, you know that, right?"

"I love you too," she whispered.

❧

"LADIES AND GENTLEMEN, we will be landing in New Orleans in about fifteen minutes. Please take your seats and fasten your seat belts. The temperature is a balmy 78 degrees with plenty of sunshine. Enjoy your stay and thank you for flying with us today."

Rafe took Jamison's hand and squeezed it reassuringly when he noticed her white-knuckled hold on the arm rest.

"I don't think your son likes to travel."

Rafe put his big warm hand on her belly. "He better behave, or he will have me to answer to." Rafe's eyes widened when he felt the baby kick. "Does it hurt?" He noticed Jamison wince.

"Not really, it just surprises me. It's not like he hollers out, 'I have to stretch my legs.'"

"We'll be on the ground soon." He continued to hold her hand as they felt the plane begin to descend.

※

AN HOUR later Jamison was laying on the big soft bed in the hotel. She curled onto her side and grabbed another pillow to hug. "So much better."

"Good. Need anything? Food? Drink?"

"No," she yawned.

Rafe leaned down and kissed her. "You nap. I'll be back."

Jamison nodded sleepily and closed her eyes. She never heard him leave the room.

Rafe stopped at the front desk of the hotel.

"Can I help you, *cher*?" The woman behind the counter enquired. She was middle-aged, Rafe guessed. Her hair was pulled back away from her face, and he thought he saw a glint of recognition in her eyes.

"I honestly don't know." He put his hat on the counter. "I'm looking for some tourist information."

"Welcome to our beautiful city. There is shopping of course. The smaller shops will have local treasures to explore. There are many restaurants that offer a variety of flavors. Music will fill the air as you stroll

along our famous streets. And our cemeteries have become legendary if you care to take a tour."

Rafe's brow furrowed at her words. Cemeteries?
He tipped his head, "Thank you." Rafe headed back to
the room. Cemeteries? Who goes to cemeteries on
their honeymoon?

Back in the room he stopped by the bed and shook
out a light blanket to cover Jamison. His thoughts travelled back over the last six months.

Jamison had come back from New York. She'd said
she loved him, and her life wouldn't be complete
without him. He remembered their wedding day.
When asked, she'd said, "We do" instead of the
normal "I do." It was her way of telling everyone she
carried his child.

The faraway look in his eyes disappeared as his
gaze focused on Jamison. She was awake and watching
him as memories replayed in his head.

"Hungry?" His voice barely above a whisper.

She poked her belly. "This one is hungry." She sat
upright on the edge of the bed. "I guess I could do
with something too."

"Well, then, come on family, let go find something
to eat." He walked to her and held out a hand.

When they passed through the lobby the woman
behind the counter smiled, "Take care of the babe. He
is special."

They both glanced at her as they walked by. The
warm New Orleans sunshine embraced them as they
stepped beyond the hotel doorway. It was a welcome
change after the cold of Wyoming.

"What do you think she meant?" Jamison reached
out to take Rafe's hand looking back at the door.

Rafe shook his head. "I don't know.".

"She kind of creeps me out," Jamison muttered.

"Forget her, we have New Orleans." Rafe pushed his hat low over his brow. They started walking down the street. "What are you hungry for? We have burgers." He pointed to a place advertising their menu.

"We can get burgers at home. Let's find something different, something local."

They continued down the sidewalk, sidestepping others as they strolled along. Jamison gazed at all the different colored buildings and the amazingly intricate ironwork on the balconies above them. She spotted a sign above a doorway, *Cajun Shrimp, and Gumbo*. "What about over there?"

"Think you're up to spicy food? You didn't have such a good time flying in. I don't want dinner tonight to ruin your trip."

"Oh, I'm fine. I think we can handle a little spice tonight."

"Your wish is my command." He winked at Jamison, the gold flecks in his eyes glowing. He opened the door to the small restaurant and allowed Jamison to walk in first.

A young girl came up to them with an armload of menus. "Just two?"

"Yes, please." Rafe said, then looked at Jamison. "Well, maybe three."

The girl chuckled. "I think we can handle that." She took them to a table, handed them menus, and with a brisk nod, "Your server will be with you shortly."

An hour later, Jamison wiped her fingers on a crisp white napkin. She sat back in her chair. "That was delicious. I think I could get used to the food here."

Rafe finished off his beer. "Can't say I disagree." He looked at the mess of empty dishes littering the table.

The server came back. "Can I get anything else for you? Dessert? Another drink?"

Rafe glanced at Jamison, who shook her head. The server looked through a stack of receipts and laid one face down on the table. "Thank you for coming. We hope to see you again." She nodded and walked away.

Back out on the sidewalk Rafe raked his fingers through his motley blondish hair and settled his hat on his head. Dusk fell over the city painting the sky with golden oranges, pinks, and purples. The gas lamps burned, giving an old-fashioned glow to the street. Street bands played softer blues music. Some people danced but most simply stopped to enjoy. The clop of horse hooves could be heard as they pulled carriages along the street.

They strolled the city streets as they headed back to the hotel. Just outside the hotel door Jamison stopped. Rafe turned to face her. He wiped a stray tear from her cheek.

"This place is so beautiful Rafe. Thank you for bringing me."

"All for you, love, all for you." Rafe wrapped her in a warm hug and kissed her forehead.

❧

JAMISON WOKE WITH A START. She had been snuggled close to Rafe until the baby kicked. She crawled out of the king size bed and grabbed a robe to cover her nakedness. Rafe had been gentle as he normally was these days but delivered on the spicy dessert he'd promised. Jamison headed toward the bathroom unaware her husband was awake and watching.

Rafe was propped in bed when she came back.

"I'm sorry, I didn't mean to wake you."

"You didn't, the lack of you did. It got cold without you two in here with me." He ran his hand across the soft white sheets.

Jamison shrugged. "You know how it is these days."

"Yes, he seems to interrupt quite often." Rafe looked at her belly with a mock scowl.

"You just wait," Jamison quipped back.

Rafe patted the bed. "This is empty." He raised an eyebrow inviting her back to bed.

Jamison shook her head. "Later."

Rafe threw back the covers and exposed his nakedness. Jamison giggled. "Just what were you expecting this morning?"

"I really enjoyed dessert last night. I was hoping for another helping this morning. But I see how this is going to go." He swung his legs over the side of the bed. "Some honeymoon this is going to be."

Jamison walked over, opened the robe, and sat down on his lap. She placed her hands on his shoulders. "Anytime with you." She leaned into the kiss. In time, Rafe picked her up and laid her on the bed then made love to his wife.

❧

"So, what is on the agenda today?" She sat at the little table in front of the window. She had pulled the heavy curtains back leaving the sheers in place to hide them from prying eyes.

"This is your honeymoon. You lead the way, I will follow."

"This is our honeymoon. We're in this together."

"Well, sometime this week I want to go out to the

bayou. I think I'll be safe out there. It won't be safe to run in the city. There are too many people."

"My wolf. Yes, you must go run. Who knows, you might make friends out there." Jamison knew if her wolf didn't run often enough, he became short tempered and hard to live with. At the ranch he could run whenever he wanted. She never knew how far he went or what he did when he turned wolf, but he would come home muddy or bloody or both, and always exhausted. "Just let me know when you head out. This is unfamiliar territory. I don't need you getting beat up by another pack."

Rafe nodded. His Jamie had come a long way in six months. It wasn't often a werewolf married outside the pack and especially with a human. He'd felt the connection from the first moment he'd seen her arrive in Smokey Creek.

"I was thinking of shopping. You know, souvenirs for people back home."

Rafe looked skeptical. "Okay. I'm sure there are hundreds of places to check out." He rolled his eyes as he crawled out of the bed.

Jamison dressed while he was in the bathroom. Rafe had no problem being naked around her or showing her how much he wanted to make love to her.

Jamison rolled her eyes and giggled. "You're going to have to strap that thing in for the moment my love."

"Damn it, I was hoping you'd still be naked and take care of it for me."

"Later." Jamison licked her lips. Rafe groaned. "Shopping. Remember?"

"Yes. Shopping." Rafe reached for his jeans. Jamison would never get tired of watching him move. He pulled a t-shirt down over his torso, combed his fingers through his hair, and grabbed his hat. "Ready?"

"Um," spying her bag hanging on a chair, she slung the small purse over her shoulder. "Yep."

As they walked out onto the street, they smelled the city waking up. They found a small cafe that touted fresh coffee and beignets. Order in hand, they walked back out to the sun-soaked street. Jamison took a sip of the strong black brew and smiled. The dark roast, full-body flavor was there, but it was a little sweeter, nuttier. "This is good. I want to take some home."

Rafe took a sip of his and wrinkled his nose. "If you say so. Remind me next time to order regular coffee, not the local stuff."

"You don't like it?"

"It's do-able. Just doesn't taste like real coffee. Too sweet." Rafe handed over his cup so he could open the bag of French donuts. He took his cup as he offered the opened bag to Jamison. She reached in and pulled out the square, sugar-covered pastry. She took a bite and groaned. Ether she was very hungry, or her taste buds were made for New Orleans food.

Rafe grinned at her enjoyment and took one for himself. He looked at it skeptically but judging from Jamison's reactions, it couldn't be that bad. He sank his teeth into the sweetness and had to agree. "These I can handle. We should get some for later."

Jamison nodded and licked the sugar from her fingers.

They walked, talked, and admired the city as they munched. When the bag was empty, Rafe crumpled it and tossed it in a trash can. He had less than a half cup of coffee left and tossed that in the can as well. He would find a place that sold regular coffee somewhere.

"Rafe, look, over there." Jamison pointed to a small shop with a wooden sign over the door that read, *The Wolf and Moon*. Skepticism written on his face, he took her hand and led her across the street. The warm smell of incense greeted them as he opened the door. It wasn't overpowering, just a gentle welcoming scent that filled the air.

Jamison stopped and tensed, then he felt her relax. The brilliant glimmer of her eyes told him she'd had one of her visions. Jamison came from a long line of very powerful witches. Although not raised by them and unaware of her heritage until recently, she was learning. She became more accepting of her gift with each vision. "Everything okay?"

"Yes." She nodded. She dropped his hand and took a deep breath. Her gaze roamed around the shop. A woman appeared from the back room. The slender dark-skinned woman hesitated in the doorway. Jamison was struck by her vivid green eyes. She seemed to recognize Jamison but that was impossible. "Welcome, *cherie*. What are you shopping for today?"

"Just looking. We've never been to New Orleans before. I wanted to take some gifts home."

"I understand. Look at your leisure. Let me know if I can assist."

"Thank you, I will." Jamison turned to look at Rafe and realized he wasn't comfortable in the store. "If you want to wait outside you can. I won't be long."

"No, it's okay." Rafe waved his hat to indicate an empty corner of the shop. "I'll be over here." Rafe watched her turn and pick up a basket.

"Hello." The slender woman walked toward Rafe. "You've travelled a long way." She turned beside him and watched Jamison.

"Yes. How did you know?" Rafe looked at her.

"Your presence is known here."

Rafe shook his head. "No, I'm pretty sure no one knows who we are. We live in Wyoming."

"The bayou will know you." She smiled. If she meant to shock, his expression said she missed. She nodded and straightened from her position beside him.

"Who are you?"

"I apologize, my name is Menyara." She answered as she walked away.

Rafe frowned, as if that explained anything. His gaze followed her as she walked toward Jamison, who was looking at a shelf of beautifully carved horses. Distracted from the shop keeper's hints his next thought was, *Cara will love them.*

"Those are beautiful, no? They are all made by a local, Quinn Peltier." The quiet voice came from behind Jamison. "I think you have found one you like?" Menyara picked up a sculpture. The horse's mane was carved wild into the air as he reared onto his back legs. A stallion to be sure. She held it out to Jamison.

Jamison looked enthralled as she ran her index finger along the grain of the wood from main to tail. She nodded. "I'll take it."

Menyara's smile seemed secretive. "Is this all for today?"

Jamison held up the basket with a few items nestled in the bottom. She glanced toward Rafe and waved him over.

Menyara checked them out, wrapping the purchases for their trip home.

"Can you have that delivered to the hotel for us?" He nodded toward the box.

"Yes, of course. You wouldn't want this damaged

before you give it to your mother." Menyara spoke to Jamison.

Jamison's eyes widened in shock. She was sure she hadn't mentioned her mother.

"Don't look so startled, little dove. We are all aware." The woman flipped her gaze to Rafe. "Your wolf takes care of his dove and the wolf-to-be."

Rafe nodded, suddenly uncomfortable being around this woman. "Yes."

"I will send these to your lodgings. Enjoy your stay."

Jamison reached for Rafe's hand. His look stopped her words until they were outside. "She reminds me of the woman at the hotel. Knowing stuff like that." Rafe nodded as they walked away from the store.

They weaved their way through the city until they came across the Cafe du Monde French Market. "Let's check this out. I smell real coffee." Rafe said hoping for a place to sit for a few minutes. He ordered regular coffee while Jamison ordered iced tea and a basket of Cajun shrimp and fries. They found a table in the sun and watched as a ship made its way toward the Gulf.

"This has been wonderful. Thank you." Jamison sipped the last of her iced tea. "Now, what would you like to do? You've catered to me all morning. The afternoon is all yours."

"I'm enjoying being with you."

"I know, but this is your honeymoon too. There must be something you want to do instead of shopping with me."

"Nope, being here with you is all I want." Rafe reached across the table and caressed her hand. He saw the glint of sun sparkle off her emerald engagement ring. His mind went back to the day she had spotted the stone in the creek. He'd carried that stone in his pocket for months waiting for her.

"You're not the only cowboy in town." Jamison nodded toward a man wearing a cowboy hat. Rafe looked over his shoulder.

"I've seen him around a couple of times today." Rafe stood and collected Jamison's shopping bags. "Are you ready to head out?" The patio had gotten crowded. Rafe wasn't comfortable in a crowd.

Jamison stood, picked up the empty containers, and dropped them in the trash. "Yep, let's see what we can find next."

They strolled through Jackson Park and toured St. Louis Cathedral. Rafe spotted the same cowboy they'd seen earlier outside the church. He kept the cowboy in his sight as he hailed a carriage. "Let's ride for a while."

When the carriage stopped Jamison walked up to the horse and petted him. "He's a beauty. What's his name?" She looked up at the driver as she rubbed her hand down the horse's neck.

"Lucien."

"Lucien, will you take me around the city and show me things only you can show me?" Jamison whispered to the horse. Lucien rolled his eyes toward her and nodded his head. He pawed at the street once as if to tell her to climb aboard. Jamison rubbed Lucien's shoulder before she stepped into the carriage.

Rafe placed the bags at their feet and put his arm around Jamison as the driver clicked his tongue and Lucien began a slow walk down the street. The talked in whispers, and on occasion Rafe stole a kiss from his wife.

He noticed Jamison hide a yawn and asked the driver to drop them at the hotel. The driver nodded and turned Lucien. Back at the hotel Rafe helped Jamison from the carriage, collected the shopping bags, and escorted her inside.

"Mr. Colstock." A young man at the front desk waved. "I have some packages here for you." Rafe looked down at his full hands and chuckled. "I'll be back down to get them. Thank you."

"That's okay Mr. Colstock, I will find someone to get them up to your room."

"Thank you, that would be appreciated."

Back in the room Jamison kicked off her shoes and sighed as she sat on the bed. "That was wonderful. Thank you for putting up with my shopping."

"Yes, well, now we can get back to the honeymoon part." Rafe sat down beside her. He caressed her cheek with his thumb. He leaned in to kiss her when he heard a knock at the door. "Damn it." He whispered against her lips. Rafe heard Jamison chuckle as he rose to answer the door.

"Your packages, sir," the young man said.

"Thank you." Rafe handed him a tip and closed the door. When he turned back into the room Jamison had curled up on the bed. He placed the packages with the rest and went to sit by the window. As he peered down at the street thought about the day. He'd never realized there were so many shifters down here. He had sensed them all day and was glad Jamison seemed unaware. He looked over at Jamison now sleeping and decided to take a shower and clean up for dinner.

In the shower, Rafe tensed when he felt a rush of cold air. Before he could turn, Jamison's arms wrapped around him. He smiled, dislodged her hug, and turned to face her. He wrapped his arms around her back. "Why is it you are always invading my showers, but I never get to invade yours?"

Jamison turned. "I can leave."

"Get back here woman. I didn't say I didn't like it. Just saying it doesn't seem fair." He kissed her hard, passionate.

"You can invade my shower anytime you want." She murmured against his lips as her arms went around his neck.

❦

"IT'S GETTING DARK. Are you getting hungry?" Rafe kissed her temple. They were cuddled together in bed.

"Yes. You zapped my calorie reserve this afternoon. It's time to replenish." Jamison moved to roll out of bed.

"We could get room service," Rafe suggested. He reached out to pull her back.

Jamison squealed and evaded his reach. "Nope, I want good food. We can go back to the place we ate at yesterday."

"Let's find some place different." Rafe threw the covers back and reached for his jeans as she disappeared into the bathroom.

❦

THE CARRIAGE ROLLED up just as they walked out of the hotel. Jamison was disappointed it wasn't Lucien. But it was another beautiful grey that glistened like silver in the lamp lights.

"We're looking for a local place with good food," Rafe said to the driver.

"I know just the place. Best food in town" The driver nodded.

Rafe settled into the carriage beside Jamison. The smell of spicy food and jazzy blues music soon filled the air. The driver stopped in front of three-story building on Ursulines Avenue. The sign out front read, *Sanctuary*.

"This looks interesting." Rafe stepped from the carriage. He turned and helped Jamison out. She walked up to the horse and whispered something in his silver ear. Rafe couldn't hear but smiled as the horse bowed his head and whinnied.

Rafe's attention turned back to the driver. "This has been a part of the landscape more years than I've been alive. Owned and run by the Peltier clan."

"Peltier. That name sounds familiar."

"You can't come to the city without running into them." The driver clicked his tongue and moved back out into the street.

Rafe read the sign on the door: *Come in peace or leave in pieces*. "Well, what do you think?" He looked at Jamison.

"Smells wonderful."

A man opened the door for them. Jamison read his name tag as they walked in: Dev. "Welcome to Sanctuary. Menyara said you were in town."

There was something about him that raised Rafe's hackles.

"Calm down wolf, all are welcome."

Rafe scowled.

"Thank you, Dev, don't mind him he's a little over-protective." She took Rafe's arm. "Menyara, the woman from the shop?"

Dev answered with a nod. "Yes, ma'am, you met her a few times today."

"Really? I remember her from this morning. I don't remember seeing her anywhere else."

"She appears differently to different people." Dev responded. "Aimee is working tonight. She'll get you all fixed up. Enjoy."

"Thank you." Rafe scowled, his body stiff and guarded. He was on full alert as he recognized the clientele as more shifters and other such beings. After seating Jamison, he sat with his back to the wall. His gaze darted around the room. He spotted the bartender. He looked a lot like Dev, but Dev was still at the door. *Must be brothers*, thought Rafe.

"Would you calm down. Nothing is going to happen unless you make it happen." Jamison changed the subject. "Menyara, she's the woman at the shop this morning. The one that sold me the horse." Rafe brought his attention back to Jamison.

A young woman appeared beside their table. "Good evening, my name is Aimee. Do you need a few minutes? Would you like to order drinks?"

Rafe looked at Jamison.

"I'd like iced tea." Jamison smiled up at Aimee.

"I'll have beer," Rafe growled.

Aimee's eyebrows shot up and Jamison frowned at her husband.

"I'll get that right out to you." Aimee left them to peruse the menu. Jamison laid her menu down on the table and glanced around the dining room. The overall atmosphere felt fun and congenial.

Aimee came back with a glass of iced tea a tall glass of beer. "Ready to order or do you need more time?"

Jamison licked her lips. "Can I start with a combo with fried broccoli, Cajun fries, and scoobies?"

Aimee nodded. "Yes ma'am. And you sir?"

"I'll have chicken fingers, French fries with cheese, and scoobies." She walked away. "Scoobies, really, they could call it cornbread and be done with it."

"Rafe, behave. This is supposed to be fun. Have fun. Lower them hackles or you're going to end up in a fight. We both know you can't take this crowd. Your son will never know his father." Jamison rubbed her belly. The baby seemed as restless as his father. "Plus, we don't want to get thrown out before we get food."

Rafe settled back into his chair. He picked up his beer and took a sip of the cold golden liquid.

Jamison sighed. "Much better."

Aimee brought out two platters and put them on the table. "I'll be back."

After the appetizers Aimee had taken dinner orders and delivered two more platters of steaming, fragrant food. Wiping his hand and face on a napkin, Rafe sat back away from the table. He had to admit whoever was in the kitchen sure knew how to cook. He smiled as Jamison finished off her last fry and sat back as well. "You look pleased with yourself."

"Mmm. It was delicious."

As if by magic Aimee returned to take up the empty plates. "Is there anything else I can get you?"

Rafe groaned, "No, I think I'm good." He looked at Jamison. Her look asked for dessert. "What would you like?"

Jamison smiled like a kid. "Simi's Banana Split." Rafe rolled his eyes.

"It's okay Daddy, she's eating for two." Aimee patted his shoulder as she left them.

"Welcome, I'm Remi. From the kitchen. I understand this is your first time."

"Yes. And you're one hell of a cook." Rafe shook his hand. "Can you do something about 'scoobies' though. That sounds ridiculous when you order them."

Remi snorted. "Would, but that's what Mama called them."

"I understand."

"Everything was good?"

"It was wonderful, thank you." Jamison spoke up.

Aimee appeared behind Remi with the massive banana split.

"I don't think I can eat all of this," said Jamison.

"Good luck." Remi left for stops at other tables.

Aimee placed two spoons on the table. "Just in case." She laid the receipt on the table before she walked away. Jamison spooned up ice cream covered in chocolate sauce and popped it in her mouth.

Jamison finally pushed the dish away. "I'm done."

Rafe drained the last of his beer and picked up the receipt. There was a dab of red sauce at the corner of Jamison's mouth. He couldn't stop himself from leaning over and kissing it away. He licked his lips and frowned. "BBQ sauce? Next time I get the banana split."

Jamison chuckled. "Okay."

Quinn looked at Rafe under his brow as he checked them out. "We'll see you back here, I'm sure."

Rafe wasn't surprised by the statement. "Probably. For the food, at least."

"Welcome home, wolf."

Rafe squinted at Quinn. "You're not the first to say that. What do you mean?"

"Stick around. Your answers are just around the corner."

Rafe was quiet on the way back to the hotel. Why would people he'd never met before in a city he'd never been before keep welcoming him home?

ENTER THE SANCTUARY

ALICE SABLE

1

L ogan's peaceful mood disintegrated as he and Coven attempted admittance to the biker bar known as Sanctuary. "Didn't you read the sign, boy?" The giant bear of a man pointed to the sign that read "Come in peace or leave in pieces" as he disarmed Logan.

"In my line of work, it pays to be prepared." Logan led a special ops unit for the government. His arsenal of weapons lay in a bin, while the bouncer frisked him one more time. Coven, his older brother looked on with amusement, having no weapons but his disarming smile. Finished with the search that stopped short of having Logan strip, the brothers were allowed to pass through a small entry into the main area of the bar only to discover three more men identical to the first one. The men were massive, with long, blond curls and flanked by a beautiful female version of themselves. They intercepted Coven and Logan in the middle of the large three-story room.

"Welcome to Sanctuary, newcomers. I'm Aimee. My husband and I own this fine establishment. These are my brothers Dev, Remi, and Quinn. You met Cherif at the door. What brings you in today?"

"Nice to meet you. Coven Sinclair. This is my brother, Logan. I own a nightclub in Las Vegas. We're in town for a few days and wanted to check out your legendary bar. I'm always interested in seeing what works with certain clientele." Remi raised a brow at the word clientele and scowled at his brothers.

"What do you mean by that," he snarled, taking a step forward. "You think our customers aren't good enough for your fancy club?" Aimee slapped an arm against his massive chest and stayed his advance.

"Cool it, Remi. You don't need to pick a fight with everyone who walks in the door!" Rolling her eyes at her ill-tempered brother, she continued, "Ignore him. He needs fed. Please make yourselves at home. I'm happy to answer any questions you might have." They dispersed to separate corners, but the brothers all continued to watch them for any misdeeds. Logan took a seat at a table with his back in a corner. He eyed the quads and kept the front door in view as the raucous sounds and tantalizing smells of Sanctuary assaulted his senses. The early afternoon crowd milled around the pool tables.

What do you think, Brother? Coven spoke to Logan telepathically. Their kind had abilities beyond human imaginings. They were Earth Elementals, but most humans would call them vampires. They did indeed consume blood to sustain themselves but need not kill. Both brothers had dark hair and bright green eyes. They could effectively glamour, control or erase a human's mind as they needed.

The Peltier's are not human, are they? I am not sure exactly what they are, but I sense their power. Logan shrugged and spoke aloud. "It's inconsequential. We came here to find Julia. This is the last place that she worked. They have to know something about her."

"I can't believe she left Toph and her grandmother to run off to New Orleans," Coven complained. "What was she thinking? After all the help you've given her and her family for these past seven years, you would think she would be happy." They first met Julia just prior to Coven's wedding fiasco, when she was spying for his kind's greatest enemy, The Society. Stubborn and defiant, Julia fought against any help Logan provided, including housing, home care, and tuition. He knew Logan feared Julia left because of his repetitive presence in her life.

"Toph was devastated when he finally called me. I can't believe he waited three months to tell us she was gone." Logan's white-knuckled fist struck the tabletop. "He must have been so lonely. His grandmother barely recognizes him after her third stroke. Julia is the only mother figure he remembers." Toph, now twelve, had been five when his parents died in the car accident. Logan's hand relaxed and flattened, palm pressed against the well-polished surface.

"You said you tracked her financials to here?" Coven asked. He leaned forward, keeping his voice low. "Is she still working here?" Logan nodded his head then shrugged.

"The trail went cold about a week ago. She hasn't used a credit card or her cell since then." A frisson of fear ran through Logan. He shoved it away, like he had all his other fears. Julia had to be okay. If only he had known sooner, he could have gotten here before she disappeared.

A server came to take their order. They both ordered a beer. Neither was hungry. They fed well before leaving Vegas, and they should be able to go days before needing more. The server, named Megan, appeared completely human. Logan captured her mind with ease. He sorted quickly through her recent memories to find Julia's beautiful but haunted face.

"I'm looking for a friend of mine. Her name is Julia. I think she works here. Do you know her?" The server warily nodded and replied.

"Yes, she did. At least until she didn't show up for her shift last week."

"Do you know where she stayed?" Logan tracked her to a long-term hotel close to the French Quarter. If they garnered no information here, they would continue their search there next. With a little push with his mind, Logan compelled the server to reveal any pertinent knowledge.

"We were both staying at Homewood in Jackson Square. Julia was hoping to get a job at the St. James Hotel. Her degree is in Hospitality and Tourism Management. She had her second interview there last week. Maybe she got the job and had to start right away." Megan glanced to see Aimee heading toward them with another stunning being in tow. This one did not look like the quads.

"I'll be right back with those beers, boys." She scurried away as if afraid of the man. Without waiting for an invitation, he pulled out a chair for Aimee. He hovered until she was comfortable, then spun the other chair around to straddle it. He put his muscular forearms on the back of the chair and leaned forward.

"Name's Fang. What are you?" Not one for subtleties, Fang got right to the point.

Coven raised a brow. Fang also was not human, but his scent differed from Aimee and her brothers.

Logan, less diplomatic and more confrontational than his older and more business-minded brother, puffed up his chest and sneered at Fang. "Look, nonhuman. You know we're not normal, and we know you're a fucking freak, too. We can either choose to get along and play nice, or things can get real ugly real fast. What's it gonna be?"

Fang growled at them, and his eyes turned yellow.

"Easy, Fang. Most of the people in here are human right now, babe," Aimee cautioned. She cocked her head at them. "You're not Daimon, Were or Dark-hunter. If you are a god, it's no pantheon I know. Help us out here, before my husband sics his Hell-chasers on you."

"It's forbidden to reveal our origins to others," Coven insisted, his voice softer than a whisper. He leaned toward the couple. "We truly mean you no harm. We're looking for a friend who worked here until last week. Julia Preston."

Aimee sat back and cast a worried frown at her husband.

Logan's sense of dread increased, and he asked, "What do you know about her disappearance?"

Unnoticed by any at the table, Megan delivered the beers and scurried away.

Aimee shook her head. "Not much, I'm afraid, but Julia seemed solid. It wasn't like her to leave us short-handed by not showing up for her shift. I'm worried that something has happened to her. We've been qui-etly looking for her, but we haven't had any success so far." Fang glanced over his shoulder at Aimee, their gazes locked in a moment. "Actually, we just decided to call in the big guns."

Just then "Sweet Home Alabama" started blaring over the speakers in the ceiling. Apart from the Peltiers, everyone blond and gorgeous headed for the door at a hurried pace. Aimee smiled up at the speakers and murmured, "Speak of the devil..."

Logan rarely saw anyone who commanded a room

better than he and his unit did. The man leading the group into the bar was well over seven feet tall with long flowing black hair tipped in purple. Dressed in gothic black on black and wearing sunglasses, he looked like an assassin. The huge guy held hands with his girlfriend or wife. She was a woman with curly brown hair and dressed in normal attire. On his left appeared to be a teenager with purple streaks in her hair. The girl wore a leather corset, plaid skirt, fishnet stockings, and platform boots. Her boots, printed with skulls, matched the ones on the man—except his were several sizes bigger, of course.

The entourage strode directly up to their table, and before Aimee could make any introductions, the man lowered his shades to reveal swirling silver eyes. He glanced around the table and then rumbled, "Let's take this meeting upstairs in a private room."

Everyone at the table vanished and reappeared in a secluded room still sitting or standing as they had been downstairs. While his kind could dissolve and move invisibly, Logan could not move other people. This being's powers made a mockery of his own.

"What the fuck is going on?" Logan snarled, standing so quick that his chair fell back. Before it could crash to the floor, it stopped and righted itself.

"Calm down, quality peoples, my Akri has the floor," the girl said in a high, sing-song voice. Logan wisely chose to sit. Aimee took a moment to make introductions.

"Coven and Logan Sinclair, meet Asheron and Tory Parthenopaeus and his daughter, Simi."

"Greetings, Elements," Acheron said, letting them know they had no secrets from him. He didn't hesitate to get to the point. "Young Julia has managed to find trouble again, it seems."

Simi cried out, "Oh no. Not Ju-Ju Bean. I like her. She's a quality people. She would bring the Simi all the BBQ wings she wanted." Simi started dancing anxiously from foot to booted foot. Her fists tightened around the chain on her coffin-shaped purse.

Acheron looked at her with loving exasperation. "It's okay, Sim. We will find her." Then those swirling silver orbs pierced Logan before he added, "Does the name Joseph Wilson mean anything to you?"

Logan had personally been hunting Joseph Wilson for seven years. This was the man who had ordered Julia raped and killed. He led a society of vampire hunters who had turned Coven's wedding into a debacle. Only Wilson had escaped after Coven's wedding. Logan and Coven both nodded with grim expressions.

"It would seem that Julia managed to find him first," Acheron said drily. There was no doubt he was calling Logan's special ops skills into question without saying a word. Not only that, but his Elemental abilities were dismissed by the huge male as well. Logan bristled but knew better than to confront this being.

"What exactly happened?" Logan asked sharply and paced a few steps around his chair. He thought better on his feet. He had a hunch this newest revelation was going to require much thought.

"Joseph Wilson lured Julia to the St. James Hotel. He is holding her there and waiting for you to show up. Now, I know you're all big and bad, and you can take care of things yourself." Acheron waited until every movement in the room ceased. The menacing silence seemed to suck out the room's oxygen before he delivered his declaration. "But this is my town, full of my people. I do not want to see any innocents injured or killed."

Acheron looked over to Fang and added, "Wilson

has also fallen in with a nasty crowd." He paused and crossed his arms over his muscled chest. The leather creaked ominously with the move. "He is now controlled by the Gallu."

"Fucking great," Fang cursed. "I hate those bastards. Should we call in Sin to help?" His voice softened a bit. "Is there any chance at all that Julia hasn't been bitten?"

"They have kept her isolated so far with only a few Gallu in the hotel. The Gallu are interested in seeing what powers they can add by feeding on The Elementals." His gaze turned to the brothers. "It is imperative to keep you two away from them," Acheron informed them and then spoke to his distracted daughter directly.

"Simi, are you paying attention?" She had emptied her coffin-shaped purse onto the table and was munching on beignets and what appeared to be diamonds and jewelry. No one seemed concerned.

"The Simi is sorry, Akri. The Simi is just so hungry. It's been an hour since lunch." She paused in her crunching. "The Simi is a growing demon and needs substanance—no, sustenance." Simi clutched at her stomach and whined.

With a fiendish smirk, Acheron patted her back. "You're in luck, sweet. I want you to rescue Ju-Ju Bean and bring her back here. You can eat any Gallu that you encounter." The squeal that followed could pierce eardrums. She immediately started cramming bottles of BBQ sauce back into her purse.

"Thank you. Thank you. Thank you. You can count on me, Akri. The Simi will not let you down." She jumped to her feet. Her coffin purse already slung around her neck. "Aimee, will you loosen my corset before the Simi leaves?" She presented her back to an amused Aimee while Logan and Coven stared dumb-founded. She let out another loud squeal, and then she was gone.

There were certainly more magnificent beings occupying this world than Logan first suspected. Ironic that his world view should be so narrow given that he was one such being. He took his seat and clasped his hands together.

Acheron pinned his gaze on Logan after her exit. Logan had the distinct impression that Acheron was sifting through his life as easily as he would flip through a magazine. Unable to stall the question that hovered in the forefront of his mind, Logan whispered, "What the hell are you?"

Acheron snorted. "I'm your best friend and your worst nightmare all wrapped up in tight leather pants."

"Mmm, sexy," Tory whispered.

Acheron grinned and kissed Tory's forehead. "Later, baby." He then redirected his mercurial gaze on Logan. "Before your mate gets back here, you need to know that you forced her to leave. She is immensely proud, and she resents your interference now. She wants to accomplish something on her own without your help." Acheron paused then delivered the worst of the blows he had to deal the Elemental. "She plans to move her grandmother and brother here once she gets established."

Realizing that his continuous involvement had indeed driven Julia away, Logan felt it like a kick in the crotch. He only wanted to help her. Her brother was like a son to him. He did not want to let them go. He... Wait, what? "My mate," he stammered. "You just told me she hates me."

"Please, I'm not telling you anything you didn't already know. She is your chosen one. Fear not." He exchanged a look with his beloved wife. "Tory absolutely loathed me the first time we met, and now she adores me." Acheron released a smile when Tory snorted and then reached for her hand before going on. "Julia is destined to love you, but you need to give her some space now."

"Or I can shoot her in the ass and lock you in a room together," a voice from the door laughingly interjected. "That will move things along faster." They collectively turned to find Eros, the God of Love and Sex, entering the private room.

"There is this little thing called free will, Cupid," Fang said snidely. Before Eros could attack Fang for the slight, Acheron flashed Fang out of the room.

Eros snarled. His sharp gaze shot up to meet Acheron's amused one.

"You won't help them if you shoot her," Acheron calmly stated. "Julia needs to find her own way back home." Acheron's expression became troubled as if recalling an unpleasant memory.

"I think that Toph needs Logan in his life now though, so I'm hoping they can come to a compromise. Right. About. Now."

Simi flashed into the room effortlessly carrying Julia, who outweighed Simi by thirty pounds.

"It is all good, Ju-Ju Bean. Those mean demons cannot hurt the Simi at all. Akri, tell Ju-Ju Bean that she is safe now." Logan jumped from his seat and rushed forward to take Julia into his arms. No one noticed the clatter of the chair hitting the floor this time. He held her close. Her eyes were clenched, her breath in puffs, her clothes disheveled. He inhaled and her sweet ginger scent went straight to his groin as always.

He had been fighting his attraction to this girl for seven years.

"Julia! Thank the fuck, you're all right." He hugged her so tightly that she whimpered in protest. He loosened his hold and placed her on the edge of the table.

"Are you hurt?" Looking for injuries, he glided his hands down her limbs.

Julia slapped his hands away. Logan was here. Again. Saving her. Again. Her anger flared. "Why are you here, Logan?" She glared across the room to include Coven in that question as well. Coven had been strangely silent since his unwilling transport through the ether.

Aimee jumped up and grabbed Coven's arm. "Now that Julia is safe, I think this would be an excellent time to compare our business models, don't you, Coven?" She dragged him, stumbling, from the room.

"Toph was worried about you. When he hadn't heard from you this past week, he asked us to locate you," Logan said quietly. Logan glanced at Acheron, who circled his hand, encouraging him to continue. Behind Acheron, Eros pulled back an imaginary bow and aimed it in Julia's direction. Tory glared at him and shooed him from the room.

"I didn't mean to chase you away, Julia. I'm gone months at a time as it is. If you want me completely out of your life, just say so."

Julia glanced around at the crowded room nervously. She took a breath, straightened her spine, and turned to him. "Go home, Logan. I don't need you here." A sigh of exhaustion punctuated her claim.

Her dismissal shattered something in his chest. It was near impossible for his kind to leave his mate once found. Logan never liked that his mate had been chosen for him long ago by the Elders. The Elders would bless a child at birth, bestowing him or her with latent power. While Logan would know almost immediately that she was his chosen one, the timing of her revelation was unknown. Until those powers unlocked, Logan and Julia alternately attracted and repelled each other like spinning magnets. The intense emotions left him reeling, and Logan fell back into his stoic military façade.

"Now that Wilson knows you're here, it's not safe for you to stay here any longer." He stepped away and tucked his hands into his pockets. "Why did you come here anyway?"

Julia averted her gaze. Logan cursed. How had she managed to find Wilson when he and all his resources had failed? "Did you know he was here?"

"I worked at the hotel he stayed at in Vegas," Julie explained. "I found a paper file with his credit card information. There was nothing in the computer system, which is why you couldn't find him. I simply tracked his credit card transactions. It led me to New Orleans and ultimately to the St. James Hotel."

While it made sense, it seemed a bit too convenient. Had someone planted those paper files for her to find? Acheron said that the Gallu, whatever the fuck they were, were interested in absorbing the Elementals' powers. Did that mean the Gallu and The Society would both be hunting his kind?

"Julia, are our families in danger in Vegas? Is it necessary I notify the Elders? Do they need to know the Gallu are teaming up with The Society?"

"The Gallu won't go to Vegas. It's Sin's territory," Acheron stated. Logan had momentarily forgotten there were others in the room.

The statement relieved Logan but didn't explain enough. "Who the fuck is Sin?" Logan growled.

Acheron's expression become colder as his eyes swirled faster, the silver mercurial to his mood. "He is my son-in-law, and you would be wise to change your tone in front of my wife and daughter." Power surged through the room and rattled the light fixtures. Tory placed a staying hand on Acheron's arm. He immediately calmed.

"I will be sure to let Sin and Katra know what is happening here. The Gallu are always scheming with nefarious beings in hopes of advancing their own kind. Fucking assholes, all of them."

"Now whose language needs improvement?" Tory chided.

"Mine. Always. Sorry, Wife." Acheron looked from Logan to Julia.

"Isn't it funny that it's often not the biggest, baddest person in the room who is in charge?" Acheron gave Julia a smile, which she tentatively returned. Then his attention moved to Logan. "Keep that in mind, Logan, when you are trying to make nice with Julia."

"Ooo-kay, who's hungry? Tonight's special is all-you-can-eat BBQ shrimp, I believe," Tory interjected. "Let's leave these two to talk. We'll be downstairs if you need us."

"The Simi is always hungry. Them mean demons were a nice appetizer though. I only had three. They taste like BBQ chicken." While Simi dug out her BBQ sauce, Acheron corralled his group out the door and closed it with his powers.

Alone with Logan, Julia snorted derisively. "I am a magnet for freaks." She lifted her arms and shook them in disbelief. "How can I fly halfway across the country and end up in a weirder situation than the one I escaped?" She hopped off the table and began to pace.

"I would have to agree. There wasn't a single person in this room that was human. You attract chaos." Logan's feeble attempt at humor fell flat with his concerns eating at his insides. "Julia, it's not safe here. Come home with us," Logan pleaded.

"Why won't you let me go," she whispered. She'd stopped her frustrated stalking and stared at the door. The truth was that Julia would do anything to keep her loved ones in Vegas safe. She included Logan on that brief list. If she were ever to feel worthy and not indebted to Logan, she needed to succeed at something on her own. She saw no way to explain that to him.

Logan raked a hand over his cropped hair, mindful of Acheron's warning. He couldn't push now, or he would lose her. He tried a different argument. "Toph needs you. Your grandmother needs you." He bit his lips to keep the next phrase inside. *I need you.* "She won't do well with a move across the country. Please think about coming back."

Logan crossed the room and turned her to face him. He pulled her into his arms, placed a kiss on her forehead, and then put his forehead against hers. "I want to be in your life and in Toph's life." He squeezed his eyes in anguish before he locked gazes with her. "I will go. Just promise me... The Sanctuary, these people here, they will help keep you safe. Please don't shut them out. No matter where you are, your demons, whether real or imagined, are not going to leave you alone. The Sanctuary, this bar, this family may help you leave some of them in pieces. Enter the Sanctuary when your demons are chasing you and try to find peace."

Logan left her to ponder his words. He planned to

go downstairs and get shit-faced, to the degree that his kind could anyway. He sat down at the bar and ordered a whiskey neat.

"Keep them coming." He slapped a fifty onto the bar top. After a few minutes, someone climbed onto the stool next to his.

"My offer is still on the table." Eros grinned at him and waved over the bartender. "Just think, how much easier your life would be then. One shot, and she would love you forever."

Logan chuckled sadly, moving on to his next drink. "Technically, she has already been struck with a proverbial arrow, she simply doesn't know it yet. Are you really Cupid?" Eros growled, and the tumbler in his hand shattered.

"Don't let that whiskey make you stupid. I wouldn't like to kill a new friend." He took a deep breath and let it out slow. "Cupid is Roman. I am Greek, asshole."

Fang cackled as he relieved the bartender and cleaned up the glass shards. He poured another round for the three of them. Fang held up his marked palm for inspection.

"This is my arrow. The gods sure like to fuck with us, don't they?"

"It's one of my favorite pastimes, Wolf. More drink!" Eros tapped the bar top in rapid succession.

Logan nodded and sighed, "I'm too old for this shit."

Fang eyed him as he polished a glass. "I take it that you are older than you look?" Fang asked, putting him around twenty-seven in human years. Logan's kind live for centuries.

"I'm two hundred and seven years old and still

considered a young adult." Julia's life would also extend once they were mated.

"Interesting. I have a few hundred years on you," Fang claimed.

"Infants, both of you," Eros slurred as he turned over his latest tumbler. "But as your elder, let me tell you something about love. It's fucking awesome. Psyche is fucking awesome."

"Speaking of your love, why don't you go see her now, Eros?" Fang helped Eros off the bar stool and into the back where he could flash back to Olympus unseen. When he came back, Logan was nursing his last drink.

"I'm not sure how helpful his words of wisdom were, Logan, but I wouldn't trade my life with Aimee for anything. Being different species, it wasn't easy for us either. If it's meant to be, it will work out."

"Thanks, Fang. If Coven and Aimee are done boring each other with business talk, I'm ready to leave." Fang left to check on them as someone once again sat down beside Logan. He turned to find Julia there, watching him cautiously.

"You're leaving then," her voice a mix of relief and confusion.

"I believe you told me to go home."

Julia winced as she recalled her earlier remarks. Her behavior around him always leaned toward volatility and sarcasm. She recognized it as a protective response but hated that she always hurt those closest to her. It was time to take responsibility for her words and actions.

"I did. I need to apologize to you. I know that you're only trying to help me. I am grateful for everything you have done for Toph and my grandmother, and I thought about what you said upstairs. It's true that Gran can't relocate. I should have thought of that before I ran off. I just thought I needed a fresh start." She picked at her nail. "I fell in love with New Orleans the moment I got here. I could see myself managing a hotel in the French Quarter." She stopped the nervous picking and placed both hands on the edge of the bar.

"Then I thought could also take care of Wilson for all of us. He's such a horrible person. I didn't want any of you near him again. I planned to anonymously report him to the local police once I located him. I wasn't expecting those demons though." She shivered. "Obviously Wilson was expecting me." It seemed clear to her now that Wilson had planted his info for her to find. She wondered if The Society and the Gallu would attack Coven and Logan before they could leave New Orleans.

"I recognize your need for independence, Julia, but life hasn't been kind to you. I wanted to ease some of your burden. Give you a chance to rise above your shitty circumstances." He shouldn't have been so blunt, but the words and tone hung between them.

"You've spent so much money on—" she started.

"The money is nothing to me," Logan interrupted. "I have more than I could spend in three lifetimes. I won't miss any of it, but I would miss you and Toph if you left."

Julia sat quietly for a moment. "Thank you for coming when Toph asked." She took a deep, slow breath. "I have decided that I would like to go back to Vegas with you. I'm needed there. New Orleans can wait a bit longer." She turned to face him. "Do you think the Gallu will try to attack you as we leave?" Coven neared them and caught Julia's last question.

"Aimee said they won't enter Sanctuary, but outside we could be ambushed. They tend to travel in rather large packs." He put his hand on Julia's shoulder. "Aimee's siblings are scouting the area now."

"We do need to find a way out of here without being seen," Logan concluded. He and Coven could dissolve into dust, becoming virtually invisible, but Julia could not travel alone.

Acheron and Fang motioned them to join them in a back hall.

"Don't worry about the Gallu," Fang remarked. "We plan to leave them in pieces for you."

Acheron shook hands with Logan, Coven and Julia. His eyes started to swirl silver. "And I can help you with your other complication. You entered the Sanctuary in peace, now go in peace."

IN ANOTHER PLACE

CECILIA AGETUN

A breeze danced on my skin and the sound of chatter reached my ears. I opened my eyes in confusion. Was I dreaming? The last thing I remembered was falling asleep next to Jax, my fiancé, in our bedroom. Butterflies fluttered in my stomach just thinking about it. Soon he would be my husband.

I willed myself to wake up, but with no luck. Maybe this wasn't a dream after all.

I had been slumped over on a bench, and now I straightened my posture and scanned the area. Nothing appeared familiar. There was a statue of a man on a horse in front of me. To my side, a castle, or a church. A fence surrounded the area, like a small park. People strolled around taking photos and chatting with each other without paying me any attention. Where was I?

The humid air caused my clothes to stick to my skin. I took a deep breath, breathing in the smell of salt water. I got up from the bench to soothe my restless legs. The long shadows caused by the sun told me it was late afternoon. My chest constricted, making it hard to breathe. I didn't think I was in England anymore. A couple walked past me, and I focused on their conversation. Relief flooded through me. Their accents differed from mine, but I could understand them. *I must be somewhere in America.* How had I ended up here?

I closed my eyes and tried to teleport myself home. Nothing happened. I took a few deep breaths to calm myself down. How was I going to get home?

I stumbled out of the park and crossed the road. A whiff of sweetness invaded my senses. A cafe was located to my left. The white and green marques spelled out *Cafe du Monde*. I didn't feel like eating but I could do with a drink. My skin felt clammy and drops of sweat rolled down my back. I wasn't sure if it was from the heat or the panic of not knowing where I was or how to get home.

I put my hand in my pockets to check if I had any change on me but sighed with the realization that even if I'd had any money, it wouldn't be the right currency. Maybe I could conjure some money up? Jax told me I would be able to conjure things at will. Being the daughter of a demon and a guardian angel, it should be easy, right? But where to start? Jax's voice echoed in my head, "To conjure something up it's important to visualize it in details." What did American dollars look like? Closing my eyes, I imagined having money in my hand. When I opened my eyes again, my hands were empty. I shrugged. *It was worth a try.*

Feeling defeated, I walked past the café and continued along the sidewalk. Stairs appeared to my left, and I climbed them, following the sounds of the waves. The sun glittered in the water and under other circumstances I would have appreciated the scenery. As I made my way towards a bench something started tugging at me from the inside. I doubled over and pressed my hands to my stomach, willing it to stop. It felt like I was being pulled by a rope.

I took a deep breath to steady myself. The intensity of the pull wore off but left my body restless. I started walking aimlessly. What should I do? How would I get home? Maybe I could board a plane?

The sun had now completely disappeared. *Maybe I should try to find somewhere to stay for the night. But where? I don't have any money.* The echo of footsteps behind me brought me out of my thoughts. Two guys in their late twenties walked behind me. My muscles tensed and I sped up to put some distance between us. Taking the first turn, I casually glanced behind me. My heart pounded in my chest. They had taken the same turn. Were they following me?

"Wait up, sweetheart," one of them said. My heart skipped a beat. I ignored him and continued walking. My gaze darted back and forth hoping to find a crowd so I wouldn't be alone with these men. A moment later, someone grabbed my wrist. An icy feeling chilled me to the bones as their dark energy radiated towards me. These people weren't humans. While I turned to face them, I tried reading their minds, but they were blank.

"What do you want? If you don't let go of me right now, you will regret it." With the adrenaline rushing through me, I struggled to keep my voice steady.

"We found ourselves a feisty one," the guy said, before turning and giving me a smile. "Why don't you come and party with us?"

The other guy stared me up and down, like he was debating whether I would put up a fight. I couldn't run, not with the guy restraining my wrist. Beads of sweat appeared on my forehead. Taking a deep breath to steady my rapid breathing, I tried to ignore the tugging feeling inside my head and concentrate on tele-porting away. It hadn't worked before when I tried to teleport myself home, but maybe I could teleport my-self back to the park. Anywhere else was better than here. It didn't work. I tried a few more times but nothing happened.

Spots appeared in my vision as I struggled to jerk my hand free. But the one holding me spun me around and pinned both my wrists behind my back. The other guy approached with a smirk. My chest constricted and I struggled for air. What were they going to do to me? Would I ever see Jax or my friends again? If only Jax had taught me how to fight, but he always treated me like I was breakable.

The guy leaned close enough that his breath warmed my face and I cringed at the stale smell. Were those fangs in his mouth? I squeezed my eyes shut, ex-pecting the worst. Everything went quiet. Only the sound of my rapidly beating heart roared in my ears. My mind raced, trying to come up with ways to es-cape, but my body went limp, betraying me. A startled sigh echoed in my head followed by a voice.

"Don't you guys have anything better to do than harass pretty ladies?"

I opened my eyes as they released my hands. My attackers stared at the newcomer with wide eyes for a moment before running off. In their place was a tall, muscular gentleman around the same age. He had dark brown hair and blue eyes.

"You okay, cher?"

He tilted his head and examined me. The air vi-brated with power. This guy was even more powerful than the other ones. *I should be scared.* However, even though I couldn't read his mind, I trusted the sincerity of his words. He had good intentions and genuinely worried for me. I could tell. Sometimes being an Empath had its benefits.

I rubbed my sore wrists and looked up at him. "Thank you."

"You're welcome." He opened his mouth, but closed it again, remaining quiet.

"So, what were those thugs? Cause they sure as hell weren't humans."

"They're called daimons. They would suck your soul out if you let them."

I raised my eyebrow. "Like, literally?"

"Yeah, they need someone else's soul to survive. Come on, let me walk you home," he said with a smile.

I let out a sigh. "You can't."

The guy examined me for a while. "Then at least let me get you a taxi."

"Thank you for your kindness, but my home isn't here. I don't even know how I ended up here. The last thing I remember was going to bed and when I opened my eyes, I was on a bench in the park, and it was evening." I took a deep breath to steady my trembling voice. "I don't know what to do." I shook my head as tears burned in my eyes, threatening to fall for the first time since I'd woken up.

He gave me a sympathetic smile. "I know just the place to visit. Someone there may be able to help you. I'm Nick, by the way."

"I'm Cassie."

We started walking. Nick was quiet, and I was too busy trying to keep up with him to think of anything else to say. The tugging sensation was still in my mind, but I ignored it.

Eventually, we got to a massive red brick building. A huge black sign with a full moon and a silhouette of a motorbike parked on a hill hung above the doors.

The name Sanctuary appeared on it in white letters with purple outline. The marquees over the entrance had, *Come in peace or leave in pieces,* written on it. What kind of weird place was this?

A broad man with long, blond, curly hair stood by the door.

Nick nodded towards the bouncer. "Hi, Dev."

"Nick," he said before letting us through.

The place turned out to be a pub. I guess the bouncer outside should have alerted me. There were pool tables and old-school video games. They even had a stage for live bands. Doubt crept into my mind. How was a bar going to help me get home?

We walked past several empty tables and made our way towards the bar. A feeling of safety engulfed me. "What is this place?" I asked Nick.

"It's a Sanctuary, a safe place for preternatural beings."

When we got to the bar, a woman in a Sanctuary t-shirt with blonde hair and blue eyes greeted us with a friendly smile.

"Hi Amiee, would you mind sorting some food out for Cassie? And call Ash," Nick said with a grunt.

My heart stopped. A phone. Why hadn't I thought of that? "Wait, can I borrow your phone? Maybe I can call Jax, and he can come and get me."

"Sure," Nick said, as he handed me the phone.

I took the phone from him with shaking hands and dialed Jax's number. "The number you have dialed is not in use." I tried again with Leah and Mark's number, but I got the same result. What was going on? Was I even in the same universe anymore?

I sighed. "Does it even do international calls?"

Nick looked at me with a frown. "Yeah, you shouldn't have any problems."

I tried Jax's number one more time before placing my head on the bar table in defeat and letting out a loud sigh. "I don't understand. It's like they don't even exist," I said as I sank down on the stool. "What should I do now?"

Nick took the phone back. "You'll be fine. Aimee will look after you and Ash may be able to help if you tell him what's going on."

I jolted up from the stool and gave Nick a nervous gaze. "You're leaving?"

He shrugged. "Yeah. Can't be here when Ash turns up."

I walked over to give him a hug, then thought better of it and offered him my hand. "Thank you for saving my life."

He looked down at my outstretched hand with a lopsided grin before shaking it. When we touched, a bitter root of sorrow and turmoil raged in my stomach. It belonged to Nick. There was darkness in him, but also light. He had a heart filled with love, fighting to keep the darkness at bay. My intuition told me that at some point he would meet someone who would tip the balance and add more light to his life.

I gave him a smile. "Keep fighting. Never let the darkness overtake your heart. The light will come."

He gave me an unsure smile before he turned and walked out. I replayed what I said in my head. It sounded crazy. I shook my head and went back to the stool by the bar.

Aimee gave me a friendly look. "He's a difficult one. His mom used to work here. He took it very hard when she died and blames Ash for it."

I wanted to ask why, but Aimee disappeared to the back. When she returned, she carried a large plate of food that she put in front of me. My stomach growled as the juicy smell of the steak reached me.

Aimee laughed. "I guess you're hungry."

Despite my stomach's protest, I didn't feel like eating. The tugging sensation in my gut made me uneasy. Supporting my elbow on the bar table I rested my head in my hand while picking at the food. A teenage girl in goth clothes came and sat down next to me.

"Akri says you're lost. Is that true?"

I glanced up at her with a sigh. "Yeah, I don't know how to get home."

"Simi can be your home for now," she said, giving me a wide grin.

Her words confused me at first, but my empathic abilities told me she was being friendly. "Thank you, I could use a friend."

Her eyes widened as she noticed the untouched food. "What you eating? Can Simi have some?

"Sure."

The grin on her face got even bigger as she opened her bag and brought out a bottle of barbeque sauce.

When I pushed the plate of half-eaten food to her, my fingers brushed hers and an image of her and someone else lying upside down watching television entered my mind. She looked different, with red horns and black wings.

"I like your horns," I said with a smile.

"Akri says only the best people have horneys. Do you have any?"

I shook my head. "I don't think so. But this is all so new to me. I didn't know what I was for a long time."

She stuffed her face with my leftovers before turning around. "Akri, Cassie likes Simi's horneys."

I followed her gaze. An even taller guy than Nick, in matching goth clothes, stood to the side of me. He had a magnetic pull to him, mixed with an energy of authority.

His eyes widened as he looked her over before relaxing. I wasn't sure why until Simi whispered in my ear. "Akri worries Simi is showing her horneys to humans."

The guy Simi called Akri turned to face me. His silver eyes bore into mine. The hair on my arms stood up. If I hadn't know any better, I would have said he was a god or something similar. It was strange looking at him. Usually, my empathy powers helped me with how someone was feeling, but I couldn't extract any feelings from him. He was a blank canvas. It reminded me of the two guys earlier. I tensed on the stool and wondered what was going to happen next.

"So, you're Cassie. I'm Ash. How did you end up here?"

"I don't know. One minute I was asleep, the next I was here."

He looked to the side. "Nothing," he mumbled to himself before speaking up. "I'm sorry, but I don't think I can be of much help. It's like you don't belong to this universe."

I shook my head as tears burned in my eyes. "I don't think I do."

Aimee came out with another large plate of food and placed it in front of Simi. "Simi likes it here. Everyone always gives her food." She got her barbeque sauce out again.

I mustered up a smile to share her excitement before putting my head in my hands, tears falling down my face. All I wanted to do was to go home and forget this place and the tugging sensation in my gut.

Simi nudged me. "If you don't know what to do, listen to your stomach."

I guess she meant to listen to my gut. Maybe I should try to figure out where the tugging sensation was coming from. I had been ignoring it since Nick rescued me, but it was still there inside, trying to pull me somewhere.

I looked up and met Simi's eyes. "Maybe you're right. I keep feeling like my body wants to be somewhere else." I started to get up from the bar stool, but Simi stopped me.

"You can't leave now. Simi just made a new friend, besides all those daimons will be out now. Better to do it in the morning." She looked up at Ash. "Akri, can she come with us?"

Ash shook his head "I don't think it's a good idea. I'm sure she's overwhelmed and prefers to stay here where it's quiet. The Peltiers can provide a room for her."

After a while, Aimee came back and had a chat with Ash before walking up to me. "Let me show you to a room where you can rest. You must be exhausted."

"Thank you. I don't know how I can repay you."

"No worries. We're called Sanctuary for a reason." Aimee led me past the kitchen and through a door that took us into another building. We walked up stairs and down a hallway before she opened a door on the right.

"Make yourself at home. We'll be down the bar if you need anything."

"Thank you."

She left me alone with my thoughts. I lay down on the bed and despite everything fell asleep swiftly.

❦

WHEN I WOKE up the next morning, I went down to the pub. There was a lean guy with black hair behind the bar. "Oh, you must be Cassie. I'm Fang, Aimee's mate."

Mate. "You're shapeshifters?" I blurted out before putting my hand over my mouth. "I'm sorry," I said as I scanned the area behind me.

Fang chuckled. "It's okay. We haven't opened yet, so there are no humans here to overhear. Let me get you breakfast." He disappeared out the back and returned a few moments later with a plate of bacon and eggs.

"Thank you."

"You're very welcome. I wish we could do more for you. It's hard to be away from family."

"Well, I grew up in foster care. I didn't know my father was alive until I turned seventeen. That's when everything changed for me." I took a seat and pulled the plate closer.

"How come?" He grabbed a cup and held it up. I nodded and he filled it with rich brew.

"I always thought I was human, but then I learned that my parents were supernatural beings and that I would have powers myself."

He cocked his head to the side, and his gaze unfocused before he gave me a slight smile. "Yeah, it's hard when things change."

After breakfast, I left the Sanctuary behind. If I was going to find where the tugging feeling wanted me to go, I needed to eliminate any distractions. I closed my eyes and focused only on the tug. In my head it turned into a bright light and then into a thin thread. I opened my eyes. The thread of light was still visible, hovering above the pavement. I followed it. What was the worst that could happen? I was already stuck in a foreign country, which could very well be in another universe, with no way to get home.

After a bit of walking, I reached a playground. Several kids were running around, laughing, and screaming. In the opposite corner from me, a little boy sat hunched over on the grass. He looked to be around ten years of age. The thread of light stopped next to him. The tugging urged me forward. There was something about him. I stepped closer, and that's when I felt it. Tentacles of darkness imprisoned him. It stretched around him, followed his every move.

I closed my eyes, hoping I could see anything that would explain what I was seeing, but I came up empty. I bent down to his level. "Hi, I'm Cassie. Are you okay?"

He looked up at me with questioning eyes and reached out to me. When his hand touched my arm, a scene appeared in my head. He was sitting at a table in a kitchen with a bowl of cereal in front of him. His mother told him to eat up, but he said he didn't like it. A moment later the boy picked up the bowl and threw it at his mother. It knocked her to the floor. The boy shook his head as a shadow flew out of him. His eyes went wide when he saw his mother and he rushed out of the house.

Instinctively, I knew what I had to do. My mother had been a Verndari, a guardian angel, providing light to banish the darkness. She had died protecting me when I was a baby. After that, my father sent me to live in the human world to keep me safe. What I felt must have been part of my mother's powers that I had inherited. Darkness had touched this child, and for him to have a normal life, I needed to give him light, a tool to fight the darkness.

I reached inside of myself, to the core of my being.

I concentrated on making light and visualized it being transferred from me to the boy, where our hands connected.

Several moments passed, but eventually the boy looked up at me with a smile. "Thank you. You made it go away." He ran over to the other kids and started playing with them.

A lightness came over me as he laughed. His entire being had transformed. He now seemed to be like any other ten-year-old, playing and having fun without a care in the world.

A woman in white appeared in front of me. "Hi Cassie, it is wonderful to see you. I have been waiting a long time."

Light radiated through her, as well as around her, creating two huge wings of light. Maybe she was a guardian angel, but how would she know who I am? "Who are you?"

A smile crept up on her face. "I'm so sorry. Where are my manners? I'm Edith, Nicklaus's mother. Your grandmother."

"I thought you died?" I said with an unsure smile.

She let out a laugh. "I did, in the human sense, but I became a Verndari, like your mother."

I raised my eyebrow. "Wasn't my mother born a Verndari?"

"She was. But there are other ways to become one." She gave me a wink.

I bit my lip. This was all or nothing. "Why are you here? Can you get me home?"

"I'm here because this was your first mission."

I shook my head slightly before lifting my head to meet her gaze. "I don't understand."

"The first mission is always the hardest. They placed you in another universe so you can learn to trust your instincts without any influences from friends and family."

She placed a hand on my shoulder. "Your mother would be so proud of you. We didn't know if you could become a Verndari because of your heritage as you must overcome all the darkness inside you. They didn't think you would be able to because of your father. I am happy you proved them wrong."

"Why would that matter? No one can help what they are born into. We all have a choice. And if you don't believe that, just look at Jax. I have never met a more selfless and caring demon."

"You are right, my dear. Unfortunately, everyone does not always see it that way."

There was a moment of silence. What did all of this mean to me? I opened my mouth to ask, but Edith cut me off.

"Ready to go home?"

At the mention of home, a light-hearted feeling filled my body. I had only been in this place for less than twenty-four hours, but it had felt like a lifetime. I nodded with a smile, temporarily lost for words. She grabbed my hand. A bright light engulfed us, and I closed my eyes. When I opened them again, we were standing in Jax's and my bedroom.

I met Edith's gaze. "Will I be able to go back there?"

"Teleportation between universes is difficult. Most beings will never be able to do it, however Verndari exist outside the normal world. As your abilities grow and you learn to control and harness them, you may very well be able to go back."

I nodded. "Would you mind keeping an eye on that child, to make sure he's alright?"

A radiant smile appeared on her face, reaching all

the way to her eyes. "You are a true Verndari. More concerned about the people around you than yourself." She gave me a hug. "There is so much to teach you but I'm going to give you some time to process everything that has happened. I will see you again soon."

She stepped back, turning into a bright light. I shielded my eyes and when I looked up again, she was gone.

The End

SANCTUARY'S
SHELTERED HEART

TRINITY BLASIO

1

In every woman, there is a warrior of love buried deep inside her. This book was written not only to help you love yourself but also to discover that which has been hidden under all that pain, beneath societies and our own ingrained beliefs.
Walk with me on your own personal journey. Let me guide you through the layers covers burying your inner warrior. Warning, each book is designed for the person that is now reading this. Do you believe? Will you take the chance to escape your personal prison?

Delia Winters, Vampire, Psychic Warrior

S anctuary snorted after reading the first paragraph of the book that had dropped in her lap, right before she traveled to one of her favorite spots to recoup, the Sanctuary. Maybe it was the name thing. But she had been drawn to this haven long ago. The first time she stepped into it, Sanctuary knew this would be her healing place.

Taking a sip of her wine, Sanctuary glanced down

at the book and snorted her wine through her nose. A coughing fit ensued, drawing attention she didn't like. A glass of water was placed in front of her.

Nicolette, also known as Mama Bear, and the owner of the establishment, smiled at her. "Welcome back, Sanctuary. You are okay?" she asked, as Sanctuary took a drink of water.

"Thank you," Sanctuary said, placing the glass down on the table and noticing Nicolette's sons keeping a close eye on their mama, as they always did. They, however, were not the only ones. Half the bar now watched the two of them, which made her nervous.

"I see things never change around here," Sanctuary said, nodding to their captive audience. "I'm good, just had a bit of a shock at something I read."

Nicolette glanced over her shoulder and sighed. "I'm afraid this is normal," she turned her attention back to Sanctuary as one of her sons moved to her side.

"You read?" Remi, the smart-ass, asked.

Nicolette reached up and slapped her son upside the head.

"Apologize now," Nicolette ordered, glaring at her son, before she turned and glanced at the book. A big smile appeared on her face as the jukebox in the background began to play and people started to move around.

"What? Do you know this person? What curse did she set upon me?" Sanctuary questioned afraid now, lifting the book and flipping it to the other side. "What's so special about it?"

Nicolette laughed. "Yes, I know the author personally. She has visited here a few times. I think you protest too much. Make sure you read her book to the end. It's not a curse to find the one that is meant for you. It seems it's your time to find your other half." Mama Bear glanced at her son. "I'm still waiting," she snarled, once more drawing attention towards them.

"I'm sorry. I was only kidding," Remi grumbled and nodded to Sanctuary.

"Not to worry, Remi, soon you will have your hands full when you find your mate. I have a feeling she'll give you hell," Sanctuary said as the music changed and everyone groaned hearing Simi's scream of happiness.

"Sanctuary, you came back. Did you write my song for me?" Simi asked, skipping to Sanctuary. Simi slid in next to her. Mama Bear stepped back, giving them room as Remi left, distracted by shouting in the pool room.

Sanctuary laughed at Simi's antics, loving how energetic and happy she always seemed.

"Yes, that's right, you're supposed to sing for us tonight. I forgot you promised Simi. Let me get the band warmed up. Do you have the music for your song?" Nicolette asked loudly, making sure everyone heard her.

"Good evening, Sanctuary. I had a feeling you would be here tonight. I can't wait to hear your song," said Acheron, his voice kicking her hormones into hyperdrive.

Sanctuary knew full well she'd be on stage singing soon because no one ever turned down Simi. Hell, Sanctuary couldn't even do it no matter what the threat. The thought of hurting the innocent demon— or whatever she was—didn't sit well with her.

But when Simi appeared, he was there. Acheron. She shivered glancing up at the god-like man. "That is so mean, and you know it," Sanctuary grumbled.

There was no way she would refuse him. Even she had the good sense to know that this one was too powerful for her to handle.

Sanctuary grabbed her water, finishing it. Suddenly, the temperature in the room rose—either that, or her body was on max overdrive with his appearance at the bar.

Sanctuary turned her attention to the book which lay on the table in front of her. Letting out the breath she'd been holding, she flipped through the pages until she came to the sheet of music she had been working on for two years.

"Here, Nicolette. I'll be ready in a few minutes," she said, taking a quick peek at the stud standing next to the table.

Acheron reached over, taking the book she had been reading. "So, Delia was successful. I knew she was having trouble with all the traveling through time for the last few years. Glad I could help," he said, placing her book back down on the table. "Make sure to pay attention to the first chapter. It will explain a lot of things," Acheron said, and left her there with Simi.

"So, my song is going to be good? I even have my video camera to tape you," Simi said, pulling out a small recorder.

"I hope you like it, but you know I don't sing that well," Sanctuary mumbled as Nicolette moved toward the stage to announce her. Why Sanctuary had to mention that she'd been a songwriter while looking for her next threat was beyond stupid. Yep, her big mouth had nipped her in the butt.

"So much for having quiet, relaxing downtime," Sanctuary sighed, scooting out of the booth. She scanned the bar, always making sure nothing or no one would attack. Although they would have a serious death wish in this place. It was another reason Sanctuary had been drawn here.

Hunting down those that had turned dark was a dangerous job, but she was good at what she did. She glanced at the woman who had created this place and smiled. No one broke Nicolette's limani rules. Not only could she kick serious ass, but too many owed her their lives.

Simi's head shot up. "Someone hunting you?" she asked, serious, a knife in her hand. "I can hunt them and eat them."

Sanctuary smiled, reached over, and squeezed Simi's shoulder. "Thank you, my friend, but I never know who is hunting me till it's too late. Plus, I told you what I do and it's not exactly safe."

2

———

L ore Nightshade stood off to the side. He knew no one could see him. At least he thought no one could, until Acheron slid in behind him.

"It isn't nice to hide, especially in my friend's establishment," the god-like man said, and instantly Lore's shield of invisibility faded.

"What if I was hunting?" he snarled and regretted it. Acheron placed his hand on Lore's shoulder, squeezing it to the point of pain. There was nothing he could do but stand there and take the punishment.

"Your next assignment is not what you think she is. In case that isn't enough warning." Acheron leaned in. "She is my Simi's friend. Watch and open your eyes, Lore. You might be surprised as to what you see."

Lore focused his attention from Acheron as music started to play. He turned towards the stage and watched as the one he had been hunting, Sanctuary, stepped up. She was hesitant, scanning everything around her until her gaze met his. Everything inside of Lore froze.

As her hazel eyes met his, Lore could see the pain, the loneliness there. He placed a hand over his chest, rubbing the ache there, knowing it was her pain. Had he made a mistake? Lore took pride in his work. Always doing twice the background information, checking to assure everything was correct and he wasn't handing over an innocent.

She broke his gaze, turning towards the table she had been sitting at. Lore followed to see Simi staring at him. Acheron whispered to Simi.

"Not to worry," Simi yelled to his stunning target on stage, Sanctuary. "He won't harm you unless you're into kinky sex."

The room grew quiet, and all eyes turned towards him. Lore so wanted to fry a demon right now, but he knew to touch Simi meant instant death. She was not only a force herself, but the man who called her his daughter, Acheron, was not to be messed with. In his travels to all the different worlds, Acheron was on the "stay far away from" list.

"Please continue with your song, Sanctuary. You are safe here," Acheron said, and the band started to play.

Time meant no matter to him since Lore was immortal. But right here was the first time in ages he needed to put up his shield of invisibility. He glanced at the stage where Sanctuary stepped up to the mike, closed her eyes, and started to sing.

Her voice wasn't what he expected. Instantly his cock hardened. It was as if her hands caressed his skin. The bar disappeared as his dragon beast inside lifted his head, caught her scent from across the room, and roared inside him. A small bit of fire escaped before Lore could pull the dragon back.

It couldn't be. After chasing this woman for the past fifty years, she was his mate. "Shit," he snarled, rubbing his right shoulder. The burn did nothing to the turning in his gut. He now knew why his body was responding the way it was.

Lore raised his head. Sanctuary's words stumbled and he heard the small grunt of pain as she reached to grab her shoulder. Sanctuary raised her head and stared at him.

Lore strolled through the crowd. His gaze never left Sanctuary. He wouldn't take the chance of her disappearing into another time period as she had over the years. If Lore had to stand on stage beside her, so be it. Not bothering with the stairs, he jumped onto the stage next to her.

Sanctuary gripped the mic, ready to use it as a weapon. He expected no less from his warrior woman.

He glanced towards Ash, who was now at the stage with Simi. "She is my mate, no one will hurt her." Lore's attention turned to Sanctuary.

"Sing, my pretty lady. I will never hurt you," he said, lowering his head and placing a kiss on the side of her neck, taking in her scent. Over the years, Lore had only caught a whiff of her but now he made sure that her scent was embedded into his soul.

Yes, she was his and the first thing he'd do is to destroy the person who'd put a price on her head. No one touched what was his and Sanctuary was his.

"I'm not going to cause a scene here, but if you think I'm going anywhere with you, think again. I don't care if there is a mark on me. I've seen enough mates to know what it means." She stepped up into his personal space. "I'm willing to see where this goes. Just remember, I'll have no man if he isn't true," she informed him, not caring that everyone in the bar heard her through the microphone.

"I wouldn't expect you to. I know your skills so I ask you to not take off so we can see where this goes," he countered, reaching up and tucking a piece of her hair back behind her ear. "You are as beautiful as you are deadly, my fine woman." He backed up giving her a little space but refusing to leave the stage, hoping to ease her, knowing his presence was daunting. If she was like him, the limelight wasn't a thing they liked.

Lore scanned the bar. Ash was back at the table with Simi. Sanctuary's stare was a weight as he glanced at her.

She shook her head and took a deep breath. She nodded then glanced back at the band. "Let's get this over with. Start from the beginning." Sanctuary turned to Simi. "Here's your song, girlfriend. *Only for You.*

She is the tornado that flies by but notices everything
not touching a thing
Her heart is that of gold, yet no one dares goes digging
to find it.
Only a true one will be her king.

LORE MOVED to the edge of the stage. He listened to the words while keeping an eye on the crowd, knowing if he had been hired to find Sanctuary, there could be others out there.

His woman had a wonderful voice. He was surprised by the amount of time she must have put into the song for Simi. He glanced over at the table and chuckled. Acheron had his arm around her, holding her in her seat as she clapped and hooted. By the time Sanctuary finished, there was no holding Simi back as she rushed the stage.

She picked Sanctuary up and hugged her tight. "Friends forever—I love my Simi song. Arki said I'm not allowed to open my chest up and see if it's gold," she said, putting her back down.

"No that would hurt, Simi. I don't want you to hurt. Plus, it was a metaphor to show how kind you can be when you like someone." Sanctuary laughed. "Thank you, Simi. I needed that hug," she said, rubbing her ribs before turning towards him.

"Yep, I'm here and not leaving. Rest assured things haven't changed. Will you talk with me?" Lore held out his hand.

Simi leaned over and whispered to Sanctuary all the while glaring at him. "I have barbeque sauce in my purse."

"No Simi, he's my mate, even though I haven't decided if I'm going to accept. I don't want him eaten, but..." she whistled, and the kitchen doors opened up. "I did order you a surprise before I went on stage. Get out your sauce Simi, it's all for you."

Remi and Dev carried half a pig in and placed it at the table reserved for Ash and Simi.

In seconds, the demon had her sauce out and rushed the twin bears, who quickly got out of Simi's way.

"This place will always be here for you, Sanctuary. Take a chance on what you have been wanting and make sure you finish the book. It was made especially for you two."

Acheron turned to walk away but stopped, staring back at Lore. "Simi considers Sanctuary a true friend. If she finds out you've hurt her one bit, not even I will be able to save you," Acheron warned him.

3

"Really? I haven't done anything special," Sanctuary said, moving towards the end of the stage.

"Oh, but you have. Safe hunting, you two." Ash strolled towards his table.

Sanctuary jumped off the stage. She looked back at the man who she was destined to be with. Beside her, he towered her five-foot seven frame. When he'd reached up and tucked her hair behind her ear, the muscles in his arms rippled from what she could see.

In her hundred years, no one had ever looked at her as if she were a sirloin steak. It was as if she meant something to him, but how could that be? Were the mating strings that strong? She shook her head and headed to the bar. "Come on, let's talk while Simi eats," she said. He jumped off the stage, joining her.

Nicolette stepped in front of them. "I have a special table for you two. You don't need anyone interfering in your chat. I'll have Aimee come out and take your order," she said, taking them through the bar and out a back door.

The warm night air and the smell of the grill hit

her, and she smiled. "Tell me you have the ribs cooking?" Sanctuary asked and Nicolette chuckled.

"Of course, with Simi here we'll need to start cooking again," Nicolette said in her French accent Sanctuary loved. She stepped to picnic table that was covered with a pretty lace tablecloth. Three candles flickered in the soft breeze, which brought the scent of bouquet of lilacs to her.

"Nicolette are you a romantic?" she asked, sitting down at the table.

"Everyone needs romance, even you, child," she said, leaving them alone.

"Who hired you to find me?" she asked, watching as Lore took a seat across from her. She knew damn well he wasn't there because she was his mate.

He smiled. "Warnmat. Why does he want you back alive so bad that he's willing to pay over a million for you?" Lore asked, reaching over, and taking her hand. "I know it doesn't matter. I'll make sure he's not a problem anymore."

His hand was twice the size of hers as he raised it and placed a kiss on the inside of her palm. His gaze never left hers as he waited for his question to be answered.

"Warnmat," she sighed and shook her head. "I thought he understood I couldn't..." Sanctuary smiled. "There was nothing there, like there is here." Sanctuary tugged her hand, but he held onto it.

"This man wants to own you. I've seen this look before. We both know he's not human, but what is he? And Sanctuary, the chemistry between both of us will only get hotter." Lore tilted his head to the side. "You know he wants to know what you are?"

"I promised Warnmat eight years ago I'd keep his

secret as long as I didn't hear about anyone missing in that area. I didn't count on him doing this," Sanctuary said, meeting his gaze. "I have a feeling he already knows too much. You're not going to be the only one looking for me. But why did you take a human job? It's unusual for you to hunt a human, isn't it?"

He smiled and nodded. "I heard word this human was looking for special help. I keep watch on the humans who disturb our lives. You'd be surprised how many humans are as evil as some of those we hunt."

Sanctuary nodded, having to admit the longer this man touched her, the more he seemed to make her body heat up. She turned toward the door for the first time, not knowing what to say. Aimee came out, followed by Vane and her brother. "Are we that bad?" she asked Aimee.

"No, Fang asked his brother to keep an eye on me today since he is busy. You know how long I've worked here. My own family has someone trailing me," she growled.

"You know the activity is up. You're special to all of us. But even in this safe zone, we take precautions," Dev said.

"Really? Here in New Orleans or in general?" Sanctuary asked. "You know I'll be here if you have any trouble."

"Correction, we'll both come if you need," Lore said, glancing at Vane. "Ash will know how to get hold of us."

"Hmm, well let's see what we have," Sanctuary said, trying to throw the conversation in a different direction. "Aimee what do you suggest?"

Aimee smiled. "Thanks. Our ribs are the best and I know momma made some of her potato salad."

"Well then, let's go for the house beer, that potato salad, and, of course, your famous ribs," Sanctuary said.

Aimee glanced over at Lore who nodded to Dev and Vane. Both men joined them at the table. "I'll have the house beer, ribs, but also place a double order of your Cajun potatoes. Those were amazing the last time I was here. Oh, and dessert. We must celebrate. It's not every day one meets his mate."

Dev snorted. "Mama has taken care of that. I swear she has ESP or something when it comes to special events."

Aimee shook her head and headed back inside. "I'll bring your beer out in a second."

The bear put his foot on the table, standing next to Vane, nodding to the gate around the back area. "We've had to close this and it's sad. Even the humans are nervous. From what Ash has told us we're buffing up security but refusing to give in to these monsters. My momma's place will be here when I pass to the next world as a haven for those that need a safe place. Both of you be careful and know you are always welcome here to rest."

"Hmm, interesting," Sanctuary said, pulling out her phone and checking in with her friend. Sure enough, Isabella had sent her an update, but what her pissed off was the area where Warnmat was from: Dearborn, MI.

"What's wrong?" Lore asked.

"Several humans have gone missing around Warnmat's home. The numbers have tripled and it's spreading outward," she leaned over showing the map that had been sent to her. "I have a friend I send all the info on people I run into who set off warnings bells in my head. Like pictures, addresses, and such to help us keep track of them. Guess there was another reason to get rid of me after all."

4

L ore watched every move his woman made. She was amazing and stunning. Her long blond-gray hair made him want to run his hand through it. The way she studied everyone... it revealed why he had a hard time catching up with her.

Up close her scent was that of roses. Lore knew that among their kind her scent would change with their mating. At the age of 640, Lore was in his prime. He had a feeling his Sanctuary was young, maybe 200's, but why didn't she remember anything?

Being here on Earth for the past hundred years, he'd given up on what the seer had told him before he left on his mission to help Earth. But was someone interfering with their destiny? One thing was for sure: He'd find out who did this and why.

He stared at his woman. The seer had been right. Sanctuary was his match—equal in so many ways.

"Well, it looks like we know where we'll be spending the first few weeks of our mating," Lore grumbled, lifting her hand and kissing it. "I was hoping for somewhere warm with a beach."

"What if I didn't like beaches?" she asked, smiling as Aimee headed towards them with two beers.

Lore frowned. "But you spent over three weeks in Jamaica. That's a long time for you."

Sanctuary laughed. "You've been following me for a while. Jamaica is okay. But I was there researching things. Yes, the beach is nice, but I always come back here. Something about the city draws me. Never really had a home, but I think this town would be it if I settled down." Sanctuary nodded to Aimee, thanking her and taking a drink of her beer.

"You ever think about going back to our planet?" he asked.

Sanctuary frowned. "I don't know anything about it. I can remember parts, but from what I can, it's not good." She set her beer down. "You might want to think twice about this mate thing with me because you're not the only one that's been hunting me."

"Who's hunting you?" Simi asked, Acheron following her. "I have lots of barbecue sauce."

Lore snorted and waited for his woman to explain.

Sanctuary smiled as Simi sat down next to her. "I don't know, Simi. I have a feeling they aren't from this world though. It's why I've kept moving. I figured I have three others out there now that I know Lore means me no harm." She shrugged. "I'm sure I'll find out one day."

Simi glanced at Acheron. "Can you see who would hurt my friend?"

Acheron shook his head. "No. Humans, hunters, and such I can touch, but her species is different. I've come across a few throughout my days and only two of them had to be put down. I am curious to your true form though."

Lore laughed. "Ash, you want all the information you can get on our kind. We're hunters, sent out to different worlds to help keep the peace. Like your hunters, but we are solitary unless we find our mates. The only way to kill us is to chop off the head and burn it. Our souls are born into the next world. And once more we must search for our fated one unless mates are blood bonded then they die together and will be able to find each other in their next journey."

Lore scanned around them. He knew of three of his kind in the area, but it was always important not to allow others to know your true identity. Knowing it was safe, Lore relaxed his shield for a few seconds.

Sanctuary reached over and touched his purple hair. "Do you know how many would die to have this color hair and, my god, you're huge. Do you feed with the fangs? Will I get fangs? Damn it, I hate not knowing," she growled.

Lore took hold of her hand. "If you haven't gotten your fangs, you're considered young in our world. For women, fangs come in around two hundred to three hundred years of age. We need to find out what happened to you because there's so much you should know. One thing to remember, we don't allow others from our world to know who or where we are from. Too many have been murdered lately. What gifts have you been granted? I know you have time travel, as do all of us, but there are other gifts that are given to us at birth."

5

Sanctuary was disgusted and pissed off that someone was messing with her life. She was flawed. It could threaten her life, but also Lore's. How could this true warrior across from her be saddled with someone who didn't know what the hell to expect? Let alone have others hunting her?

When he'd shifted, she had been in awe. His hair was light purple, long down his back, but what had captured her attention were his dark purple eyes. The fact that he'd allowed others a glimpse of his real self was impressive.

"Sanctuary," Lore called her name, breaking her out of her fog. "We'll find out the answers together, my woman. As to those that hunt you, it would be my honor to find them and see what they know. To be taken away from your family is a death sentence from our world. Whoever did this will not be allowed to travel to the next life. They have taken too much from you and your family," Lore said.

"You can prevent this person from moving to the next life? How?"

"There are many species showing up on Earth. My hunters need to know about each of them. They need to know if they're here to harm those that live here or what. The fact that even I had no clue about this is a little upsetting," Acheron stated. Sanctuary knew he'd done so to ease her worries.

"There are many worlds out there," Lore said, turning to Acheron. "Your Atlantean gods are just a blip on the radar to many."

"Really interesting. We'll have to chat later, but for now, your food comes. Simi let's give these two time to eat," Acheron turned to leave. "Sanctuary, you have a good heart. Allow your man to help you learn these new things about yourself. This is what you needed instead of skipping from time to time."

"We shall see, weird one," she grumbled. He laughed.

Aimee came out carrying a large tray of food, followed by Vane and her brother.

"I believe that would drive me crazy," Sanctuary offered. Aimee nodded as she placed the food down.

"You have no clue. Fang is three times worse than Vane, and my brothers," Aimee pointed to one brother. "I won't even go into it. Now, you two eat and we won't bother you again," Aimee said, followed by her guards.

Lore ran his finger down her cheek. "I see much need there. Soon, we'll find your family, until then, you have me. I won't leave your side, Sanctuary. We will hunt together. One day, when things settle down, if you want, we can settle here if it makes you happy."

Sanctuary turned her attention to Lore. She could hear the honesty in his words. "We have so much to do and to find out. Can we do this?"

"I know we can. You're not alone anymore," Lore said, leaning over and placing a small kiss on her lips. "You are mine, my warrior woman."

AWAKENED BY THE DARK HUNTER

DAWN CHARTIER

1

Alyssa tripped on the curb. *Don't stop now.* There wasn't time to inspect her injuries. She jumped to her feet and ran a few more blocks.

Abandoned businesses lined the French Quarter street. *Keep running.* Ahead she spotted a lit sign that read *Sanctuary.* She could call the police there, then go home to her brother.

The bouncer at the door went inside without noticing her behind him. She slipped inside and froze.

The abrasions on her palms grew clammy. Several dangerous looking men at the bar studied her. She should've run right back out, but this seemed a fraction safer.

The bartender flashed a smile. "Sugar, this is a private party. We're closed to the public."

She forced her feet forward. "May I use a phone? Then I'll leave."

"There's a hotel a block away."

"Please," she pleaded. "It's an emergency." A cool breeze grazed the back of her arms.

The bartender glanced behind her and nodded once. A strong hand gripped her elbow. The bouncer must've returned. "I'll show her the way."

"I can't leave—" she began, turned, and caught sight of the man holding her. Oxygen fled her lungs. *Not the bouncer.* She jerked to run, but the man she'd witnessed murdering someone only tightened his grip.

"I didn't see anything!" she shouted. Her heart pounded. "I promise I won't tell. Just let me go." She should've stayed home tonight. Bachelorette parties weren't her thing but mistaking the rear exit for the bathroom door at the Brewery pub changed her life.

She didn't know the victim or the man holding her captive, and prayed he'd let her go.

He bent forward and whispered, "You saw everything."

"Take her out of here, Hunter," the bartender advised.

"Wait! Call the police! He's gonna kill me." Her gaze darted from person to person.

The man shoved her into a dark corner of the room. "Sit!"

The back of her legs collided with the booth and she fell into the seat.

He hunkered next to her, and she slid as far away as possible.

Cole rubbed the back of his neck and faced her. "I won't hurt you."

She folded her arms and glanced up, taking in his features. She'll need to remember him if—no, not if —*when* she escaped. He had a face that didn't fit in this time. Viking-like angles. Velvety moss green eyes.

Alyssa had to focus on what to do next. But the way people had moved out his way when they walked past, it was as though everyone knew him or was afraid of him. Did they know he was a killer? "Maybe you won't hurt me, but you didn't say you won't kill me."

His jaw set and he shoved a hand through his wavy, brown hair. "That's up to you."

A bitter taste filled her mouth. "How is it up to me? If I keep quiet? I promise I will."

He leaned closer, black jeans brushed her thigh.

She scooted away.

He glanced to where their leg touched. "You won't remember any of this tomorrow, if you do what I say."

She would've laughed at how insane he sounded. "My friends are searching for me by now." She cleared her throat. "With the police, no doubt."

"No one is searching," he said, sounding unconcerned. A beer landed in front of him.

"What can I get your human, Cole?" The barmaid waved at her.

"Nothing," Cole chugged his beer.

"What if I wanted something?" Some insane urge made her want to argue with the sexy killer. And why did he say her friends weren't looking? "I'm all my brother has left. He depends on me." Although she'd told Dallas she would be home late tonight.

"I took out the Daimon before he attacked you and took your soul, but other Daimons followed you. They have your scent. They will find you. They will kill you."

"My scent? Daimons?" A nervous laugh escaped her. "Okay buddy. I'll take my chances with the soul thieves. Let. Me. Leave."

He pressed his lips tight. "I can't. You're under my protection," he said. "I'm Cole, and you are?"

"Why should I tell you?" Her goal was to get the hell out of here, find a phone, and call the police.

He reached under her arm and pulled her to her feet. "Let's go."

She followed along while searching for a way to escape. If only she had her car, but it was at the Brewery.

"Forget your car, Alyssa." He didn't release her arm.

Her breath caught. "If you knew my name, why'd you ask?" But how did he, and had she wished for her car out loud?

He shrugged and guided her forward. "We have your things. Dalton will return them when it's safe."

She dug her heals in and glanced at his face. "How does Dalton have my things?"

"We have our ways." He stepped beside her and steered her out the door.

"Who is 'we'?" None of this made sense. "Where are you taking me?"

"You ask too many questions." They rounded the corner then he pulled her into a dark alley, just like the one behind the Brewery.

Oh God. This was it. *Scream now before it's too late.* She opened her lips and his hand covered her mouth before she could cry out. His hard body pressed against hers, making it difficult to breathe. Her head bumped against the brick wall.

He dipped near her ear. "Daimons."

Daimons? Good or bad guys? How could she know?

His thigh slid between her legs as he moved a fraction to inspect over his shoulder. Sparks she hadn't felt in ages flickered below. What was wrong with her? How could she even think about that at a time like this? Her hormones were totally confused.

Cole released her mouth then reached behind her. She lost her balance and stumbled backward into a dark room, pulling him with her.

2

C ole hadn't expected to find himself on top of a woman tonight. He'd come to New Orleans for the summer to help rid the city of Daimons. To help an old friend. Ash was as close to a friend he had.

Now he stared into the wide, golden-brown gaze of the loveliest woman he'd seen since he'd arrived in the Quarter a year ago. Her supple curves created all kinds of wicked ideas he had no right to imagine. He hardened even more, and she must've noticed, as she tried squirming from beneath him. He pushed off and helped her up.

"You hurt?" he asked, then closed and bolted the door behind them.

"I... I don't think so. Do you have lights?" she asked.

"Of course." He'd forgotten humans couldn't see as well in the dark. He flipped the switch. "Food? Drink? Bathroom?"

"Now I'm allowed a drink?" she uttered beneath her breath, then took in her surroundings. "This your place?"

"Temporarily." He strode into the kitchen and filled a glass with water. "Drink."

"If this is my last drink, can I have something stronger? Much stronger."

"How strong?" He strolled to the fully stocked wet bar. Living behind Sanctuary had its perks.

"Something to dull the pain."

He narrowed his eyes. "Listen closely, there will be no pain. You'll remain here alive and untouched until the Daimons are found and handled."

She frowned.

"Unless you want to be touched?" He quirked a brow.

She stared in disbelief. "Of course not."

Cole hid his smile and turned to pour whiskey over the ice. He made another for himself. No ice. He handed her the glass. She hesitated, then took a big gulp, coughed, then cleared her throat.

He snorted. "You did say something to dull pain."

She cleared her throat again. "I... I don't drink."

"No shit." He threw back the whiskey in a few swallows and proceeded to the living area. "Sit. Get comfortable."

She followed him and sat on the opposite end of the creamy white, leather sofa. "Why?"

He settled deeper. "Why get comfortable?"

"No. Why'd you kill that man?"

He leaned his head back against the sofa and crossed his ankles, slouching into the cushion. "Would you rather he killed you instead?"

"No, but you could've knocked him out or tied him up," she explained. "Not kill him."

She had no idea of the world he lived in. A world he protected humans from. Unfortunately, a world she was caught up in. Staring into her eyes did something to him, so his gaze lowered to her pink lips, making it worse, especially when she wet them like she did just now. Oh, hell. "You shouldn't have witnessed that, but you stepped into something you know nothing about."

"I stepped out the wrong door. I was heading to the bathroom, but somehow ended up outside."

"Probably a trap," he stated.

She rested her glass on the end table, scrubbed her face, then winced. She raised her palms and stared.

He leaned forward. "Let me see."

She held them up. He frowned. Without thought, he reached out and inspected the abrasions. Her flesh was warm and soft.

"They need to be cleaned." He stood, walked into the bathroom and returned with a damp towel.

She wrapped her arms around her waist and blinked up at him.

His gaze searched hers. "Your hands."

"I can do it." She reached for the cloth, but he seized her wrist.

She clinched her fists. She didn't trust him.

"Let me help," he said, not used to begging.

She bit her bottom lip, then spread her fingers open, her breathing labored.

"You aren't used to someone else doing things for you?" With his other hand, he grabbed her glass and offered it to her.

"No." She sipped. He finished cleaning one palm and she reluctantly offered the other.

"Wasn't too bad, was it?" He wasn't sure what came over him, but he took her whiskey then pressed gentle kisses in each palm.

Her cheeks flushed. "No."

He forced himself to let go then noticed dirt stains on her pants. He reached down and raised the leggings over her knees. She tried swatting his hands away, but he ignored her. The abrasions weren't bad, but he wanted this closeness. He took his sweet time with each knee. He began to ask if she hurt anywhere else, but discovered her eyes closed. Her breathing was heavy. He stood to grab a blanket, but her gaze flew to his.

"Were you asleep?" He hadn't expected to find such heat in her stare. He thought he'd been the only one affected by his ministrations.

She shook her head. "I'm very much awake."

An unexpected tug pulled on the corners of his lips. She'd looked so innocent. He cleared his throat. "I need another drink." He refilled their glasses, turned, and found her standing, swaying slightly. He left her whiskey on the bar.

"Restroom?" she asked.

He pointed behind her. "No windows, if you were thinking about escaping."

She scowled. "Maybe I was, but I honestly need the facilities."

The door clicked behind her. He took out the gumbo his Squire had left behind and heated it. Alyssa would need something to absorb the whiskey.

"Am I your prisoner?" she asked when she returned.

He set the bowls down, took a seat, and rubbed his stiff neck. "It depends on how you look at things."

She slumped into a chair across from him and tapped her fingers. "For how long?"

"Again, it depends." He took a bite.

"On what?"

He slapped the spoon down. "When we kill the Daimons who are after you."

Her shoulders dropped. "I don't normally leave my brother alone overnight."

"Should I send someone to get him?" He exhaled. Hell, he wanted her to himself for tonight. Stupid idea. *You cannot get involved.*

Her eyes widened. "No! Leave him alone."

The fear in her gaze twisted his gut. He could insist until he was blue in the face, but she still wouldn't trust him. He didn't blame her. Trust didn't come easily for him either.

"Let me call my neighbor. I'll ask her to watch him." She pushed her gumbo away.

Her intense eyes followed his every move. He dropped his cell phone in front of her. "Make him stay with her until you return."

She nodded. "She'll ask questions."

"You met a guy and you'll be spending a night or two with him. Act normal," he suggested.

"Act normal. I'd never leave my brother alone to be with a man." She lifted the phone. "Much less a man like you."

That stung. He grabbed the phone back, forgetting it was locked, but her fingers brushed against his. Heat shot up his arm and landed smack in the middle of his groin. From a mere brush?

"It's locked."

"Oh." She stared at his hand.

"Oh." The need to touch her again was all he could think. He laid the cell down not understanding this powerful sensation.

She grabbed it and dialed. "Umm, Lesley, I... I need a favor," she paused. "Sound funny? No, I'm fine. Uh, can Dallas sleep over?" she paused again. "Yes. Fine. No, my battery is dead. I borrowed a friend's." Crimson bloomed across her cheeks, and she stole a quick glance at him. "Not that kind of friend." She bit her lip. "I owe you whenever you need a night out from Shelby. Tell him I love him."

She deposited the cell in front of her. "Wouldn't you rather be out there killing?" she asked.

"No." He much preferred her company.

She stood and drifted toward the sofa. "I can't sit here and do nothing."

"What do you normally do on Friday nights, other than go to the Brewery?" He poured himself another drink. It took a lot to dull his senses.

"Normally I'm safe at home. I don't live a dangerous life like you."

"Not many people live a life like mine." It wasn't as exciting as one would think. "Try to relax." He sank into the sofa and patted a spot next to him. "Try." She settled close, but not too close. It had been a long time since a woman intrigued him like this.

"If I hadn't killed the Daimon, he would've killed many others tonight." Her thigh brushed against him.

She studied him for a moment. "So, you're some kind of vigilante?"

"More like an exterminator." He couldn't explain everything, but for some reason he wanted her to believe him.

She frowned. "I'd rather believe you're a vigilante."

A deep laugh escaped him. Something he hadn't done in a long time. He wasn't sure what possessed him, but he reached up and cupped her chin. "I'm no dark hero, Alyssa Brooks."

"So, you got my name from my license in my purse, which I still don't have back yet."

He pushed her hair behind her ear. "You'll get it back. I promise."

"You went through my personal belongings." She didn't sound mad, more surprised.

"For identification. Nothing more." The back of his knuckles eased down her throat, and she rolled her head to the side. Exhaustion poured off her in waves.

She sighed. "I need my cell phone, too."

At this moment, he wanted nothing more than to curl up next to her on his bed, but he'd take being next to her. "Alyssa, you're exhausted. You take the bed. I'll take the sofa."

Her gaze shot across the room and landed on the bed. "I can sleep right here, if I'm able to sleep at all." A muffled yawn escaped. "Did you drug me?"

"Of course not." He stood, and offered his hand. "Don't make me carry you to the bed, cause if I do, I'll climb in with you."

"No." She jumped to her feet. "I'll go."

Her response was exactly what he'd expected. He veered toward his dresser, grabbed some clothes and handed them to her. "You might as well get comfortable. You can change out here, while I take a quick shower."

She observed the front door. "You aren't afraid I'll run?"

He cupped her chin and forced her gaze to meet his. "Are you going to?"

She regarded his mouth and licked her lips. "I should."

Was she aware of what she just did? Fuck. He wanted to taste that mouth. He dropped his hand, dug into his pocket, and jiggled a key in front of her. "You should, but you can't."

"We're locked in?" She took a step back.

"No. Not 'we'." He shrugged, then closed the bathroom door behind him.

3

Alyssa rushed to the table where she'd put the phone. Gone. "Dammit."

Choice one: Stay with the sexy murderer who didn't appear to want to harm her. Choice two: Try to escape when so-called Daimons are hunting her. Insane. For now, it would have to be choice one. She changed into his Metallica t-shirt and cotton shorts.

The shower started and images of Cole wet and slick with soap filled her mind. Bubbles glided down his muscular arms, chest, back, and down his round ass. She swallowed. *What's wrong with you?*

A muffled moan came from the bathroom. Then another. A grunt. A growl. Another groan. Whatever was happening didn't sound good, yet it did something inside of her.

She approached the door and leaned against it. "Cole?"

The noises abruptly stopped. "What?"

He sounded annoyed. "You okay?"

"Almost," he bit out.

She backed away when another moan came, less muffled this time. What the hell? Nooo. He wouldn't. Would he?

Her stomach clenched and electric pulses tingled between her legs. She plopped down on the bed. The pressure between her thighs grew with each grunt. A vision of him with one arm braced against the shower wall and his other large, strong hand stroking himself. Those muscular hips thrusting. Then she imagined being in the shower with him.

She exhaled and shook her head. What kind of woman would imagine her kidnapper naked, wet, and pleasing himself? "The alcohol. Has to be." She scrubbed her face. "No sex in three years will make a girl desperate," she said to herself.

"Does it?" he asked.

Heat rose from her chest and burned all the way to her ears. "What?"

"I guess that makes us even." Black gym shorts rode low on his hips and her gaze traveled up his flat stomach toward his chest.

"Even?" She bit her lip hard.

"Eavesdropping." He narrowed the distance between them.

Why did it arouse her even more? She craned her head, not wanting to have his, um, directly in her view. "I... I wasn't. I heard...something, thought you hurt yourself. I wasn't—"

"Did you enjoy listening at the door?" He grazed the side of her face and slid his fingers through her hair.

She should lean away from his touch. "I... I told you. I thought something happened." *Keep digging yourself a hole.*

"Something did." He touched the pulse in her neck. "Your heart is racing, I think you knew exactly what I was doing." His fingers trailed along the V of her shirt which she realized hung loosely down one of her shoulders.

She swallowed. "You're wrong."

"Am I?" He bent forward, his mouth less than an inch from hers.

She wanted him to kiss her.

He growled in the back of his throat and pressed his lips to hers. She opened for him, and his tongue swept inside. She sighed, and he deepened the kiss.

He leaned back and asked again. "Am I?"

What? She'd forgotten what they were discussing seconds ago. "Yes," she whispered. He kissed her again. Slow. Long. Deep. Liquid heat bubbled up through her like a volcano on the verge of eruption. Her back arched, pressing her breasts higher.

He broke the kiss and knelt, then pinned her with a stare. "Tell me to stop, Alyssa."

She wanted Cole like she'd never wanted another. "I can't."

"You can't do this, or you can't tell me to stop?" He pressed a light kiss over her red palm.

She clutched the bedspread with her free hand, torn between her options. "Both."

"You can. Let me pleasure you."

"Pleasure me." Her breath caught. This wasn't happening.

"Is that a question or permission?" He caressed her wrist with his mouth. Then he gently sucked. "You denied yourself for too long."

God, had she, but responsibilities came first.

He stroked inside her thighs with his fingertips and jolts of desire shot through her.

Cole pressed a soft kiss to each injured knee. "Can I remove these shorts, love?"

Her heart galloped. She nodded.

She reached for him, but in seconds he had her flat on the bed. His fingers tugged then pulled the shorts completely off. Her cheeks heated.

"Take off your shirt." His voice sounded thick.

He swiped his tongue over his teeth, as though he was about to feast. On her. He slid down. "Open for me, love," hands firm on her inner thighs. "I know you need this almost as much as I need to give it."

She nodded. "Why do you want...me?" An average school librarian with a few extra pounds.

He observed her body from head to toe. "Seriously?"

Heat rose up her neck and landed across her face. "I don't normally—"

"I've wanted you since the moment you walked out of the Brewery." He nipped her leg, she jumped. "You deserve some fun. Give in to it."

"Give in to it," she repeated.

His voice lowered. "Let's explore this connection between us, and the physical side of it." He blew warmth between her legs.

Every nerve ending burned with need.

"Can I taste you sweet, Alyssa? Take you over the edge?" Sincerity filled his tone. Desperate even. But he was right. There was something there.

She nodded.

He opened her legs. His gaze locked between her thighs, then he licked his lips. "I'm hungry for you, love."

A blush grew across her cheeks.

He pressed a soft kiss to each thigh, then parted her with the swipe of his tongue.

She bucked beneath him, but his hands clamped down. He pressed his tongue into her softness with slow circles.

She fisted his hair as his tongue stroked over her swollen center. The ache between her legs grew and her back bowed. Her grasp increased, holding him against her. She closed her eyes and groaned as pulses of pleasure washed over her.

"Cole," Alyssa cried out, and released him, but he remained there, savoring her.

Cole lifted his head and smiled. "You're relaxed now. I can see it in your face."

"Who wouldn't be? I never knew it could be so—"

"Delicious," he finished for her, and climbed on the bed.

"That wasn't the exact word I was searching for," she smiled. "I floated to heaven, and burst apart."

"As did I." He gave her a mischievous look.

"How? I haven't done anything for you." She blinked confused.

"Oh, Alyssa. You have."

She laughed. Was it normal to laugh after such a wonderful moment? "I've never felt like that before. I want more. I want you."

He closed his eyes for a few seconds, not saying a word.

She stiffened. "You don't want more?"

He swore. "I desperately want more, but Dark-Hunters aren't delicate lovers. I could lose control, Alyssa. I don't want to hurt you."

Dark-Hunters? She was curious of the term, but for now she only had one thing on her mind. He'd released her desire, and she didn't know how to reel it back. His warning excited her more. She ached deep. "I'm not a virgin, Cole. I won't break."

His eyes darkened. "Yes, but after three years you need a delicate reintroduction. I'm not—"

She reached for him and kissed him. He rolled

them, pulling her on top. The kiss turned fierce. Demanding. He bit her lip, she tasted blood. He sucked her lip into his mouth, groaning seductively. The pressure hurt and she cried out.

He jerked back, releasing her, burying his face next to her head. "I'm sorry. We should stop."

"No." She couldn't.

He hesitated, but kissed her again, tongues mating slow. Taking and giving. She leaned back. "Your shorts?" she dared ask.

This magnificent man made her bold. The lonely, shy librarian was gone.

He lifted his hips, tugged the clothing off, and flung his shorts to the floor.

She laughed at his haste, then inspected his body. Her jaw dropped.

He rested his hands under his head. "Alyssa?" He frowned. "You're giving me a complex."

She blinked. "Oh, umm. Your...um...is a little intimidating."

"In a good way, I hope."

"In a very good way." She touched the length of him, and he sucked in a deep breath. "That couldn't have hurt," she teased.

"In a very good way," he hissed then glanced to where her fingers closed around him.

She was in control, and powerful. "Steel and silk melded into one."

"Take me, love. Guide me inside you."

She eased the tip inside her core and took him inch by wonderful inch.

He moaned. "So, damn tight, Alyssa. Go slow. I don't want to hurt you."

Arching her back, her palms dug into his thighs, and she began to move. Her body adjusted, but a deeper place within yearned for more. "I'm on fire. I need more."

His eyes changed color. Glowing, yet darker. Strange, yet erotic. He rolled her beneath him. "Legs over my shoulders." He took her deeper, leaving her breathless.

Her ears pulsed and her toes tingled. Pressure built until she cried out and bucked beneath him. He hadn't lost control, but she had. It was the most amazing thing she'd ever experienced.

When her orgasm finished, he withdrew, spending against her stomach. He cleaned her with his t-shirt, then collapsed next to her. "Damn. That was the hardest fight. I nearly lost control."

Her insides still hummed with pleasure. "It was exquisite. Slightly painful, but the most satisfying moment I've ever experienced. It took a moment, but then I just... let go. I never let go."

Cole kissed the back of her other hand. "You're most welcome." He smiled. "You should let go more often."

"I agree," she paused. "I never thought in my wildest dreams that I'd end up here. With you. In your bed."

"Do you regret it?" Concern shown in his eyes.

"Not one second."

He watched her intently. "Can I ask why you usually don't let go?"

She massaged her forehead and released a deep breath. "It's a long story. I don't want to douse this moment."

He nodded, then pulled the sheets back for them. "Get some sleep, Alyssa."

4

Cole couldn't sleep. Alyssa surprised him. She knew what she wanted and asked for it. Holding her like this felt right, but it wasn't. It couldn't be.

She didn't belong in this evil world he lived in. Unfortunately, he'd have to wipe her memory of him. It would be better for her that way.

A knock on the door and he eased out of bed, slid on his shorts, then glanced over his shoulder. She never moved. He swung the door open, motioning to the Hunter to be quiet. Then he stepped outside, leaving the door opened a bit.

Dalton threw a purse at him and grinned. "That's some protection you're doing in there."

"Shut up," he snapped. "Is it taken care of?"

Dalton nodded. "Toasted and roasted."

"Good." Yet, he wasn't ready to let Alyssa go.

Dalton peered at him. "Bro, you look like your dog died. What gives?"

Colt shoved his hand through his hair. "I haven't enjoyed a woman's company in a long time. It's a strange feeling."

The Hunter nudged his arm. "Keep seeing her then if that's what you want."

"My assignment here is temporary." He couldn't get involved and then hurt her like that.

Dalton cursed.

"Quiet, man."

Dalton leaned nearer, lowering his voice. "Ask Ash to make NOLA permanent."

As much as he would like that, she deserved normalcy. "Nah, she doesn't mean that much. I'm ready to bolt." *Liar.*

"Whatever, man." Dalton's cell rang. "Duty calls. I wouldn't mind seeing you stay." He ran off.

Cole pushed the door wider and found Alyssa pouring a glass of water.

"Your purse." He handed her the bag, but she wouldn't look him in the eye. Had she heard what he'd said? "You're safe to leave, if you wish." He went to the dresser and pulled out a t-shirt and slipped it over his head.

"Yes, that's what I want." Hurt laced her voice. She grabbed her clothes and turned toward the bathroom.

What was he doing? He didn't want this. He wanted her. He reached out for her hand and pivoted her back in his direction. "Wait," he paused. "Is something wrong?"

She focused on his hand holding hers. "Nope. Just ready to check in on my brother."

"I'll take you home, but can I see you again?"

She blinked. "Why? Your job is done. This meant nothing, right?"

He squeezed her hand tighter. "Listen, I lied to Dalton. I want to be with you. However, being in my life could get you hurt."

"Shouldn't I be the one to decide what I want? Because what I had before wasn't a life." She paused. "What I'm feeling toward you seems unnatural and fast. I can't explain any of it. But it feels right. You feel right."

"I'm glad you think so, Alyssa, because everything about me and the Dark-Hunter world is unnatural. There's so much you don't know. More than killing Daimons." He paused. "I possess Supernatural powers." He tilted his head. "Are you still sure?"

She offered him a smile, cupped his cheeks, and kissed him. "Did that answer your question?"

He wrapped his arms around her. "I'm unsure. Let's try that again."

HOW A DEMON MADE A FRIEND

EVA NELA

1

NEVADA DESERT, 2006

"Run!"

Her legs failed. Her hunger gripped her. The light annoyed her eyes, they hadn't been able to adapt to her surroundings. The only sound in her ears was the cry of her sisters before that door closed.

"Run! Don't stop, if you stop you won't have a chance, you must run. Run! Run!"

She moved as fast as her legs allowed. She fell to the ground, got up, stumbled, fell again. Despair was her only company—she was alone, no more sisters, alone in the world.

She fell again. She looked at her small and delicate hands buried in the hot sand. A completely different feel from the one that surrounded her for years, millennia locked away.

There would be no more hands equal to hers to hold when she was afraid, when she felt sad, no more. Never again. Unless she returned. She glanced back and only saw the desert. There was nothing but desert around her. The pain of her loss came so strong that she could not even hug herself. It invaded her so deeply, so strongly that she could only scream.

And she screamed.

She screamed at the top of her lungs until her throat was shattered. She screamed until she couldn't feel the difference between the pain in her heart and in her neck, her burning hands or her blistered feet.

She got up painfully, looked in all directions, searched for a place to hide. There was nothing, just dunes and more sand.

The direction of the wind changed, bringing familiar scents to her. How could she know anything if she had just left a cave? What was this strange scent and why did it feel familiar as well as terrifying?

Her doubts and fear got her moving, this time more calmly. The aroma came from far away. Suddenly there was a memory in her head, a vision of the day they were born. Her eyes widened in surprise. She hadn't thought of that in many years. Why was it coming to her mind now?

She fell to the ground. This time hunger, thirst, and fatigue prevented her from moving. With tears in her eyes, she let those memories carry her away.

&

"MADNESS, doom, nightmares, deaths, plagues, poisoned water, destruction of crops, diseases... our final revenge is ready." Laughter echoed from the vaulted arch of the ceiling.

Her ears were too sensitive to bear that sound. A low growl escaped her throat, and she raised her hands to cover her mouth. They shouldn't realize that she was awake, but she needed to hear everything.

She looked around cautiously. Beside her, other female beings slept while some began to wake. She remained still. She didn't know who these beings were, much less who she was.

More laughter—it made her want to shrink. The voices were so cold, distant, evil. Other voices were very soft.

Her body twitched, touching another being. She opened her eyes and closed them again. The eyes were red... What color were hers? She looked at her long blond hair and it made her want to touch it. Wait. She told herself she should not move. This time the voices started to argue. The sour tone of someone's voice began to rise.

Suddenly, a sweet voice sounded, different from the rest, delicate, subtle. It declared, "They have just been born. Please, we must see first how they act before deciding. We cannot lock them up without giving them a chance." The delicate voice was speaking for them.

They were the ones who had just been born, meaning that they were all sisters. Happiness bubbled up in her body while her mind hoped she was equally beautiful as the beings that accompanied her. Despite her intense joy, she could not stop listening.

Another voice rose, this time angrily. "They have all the necessary resources to be able to destroy humanity completely. We gave them all the gifts related to destruction, they could even destroy an entire pantheon. There is no way to control them, so it is best to lock them up. Should we ever disappear then they will be our final revenge, plunging the world back into the Bronze Age." The enraged voice began to laugh. "Can you imagine the shock of the others when they find out that they're going to die by our hands despite our disappearance? Nothing will stop them. It's better that we keep them hidden.

Just think about it," The hateful voice continued. "Enil endowed them with explosive temperament— extremely irritable. Unni gave them exceptional beauty—nothing can resist them. Ann gave them intelligence—they will be able to defeat even us who created them. Their father is the demon of total destruction. They will have no other interests when they awaken."

The subtle voice that had spoken at the beginning, spoke softly again, as if everything that the irritable male voice said was superfluous. "And me? You have forgotten me, Zakar. Do you think there is nothing I can provide them? You go too far and think you can speak to me like that because you are my uncle. May I remind you that I can also bestow gifts. I have given them the ability to discern both good and evil, and more importantly, I gave them compassion."

"You what?" The male voice shouted furiously. "How is it possible that you have done that? Do you not understand the mission they'll have at some point? Your sentimentality has led you to commit such madness, now more than ever we must lock them up. You do not comprehend that they have no limits, they are uncontrollable, together the seven are all we wish for in the event of a war, but they cannot live with us in peacetime."

She began to fear for herself and the others. She tapped her companion with her foot. She realized that her companion—her sister—was looking at her with wide eyes. They were all listening to the shouts, the claims that were rising in an endless altercation.

"If we're going to escape, this is the right time to do it." She shifted her head, trying to observe the place, looking for an exit. A light warm touch caused her to look across, yet another sister smiled fondly at her. This one moved her hands slightly to the right, pointing to the exit to a tunnel. She looked back to the other side and repeated the gesture to her companion and saw how the companion repeated it to the others.

Taking advantage of the discussion, they began to get up.

Their feet touched outside a golden line that surrounded the stone bench where they had awakened at that instant. They were halted in place, collapsing to the ground in a heap, prey to the pain. The electricity rose from the ground, forming an arc that enclosed them while draining their powers. It made them weak. Together they all held hands. If they were going to die, it would be as they were born, at the same time.

They suddenly let go of the powers they possessed. They tried to provoke nightmares in the mind of the god who sneered at them from the corner.

"See... I told you they would try to escape the first time. There is no more discussion, they will be incarcerated."

The young goddess at his side looked at them sadly, admitting her defeat. "I would also try to run away if all I hear as soon as I open my eyes is that I am a threat and that I must be controlled." A sad smile tugged at her lips.

Beside them the demon Asagg, inside his own golden circle, among the hundreds of chains that held him on his knees, waited to be returned to the underworld. He raised his gaze to see his daughters, his red eyes glowed with amusement as if he saw something the others could not. He waved his hands, immediately earning a slap from the gods guarding him.

"What do you want? Speak now, before I tear you

apart with my hands, you filthy garbage!" Zakar's voice was irascible.

Laughter fell from the demon's broken lips. His low, guttural voice expressed the most demonic amusement. "Nobody will be able to control them. They will wipe out everything and everyone, including you. My blood is in them, and they are exceedingly powerful. Your revenge." He kept laughing at them. "They are my revenge. They will ravage everything, and they will give it to me."

The blows rained down on him. It didn't stop his laughter as he crawled on the ground trying to protect himself from the beating he was receiving. He stopped to catch his breath and looked at the sisters.

"One day, you will be free. Remember this moment. They are not interested in you. They are interested in what you can achieve. Once they've got it, they will end you. Do not stop, ruin everything and resurface from the pain and misery of others."

"I've heard the last of you." Pouncing on him, Zakar removed his heart, held it in his hands while it was still beating and threw it into the nearest fire. The flames turned green. Zakar's body began to glow as he absorbed the demon powers.

He turned and stared at the sisters as they held hands, their red eyes ablaze with fury, their sharp teeth visible as their mouths gaped in pain, surprise, and fear.

"You will never see any light but the fire here. You will be thrown away into eternal darkness. You will never see the world or know its pleasures." With a wave of one hand, he opened a hidden wall, exposing a deep and dark cavern. With the other, he lifted them from the ground and threw them inside. As soon as they fell to the ground, the wall reappeared, and they were left in the deepest darkness, alone.

❧

SHE OPENED HER EYES. The sun hid behind the horizon and the aroma she had perceived before fainting became sharper. Closer. She sat terrified. She knew how she recognized that smell. It was Zakar.

Where can one hide in the middle of the desert? She looked frantically around. She could not see anything.

She climbed the next dune and fell to her knees in front of what rose before her eyes. She had never seen the stars before, let alone witnessed them exploding in colors. Some of them rose from the ground and burst into different combinations of hues. Following the reverse path of one, she could spot the reflection of other lights in the distance.

What could be so luminous that it would outshine the stars and the moon?

She stared at the horizon for a long time. To hide, she decided, there was nothing better than a well-lit location. Dragging herself sluggishly, she made her way to that strange area that glowed so much.

Las Vegas, Nevada, 2006

Hiding in an alley, she panted for breath. Hungry and thirsty, she had been able to cover herself with what she assumed was clothing hung across wires that stretched between two tall structures.

Thanks to her skills, she had managed to jump high enough to pull down the strange orange garment that now covered her to her knees.

The sleeves were so long they went past her hands and made her look like a stray child. She was out of place with her dirty appearance, and it was striking that she was barefoot. As she ran closer to the curious lights, she noticed the ground change from sand to a grey substance. While compact, it was warm to the touch.

Strange devices emerged at high speed. The glare of the lights was intense and they almost ran her over as she stood in their path. There were massive structures around her, each one more beautiful than the other.

Her scent blended with that of hundreds of beings around her. Many stared at her with interest, given the precariousness of her clothes and the brightness of her red eyes.

Running away from people was how she ended up in the alley. She was grateful that her scent got lost, mixed with that of an innumerable variety of creatures. That would make it more difficult to find her.

She sat on the floor, closed her eyes, and tried to rest. A shadow cast over her, blocking the faint light behind her eyelids. She half-opened her eyes.

The man approached her and spoke to her in a language she didn't understand. He eyed her expectantly. He repeated the words and held out a hand for her to take it.

She looked at him questioningly. Something about the man's tone and posture indicated that she shouldn't trust him.

The man's tone turned threatening. He approached her, grabbed her arm, and lifted her off the ground. The man held her shoulder and hit her in the face. She fell to the ground with split lips. Blood dripped from her mouth. She looked up at him from the ground.

The guy stomped over and lifted his leg to kick her. The impact knocked the air out of her. Fury pounded in her veins and the control she had been holding in so tightly finally snapped.

She needed to eat, and nothing seemed better than the human in front of her. She allowed her powers to emerge. Her eyes began to glow a vivid red. She entered the man's mind looking for the things that frightened him most. She recreated his fears and insecurities. The laughter of women in the past, the scorn of his mother, and she observed how, in his eagerness for revenge, he had hurt many women. Some mortally wounded or lost forever in fear.

She used her powers to transform those victories and defeats. In his mind, all those shattered women now rose, beating him in turn. The pain caused them returned to him multiplied by a thousand. The agony of their suffering enriched the man's blood. When she fed amid screams of pain, the strength came to her like an avalanche.

All that fear provoked renewed her. The death throes made that final, the souls of those lost women could rest in peace.

She seized his knowledge of the modern world, the use of language and contemporary culture. At last, she understood what she saw. The buildings, the cars that nearly killed her, and the sweater that covered her. The most important thing came at the end. Fireworks, the exploding stars were fireworks.

She licked her lips feeling her powers return to normal. The man's blood now run through her veins.

She looked at her legs, which were covered in blood. The limp corpse of the man was at her feet. She tapped it lightly, smiling to see that it didn't move. He could not hurt anyone anymore.

She looked around, searching for where to hide the body, how to make the traces of her actions disappear. She thought of leaving it abandoned. In the end, countless cases of bodies disappeared in the middle of the night. She was doing the world a favor and they should thank her for it.

She was about to leave when a voice stopped her. A man stood at the end of the alley. Tall, with blond hair, blue eyes, and a big smile.

"You can't leave that there." He made a gesture with his hands as if it was a pile of garbage. "They're going to discover you soon like that. Come, let me help you." He approached with slow steps, trying not to scare her.

Something inside her told her that this man was different from the one she had killed. She stepped back a little to let him get closer to the trash on the ground.

"My name is Kyle. What's your name?" He popped the body off the ground with one hand and extended the other toward her. "I know where we can get rid of this." He shook the body with amusement. "The alligators will be satisfied, and you can tell me your story." He looked down at his hand and looked at her. "Are you coming? I'm sure I couldn't hurt you."

She approached him and smiled. "I'm Kerryna. Nice to meet you." She took his hand and they both disappeared from the alley.

New Orleans, the Bayou, 2006

They were in the middle of a vast swamp. She smiled, knowing what she was seeing. This starry sky was different from the desert. It was a darker blue, almost purple. The stars sparkled. The salty scent of blood went very well with the stagnant, green water.

Some logs began to move in their direction. She clung to the hand that held her, hearing a soft laugh. "They are only alligators, and we are going to give them a gift." He threw the body in the direction of the logs and watched as the remains were torn to pieces.

She turned around, not wanting to observe what was happening. A little squeeze made her look up. Blue eyes stared at her with curiosity.

"May I know who you are and how did you get to New Orleans without anyone noticing you? Besides that, you killed a man without blinking an eye. Now you turn around so as not to see how the alligators eat him."

She pulled away. "That was an accident. I wasn't trying to eat anyone, I just wanted to be alone. Why is your smell different from the rest?" She looked at him. "You don't smell like the gods, neither like humans, nor like us." Her smile lit up for a few seconds to fade instantly. "By us, I mean the Dimme demons."

He smiled a little. "That's because I'm a Katagarian bear. What's a "Dimme"? Why do you say us? I only see one." He began to walk away from the water's edge.

"I am a demon. I was born along with my sisters a long time ago. We were locked up for millennia and had no chance to know anything. Recently we had the opportunity to escape, but only I managed to get out." Tears stung her eyes. Every time she thought of her sisters, the pain returned. "Now I'm alone in this world with no place to live, no family, and no idea what to do." She looked at him sadly. "I guess this is where our path's part. It's been a pleasure, Kyle. I guess one day we'll see each other again."

A hand on her shoulder stopped her. "You can't walk down the street like that. You can get into trouble. Besides we must do something about your self-control and the color of your eyes. You draw too much attention." He pulled her close to him again. "Come, let's meet Maman. She is a little scary at first, but she can guide us."

She looked at him with doubts in her eyes, he sighed. "Cher, if I wanted to do something to you, you'd already be with the alligators. Let's eat properly and talk."

New Orleans, The Sanctuary, Peltier Bar - 2007

Bookkeeping was the most peaceful thing. It eased her nerves and gave her the necessary calm to cope with the feeling of being constantly watched.

She checked the numbers one more time. Everything was correct. Maman would be pleased.

A slight crack in the air alerted her to the arrival of someone. She sighed tiredly and remembered the day she arrived at the bar, hand in hand with Kyle. They had eaten, talked and she had explained everything to him. She saw the fury in the puppy's eyes. She knew now that the man she had met was a puppy still. He took her to see Maman. After she talked to Papa Aubert, they had agreed to let her stay at Sanctuary.

Adapting to her new lifestyle, she started with the basics. Elemental things to get by. She trained in fighting, mastered magical powers, and began to make a living. She tried everything from waitressing to cooking through all positions until she reached administration. It turned out she was good with numbers. She became an accountant.

She worked with the Sanctuary regarding her sisters. They concluded that if she freed them, it would be the destruction of the world. Many of them—through the long years of confinement—had sworn that if they managed to get out, they would destroy absolutely everyone without stopping for anything. How to explain to them that the Sumerian pantheon had disappeared, prey to their own greed?

Amidst these investigations, she discovered that her father had given rise to the terrible Gallu demons. One of these demons had escaped from its service and had mated with a mortal. There were two children before his death. One remained, a female. This woman was a doctor and worked in the city's forensic department. She also taught at the university.

Since Kerryna learned this, she began saving as much as possible to pay rent for a house where her cousin lived. Dimme demons were social by nature, and they liked to be in company of their kind. She was afraid of being alone, so she had asked the puppy for help in tracking the cousin.

Now he came with what she hoped was good news.

A tight hug made her grin, she really liked that puppy a lot. She returned the embrace with affection.

"How is my favorite accountant?" He smiled as he saw her blush. "Let's go for a walk. I know where your cousin lives. The good thing is I found an apartment right next to hers. Let's go see it." He took her by hand, as he always did since they met, and pulled her out of the house.

They passed Dev, who gave them a warning look. "It's not time to go for a walk." He scolded them with a low sound. "The clientele will be leaving soon, and we need all hands-on deck to get the place ready for tomorrow."

Kyle walked on as if he hadn't heard anything and ducked his head in time to avoid being hit with the kitchen towel.

Outside was the puppy's favorite black motorcycle. Kyle handed her a helmet and nonchalantly mounted it. She climbed on the back, and they sped through the streets. She was sure they had committed at least three infractions when another motorcycle intercepted them. Kyle picked up speed, sure that his bike would outrun the chasing junkers.

"Hold on tight," He yelled through the headset intercom.

They were about to turn the corner to return to the Sanctuary when one of the motorcycles hit them on the rear tire, causing them to skid dangerously close to the sidewalk. The fall was not good. She felt the impact on one of her ankles. This would prevent them from running.

She noticed that the puppy was on guard, doing his best to keep her at his back. She tried to look past him, aware of the evil presence emanating from the beings around them. She tried to grab Kyle's hand. She was determined to disappear with him when several attacks came from various angles. She let power wash over her. She blinded her opponents, causing visions that would have driven them to madness if she hadn't stopped. The memory of those visions would surely torment them for months.

She grinned but her smile disappeared when one of them sent back the nightmares and tried to invade her mind. The attack took her by surprise.

She heard a voice ask, "Who are you? How did you

obtain those powers?" She tried to secure her mind, but the creature managed to break her block.

There was a sound of surprise in his tone as he said, "You are a Dimme. Kessar should know this."

As he was about to grab her arm, she felt more than saw how powerful a presence he was as he lifted her off the ground, placing her on her back. The low growl that followed the movement would have terrified her father too.

The creature had a deep, low voice, tanned skin, and black hair. That was all she could see at that moment.

She gawked as the newly arrived creature pounced on the other, avoiding at all costs to be bitten while still attacking him with fierce blows. The Gallu tried to hit him. This irritated him for his skin turned blue and black, large horns emerged on his head, and his voice became more profound. He grabbed the Gallu by the throat and slammed him to the ground. Then he simply ate it. Finishing the matter, he spun around to look at her with big yellow eyes.

"You shouldn't be walking alone if you can't defend yourself properly." He growled aggressively. "But... Well, that also gave me a chance to meet you." He smirked, flashing his sharp teeth. "I'm Xedrix." The lovely grin he displayed vanished when he noticed that she wasn't smiling. He approached slowly.

Her whole body ached. She resented the hits received. Kerryna got up, carefully doing her best to ignore how fast her heart thudded against her sore ribs. Who was this being? She looked for Kyle without finding him, then she saw him lying on the sidewalk with a profuse wound on one side.

"No! No! No!" She screamed desperately. Out of all the Peltier brothers, he was the closest to her.

After all this time, he couldn't be hurt. She tried to stop the bleeding. Despair prevented her from focusing.

A hand settled on her. "If you continue like this, you won't be able to transport yourself, and your friend will die." Xedrix had returned to his human form, and his dark gaze filled with concern. "I'm sorry I didn't get here any sooner. Kyle is also precious to me."

The low voice caught her attention.

"Look at me, Kerryna!"

His command roused her emotions. "Concentrate. When he's okay, tell him to take you to the Vampire club. We can talk then." He stroked her face. Looking at the puppy on the ground, he reluctantly turned away from her.

"You're ready now."

She shook her head affirmatively.

"Go then," he commanded.

She gathered her energy and transported them both to the Sanctuary.

Leaving Kyle in the medical room, she rushed for Carson and brought him to the boy, answering his questions regarding how he got injured and what had caused it.

"It was a Gallu." Concern showed in her voice. "It didn't bite him, but that thing hurt him in the chest, apparently with a dagger. Do you think he'll be okay?"

"Of course, he'll be fine. He's strong." Maman's voice came from the door of the medical room. She looked at her son with troubled eyes that were full of love and concern. "It is your fault he's like this. I told you the first time you came here, and when we agreed to protect you, if anything happens to my children, you must leave. I can't have you here posing a risk to mine. You have until dawn. *C´est dommage*, we were used to having you here.

"Can I wait until he's out of danger?" She agreed with Nicolette's decision. She would not endanger those who had done her so much good. "I'll be leaving in the morning. Merci beaucoup, Nicolette."

The bear turned to her with a sad smile. "I can't afford to lose any more children in this nameless war. *Au revoir, ma cherie.*"

New Orleans, The Sanctuary, Day of the Dead, 2010

The weather was changing, becoming terribly cold. Kerryna stood outside the bar wondering if she should go in or not. It had been a while since the last time she was there. By now everyone knew how to deal with the Gallu.

As she struggled with her thoughts, a large shadow covered her, followed by a chuckle. She turned and a big smile appeared on her face. She threw herself into Dev's hug.

"You shouldn't be standing there in this weather." The bear's low voice made her lips tremble. "The best thing is that you get to the bar. I already told Aimee. She will make sure you get warm quick."

"Thank you very much Dev, I will, but I have to do something first." She climbed the stairs and pressed the password that took her inside the Peltier house. In the great hall, there were the wakes with the names of each one of those lost in battle. She looked carefully for a particular one. When she found it, she fished in her pocket for the candle she carried. She lit it and took it to the receptacle. After a moment of silence, she turned and left it there.

Leaving the hall, she collided with Kyle. "What are

you doing here?" He smiled and squeezed her in a strong hug. "This day is to be with yours, remembering those who are not."

"I'm doing it, just being here." She turned and showed him the lit candle. It was placed over Nicolette Peltier's name. "I always remember those who were good to me, especially in difficult times, it helps me calm my mind."

PLAGUE OF PANTHEONS

SARAH COMPTON

1

I chose a table near the window to get a better look at my surroundings. The warm aura of Sanctuary enveloped me like a blanket. This was a good meeting spot. My name is Gwendolen, and I'm twenty-three years old. That's young in terms of an immortal.

My mother, Cerridwen, is from the Celtic pantheon.

My father, Saturn, is from the Roman pantheon.

No one knew I existed. Why, you ask? Because in most cases pantheons do not mix. Gods and goddesses from other pantheons are constantly fighting with one another. But my parents were one of the rare few to find true love.

I'm here because of a darkness that has set in. Not only with the harvest but with people's emotions. They've been acting out of character with anger. My father and mother never once fought or said a cross word. But this darkness is like a boil that's festering. When the people fight, they don't realize what they're saying or doing because of the black fog that seems to come over them. It surrounds people like a thick blanket and hides their memories.

Some have said they can see it swirl angrily around others and infect new people.

The crops are rotting in the fields as they struggle to keep the plantings alive. Nothing was left of my father's field. What were we to do? The people pray to my mother and father, begging the gods and goddesses to help them and to feed their families. I knew it was time I went and got help.

I had often heard tales of Acheron and his Dark Hunters. Legends of him had spread like wildfire. His brother Styxx also has a reputation. I knew if anyone could help it would be them. I had no one else to turn to. The problem was, with no one knowing I existed, would they believe me? I had to help my family and my people no matter the cost. I snuck away in the dead of night leaving a note telling my parents how much I loved them and how I would fix everything. That this darkness, and whoever is causing it would be eradicated.

My hands were sweaty, my nerves getting the better of me. What would Acheron think of me? Even if he did believe me, would he help me? So many questions ran through my head.

I left a note on the doorstep where Acheron lived with his wife, Tory, and their two boys. My only hope is that, one, he reads it and comes. Two, he doesn't perceive me as a threat and try to kill me.

My mother often speaks of Bethany, Styxx's wife, with fondness. She's one of the few goddesses my mother likes. My mother wanted Bethany to meet me but Cerridwen was too afraid of what people might think. I don't know why since I'm completely unremarkable.

Nothing about me is spectacular. I'm a regular

plain Jane. Except, of course, for my ability to shape shift. Turning into any kind of animal I want or need to be at that time has its perks.

Sighing, I glanced down at my watch. I left the note on his doorstep two nights ago. I've been staying in one of the rooms at Sanctuary waiting for an answer, any answer.

I was approached this morning by a man wearing a cloak that covered his physique and face completely. He had a very deep voice, soothing, yet with an edge to it. Like he wouldn't hesitate to kill me if I moved the wrong way. The only thing he said to me was that Acheron and Styxx would be here to meet me at noon. Then just as quickly as he appeared, he disappeared.

Looking around the bar I watched as the werebear siblings run the place. The tall, beautiful one they call Aimee smiled at everyone. She took orders as she went around the room greeting guests. Her brothers guarded the door and looked so serious and incredibly moody.

Aimee glanced at me and smiled. Making her way towards me, she opened her order pad. "What can I get for you?"

Smiling at her I politely replied, "Nothing I'm good, thank you though." She patted me on the back.

"Don't look so nervous, you'll be fine." Aimee was the first person here to befriend me. I felt like I could tell her anything. She said if anyone could help me it'd be Acheron and his bunch.

I was glad to have Aimee's friendship. Her brothers and mate certainly didn't trust me. Hopefully with time they'll see that I'm grateful for her friendship. There were many types of people in the bar today. Demons, were-people, even humans. Though the humans didn't know what this place truly is. But they were here with the others, in peace and harmony.

The doors opened and Acheron, Tory, Styxx, and Bethany all walked in. I knew Acheron and Styxx were coming but I didn't expect their wives. Behind them stalked the tall stranger from this morning. My heart began to pound as his gaze landed on me.

Acheron looked at the cloaked man and said something. He lifted his hand and pointed to me. Acheron and the others made their way towards me. Pulling out the chair in front of me, Acheron sat down.

"Who are you, and explain why you asked for us, specifically?"

Looking down at my hands, I took a deep breath. "Look, I know you don't like other pantheons. In fact, I've heard that you don't like other gods. Especially with everything that has happened to you. But my family, no not just my family, my people and other pantheons need your help. I asked for you specifically because I don't know who else to turn to."

Crossing his arms and huffing, Styxx replied. "What kind of help are you talking about?"

Tearing up, I lifted my gaze. "There is a sickness infecting the land and people. A darkness that infects minds and hearts. It's like a thick dark ooze that cannot be cleared. The crops are rotting away. My people are going hungry and I don't know how to stop it."

"You didn't answer my question. Who are you?" Acheron asked in a threatening tone.

"My name is Gwendolen. I'm the daughter of Cerridwen and Saturn. My parents have kept me hidden, fearing what their pantheons would say about their love and what was created from it."

Bethany's eyes began to tear up. Coming over, she hugged me tight. "Your mother and I are good friends and I bet she's worried sick about you."

"Yes, they're worried, but I had to do something. Whatever this is, it's affecting them too. They fight each other, then when the fog passes, they don't remember the awful words they spoke."

The stranger leaned down and whispered in Acheron's ear. Nodding, Acheron stood up. "We will help you any way we can. I'll send word to your parents that you're with us and set up a meeting to find out what's going on. You'll stay in Sanctuary until everything is resolved. Gawain here will be your guard."

The cloaked man lowered his hood. A mass of dark curls appeared. Eyes the color of molasses were surrounded by dark lashes. A shadow of hair covered his jaw. A strong, straight, prominent nose, dark eyebrows, and full, soft lips completed the picture. I couldn't help but stare. He was the most gorgeous man I had ever seen. He smiled and my face burned with a blush.

Looking down at the floor, I took a few deep breaths. "I don't need a bodyguard. I can take care of myself."

Acheron crossed his arms. "You will have Gawain as your bodyguard." A glance at Gawain then he tilted his head toward the door.

Shutting the door, Acheron turned to Gawain. "Did you read her mind?"

"Yes, I know exactly who she is. She's not here to harm you. She is genuinely concerned for what is going on."

Acheron opened the door and gestured me to

follow him. I crossed to the stairs, Gawain at my heels.
He nodded his head at me, then placing his hands on
the door, he closed his eyes. After a few seconds he
stepped back. "This is where you will be staying,
Gwendolen, for the time being."

I opened the door and gasped in shock and de-
light. The room was gorgeous. A lot bigger on the inside than the outside. The bed was huge, the sheets
were dark grey. The canopy was white and had little
twinkling lights embedded in it. The floor was a beautiful white carpet. There was a large bookcase filled
with books. The walls were a light purple, and a TV
hung on the wall.

Looking around in wonder, I glanced at Acheron
in shock.

Acheron cleared his throat. "Gawain told me that
you liked things like this. We all want to make sure
you're comfortable."

I looked at Gawain and asked, "How could you
possibly know I liked all of this stuff?"

"I can read thoughts and emotions. It's a little gift
of mine."

I smiled at Gawain. "Thank you all for being so
warm and welcoming, but please don't go through my
head Gawain. That's rude."

Aimee came to the room with extra towels in her
hand. Looking around the room in shock, she glares at
Acheron. "You changed our room?"

"Relax Aimee, it's only temporary."

I thanked Aimee for the extra towels then she and
Acheron left the room.

Only Gawain and I remained. I knew nothing
about this man. Yet he made my heart pound with
excitement and fear. Gawain shuffled his feet
nervously.

"Well, I'll be outside your door should need me." He spoke quietly.

I took a deep breath and went to the bathroom that was attached to the bedroom. Taking a hot shower, I tried to clear my head of so many questions. Would Acheron be able to help? Who was causing such catastrophic ruin? Stepping out of the shower, I dried off and put on my pajamas. I headed to the bed and lay down. Taking a small nap might help clear my head. Letting myself relax, I fell asleep.

🦋

"WHAT ARE we going to do? It is now not only our pantheons suffering. Demeter contacted me saying her fields are decaying and nothing is growing. People have been acting out of character. She also stated there has been a dark aura around of lot of the people. Food will soon become scarce. They'll start fighting each other for it." Cerridwen continued.

"My husband and I have not been prayed to in a long time. This new age and all its technology have done away with the people's belief in us. But since this disease has made itself known we've been getting prayers. People beg us to help their farms and their families.

"Our daughter came here hoping for a miracle. But we can't let her get involved. Not many people know of her existence. If we are to work together, she has to stay here where it is safe." Saturn's tone seemed to scold the assembled team.

The hushed voices woke me from a deep sleep. The voices familiar to me, I jumped out of bed. Walking to the door, I opened it. Stepping to the banister, I listened to the hushed conversation. Sitting at a large table were my parents, Acheron, Styxx, Tory, Bethany, Gawain, Aimee, Fang, and the Peltier brothers. I had to hear what they had to say.

"Gwendolen is a grown woman. She should have the right to decide for herself what must be done. She doesn't seem like the type to stand in the background." Aimee said fiercely.

"She's our daughter. Just because you're okay with mixing pantheons doesn't mean others will be pleased. We've been protecting her from those who would do her harm or use her."

I knew my father and mother were trying to protect me. But sometimes it can be infuriating to be treated like a child.

"We have suspects we believe are causing this. What better way to start a war with other pantheons than to get them thinking we are hurting each other's crops and harvests?" Cerridwen added.

"Do you believe that is what's happening?" Tory asked worriedly.

"We believe so, but we're also worried that whoever is doing this is trying to draw us out. Find out our weaknesses." Saturn's gruff tones didn't reassure anyone.

"We need to warn the others. Whatever this is, it's spreading quick and silent. Like a dense fog." Gawain pitched in.

I took a deep breath and started down the stairs. "What you're not going to do is lock me away and keep me hidden. Especially when I can be of use," I said as I headed towards the table.

"Oh no, young lady. You will not be involved," my father said in a stern voice.

"Father, I'm not a child. I know I don't have great

powers but there must be something I can do," I replied as my voice started to crack.

"I don't find you useless daughter, but I wish you wouldn't risk yourself. Your mother and I have done everything we could do to protect you. I don't want to lose my only daughter, who I love and cherish." He rose from his chair and embraced me.

"You will stay here with Gawain. The barriers I will put in place will prevent you from leaving." He kissed the top of my head. "I do this because I love you. And your mother and I do not want to you to be harmed." Saturn pulled back.

He put his hands on my face as tears ran down my cheeks. Kissing my forehead, he then hugged me tightly. Stepping back, he grabbed Cerridwen's hand and smiled at me. Nodding at Acheron, everyone disappeared. And I was alone with Aimee, Fang, the Peltier brothers, and Gawain.

NOT KNOWING what to do with everyone gone, I stood there in shock. Running to the door, I threw it open. It appeared normal. I tried to walk out. Unfortunately, the barrier my father said he placed was indeed there. I cried out in frustration, anger, and hurt. I wanted my parents to see me as useful. But there was a part of me that also understood why they did it. I had no choice but to accept the situation I was in.

Waking up the next morning in this room was still new to me. I loved it. The colors, the feel of the bed, the smells, the way the lights twinkle in the canopy. What I did't like was the fact that I was stuck here. Sighing, I sat up, intending to get out of bed when I heard a knock. "Come in." The door opened and in came Gawain. Pulling the blanket up higher, I started to blush. "Good morning, Gawain."

"Good morning, Gwendolen." Gawain smiled. "Would you like to join me for breakfast? I figured if you're here and unable to leave then why not have some company."

I nodded my head at Gawain and smile. "I'd really like that." Jumping out of bed I rushed to the bathroom. After taking a quick shower, I brushed my hair and teeth. I got dressed and headed out of the bathroom. Gawain stood in front of the window, looking out. As soon as I came out of the bathroom, he turned towards me. Grinning widely, he held out his hand. Nervously, I took his hand and he led me out of the room.

The sounds and smells of Sanctuary flooded my senses. The smell of sausage and bacon made my mouth water. Heading down the stairs we sat a table near the window. Aimee headed towards us. She had a big grin on her face and a notepad in her hand. One couldn't help but smile back. Aimee had such a big heart and great personality.

"What can I get for you two this morning?"

Gawain looked at me and grinned. "Ladies first."

Smiling shyly, I respond, "I just want bacon and sausage."

Gawain grinned at my short order. "I'll have the same thing, thank you, Aimee." Writing in her pad, she smiled and nodded her head. Turning away, she heads towards the kitchen.

My heart began to pound wildly. I was stuck here alone with Gawain again. Just being around him made my heart race. Taking a deep breath, I inhaled all that was Gawain. An earthy smell like the forest and of leather, that was Gawain. He was utter perfection. Not a hair out of place. I wanted to run my fingers through it and tussle it. See what he would look like wild and uninhibited. Looking down at his hands, I memorized every crease and line. I imagined what they would feel like on my body. My face turned red and I shook my head. I didn't need to be thinking those things. He was my guard, nothing more.

"So, tell me about yourself Gwendolen."

Clearing my throat, I took a sip of the water. "I grew up in a section of the fairy realm that's in Ireland. My parents thought I would be safest there. That no one would discover me there unless they really tried. We live in a cottage, big enough for just the three of us. My mother and I have a garden there. Both crops and flowers alike. A great big willow tree that my father planted was in our backyard. We would sit under it every day and read a book or simply talk.

"My father wasn't always able to be there. He has so many responsibilities, but he always made time for mother and me. I have so many great memories there," I said with a smile on my face.

Gawain nodded. "It must be amazing to have such great memories with your family."

"What was your childhood like, Gawain?"

He looked away and sighed. "It wasn't the greatest childhood. You don't know this about me but I'm a freed Dark Hunter. I got my soul back from Artemis. Before that, I was a member of the round table during Arthur's reign in Camelot." He paused and nodded. His dark eyes were full of mirth. "Yes, Camelot was real, and Arthur was real. Being a knight had given me purpose in life. After everything was destroyed, I had nowhere to go. I couldn't deal with having lost everything. As I lay dying, I begged for something, or someone to help me. I wanted revenge. That is when

Artemis approached me, and I never looked back." He leaned back in his chair.

"I became a close friend to Acheron and fought by his side just like I did Arthur's. My life had new meaning to it. I'm glad I've gotten my soul back, but I'll always remain loyal to Acheron."

Gawain and I talked for more than two hours. Neither one of us noticed Aimee bringing our breakfast or the noises from other customers as they came in. At last, realizing our cold breakfast was on the table we ate everything and parted ways. I headed back to my room. Gawain went and patrolled. Waiting for a message from Acheron or the others I fell asleep.

Every day was the same. Gawain would wake me up each morning. We would eat breakfast together and talk about our pasts. His stories were fascinating, better than the books in my temporary room.

Then we would part ways and do other things. I hated being cooped up without knowing what was going on outside. But I was glad I had Gawain to keep me company. Some days we would mix it up by watching a movie together or playing a board game. We even got Fang, Aimee, Dev, Remi, and Samia to play as well. Though Dev and Remi just growled at one another over who was cheating.

Every day I grew closer and closer to Gawain. And every day my feelings for him grew stronger.

I also worried about what was going on and if they had found the culprit. Gawain and the others would hear word from Acheron but never would tell me what was said. I know they were trying to protect me, but I felt so left out. I didn't know if my family was okay. Or if the other pantheons were being affected. I just wanted a sign that everything was okay.

Today was turning out to be like the same as the

days before it. Gawain woke me up. Gave me his heart stopping smile and took me downstairs. We had our usual breakfast of sausage and bacon. We talked about our favorite characters and what our favorite food was. Gawain said his favorite food was by far pizza. It was the same for me. Who doesn't like pizza? Unfortunately, our similarities on liking pizza ended there. Because he liked pineapple on pizza. Uggh!

We started to part ways after our long talk over breakfast when someone came barreling into Sanctuary. It looked like a Charonte demon. She was slender with red and black skin, and her horns glowed red. She was dressed in all black. She looked at Gawain and squealed.

"Gawaini." Running towards Gawain, she hugged him tightly.

"Gwendolen, this is Simi. Acheron's second daughter/ Charonte demon. Simi, this is Gwendolen," Gawain said as he took my hand and held it.

"Hi, Gweni. Can I call you Gweni? It sounds like Gawaini. Hey! Gweni and Gawaini!"

Simi talked a mile a minute. I started to laugh. "Sure Simi, you can call me Gweni."

Gawain pulled out a seat for her to sit down. Aimee came over with fries covered in BBQ sauce and handed them to Simi. She squealed in excitement and began to eat the fries frantically.

"So, Simi, why aren't you with Acheron?" Gawain asked her.

Simi looked up from her plate with BBQ sauce all over her face. "Akri sent me here to tell you something in person. Said that they have found out is causing that icky black stuff to kill food and hurt people. They are dealing with a bad god. Her name is Morta."

I shot out of my chair. "Morta? She's been after my

father for years. Why would she attack his crops and hurt the people?"

Simi looked at me sadly. "She knows about you and your mama. And is all mad and trying to rally other gods and goddesses against your parents. They are dealing with her now."

Tears falling down my cheeks, Gawain pulled me into his arms and held me tightly. "Oh Gawain. This is all my fault. She found out about me and is trying to hurt my father and my people," I sobbed into his shoulder. He cupped my face in his hands.

"Sweetheart, this is not your fault. This is the responsibility of a woman jealous of your mother. Why does it matter your parents aren't from the same pantheon? All that should matter is that your mother and father found true love and companionship. We will do everything we can to stop her and to keep you safe."

Gawain leaned down and kissed me on the mouth. Moaning softly, I moved to deepen the kiss. Wanting this more than anything, I ran my fingers through his hair. Gawain deepened the kiss, and my lips parted slightly, allowing his tongue to slip inside. Our bodies pressed together excitedly. I could feel his heartbeat against mine.

Breaking the kiss, Gawain picked me up. Not noticing all the eyes looking at us, he went up two stairs at a time. Sitting me down on the bed inside the room, he turned to close and lock the door. He tore off his shirt as I began to tear off my clothing as well. Gawain approached the bed and helped me with my pants. Kneeling on the floor, he slowly kissed upwards on my leg. Soft, sweet kisses. I shivered in anticipation. I tried to get him to hurry but he stopped me.

"We have all the time in the world, Gwendolen." He said with a smile touching my body as if I were fragile. He looked at me like I'm the most beautiful woman he'd ever seen. Gawain got on the bed and kissed me softly. "Your skin is like satin." Our love burned between us as we became one. Pleasuring one another and baring our souls.

❧

LYING in Gawain's arms felt like heaven on earth. A tuft of chest hair tickled my nose. His hand drew lazy circles on my arm. I wanted to tell him I was in love with him. That I no longer felt alone. But I wanted him to say it first. After what seemed like forever in our comfortable silence, Gawain finally spoke.

"Gwendolen?"

"Yes?" I looked up at him so I could see his face.

"When all this is over... When you're finally safe and out of harm's way... Would you like to live with me?"

In surprise I asked, "Why?"

Confusion set on his face he replied, "Because I love you Gwendolen. Being here at Sanctuary with you, getting to know you, seeing you every day I realized I want to spend the rest of my life with you. Not knowing what the future may hold but willing to take the chance with you. I want to grow with you by my side. That is, if you want that too."

Tears formed in my eyes. "Yes. A thousand times yes! I love you too Gawain. I want to be wherever it is you are. I know we must remain here for the time being. But home is wherever you are. Eventually Morta will be caught, and hopefully it will not come to war."

❧

Staring at the blurry image of Gwendolen and Gawain through the water, Morta's evil smile reflected in the surface. "Let her have some happiness today. For it will all be taken from her in time."

She walked away into the shadows, disappearing into a thick fog.

SECOND CHANCE FOR A FOREVER MATE

C STRIPES

1

The kick caught him hard in the ribs. His feet left the ground. The air left his lungs. Blackness crowded his vision and he waited for the body slam. The ground was mushy in the bayou, but that wouldn't stop the hurt.

He forced his muscles to respond, twisting and arching his back to come down in a crouch.

"When you gonna give up, boy?" Two other chortles joined the speaker.

Beau had to hold on for a few more minutes. A stray breeze brought him the scent of his pack. They were close but not close enough for him to escape the trio of drunk swamp hunters who'd caught him with his dick in a bitch. As soon as the knot subsided, she'd run. He'd stood his ground to give her time to get away.

Surrounded and outnumbered, he'd kept them busy. They'd stacked their rifles beside the tent. One wore a machete but that hadn't cleared leather as they were happier to kick a dog around.

He was brought back to the fight as the heaviest idiot tossed the rest of his moonshine over Beau's coat.

"We could light this mutt up." He flicked open the lid of an old lighter.

"Donnie, put that shit away. Somebody will see the light. 'Sides, he could set the place on fire."

"Leon's right, numbskull. Ain't no need to set the swamp on fire. We have bounties to load up. This here's just a little diversion."

"No need to call me names." Donnie snapped the lighter closed. "I hate the smell of burnin' hair anyways."

A low growl took their attention from Beau and to six other wolves. Their eyes reflected in the fire light. Gold, green and red stared from the deep shadows.

"Caleb, thems more dogs."

Beau straightened from his crouch. It took some doing, but his muscles followed orders. He shook out his coat and looked around him. Pride swelled his heart and in appreciation he gave a soft howl. It needn't carry far. The others took up the softened wild song. Each voice tempered to meld into a feral chorus like no other in the world.

Beau let his vocalization die off, the others trailed down to a lone note. When it died silence ruled the bayou. The humans were mute until the alcohol gave them courage.

"We'll kill you all."

Everyone was distracted and Beau slipped into the shadows. He shifted forms, taking a selfish moment to enjoy the painlessness. He stepped into the light. "That'll be enough fighting tonight." He marched to the jug of rot-gut moonshine and kicked it over with a bare foot. The liquid glugged from the mouth, sparkles in the firelight.

"Hey, you kain't do that. We paid good money for that." Leon took a step toward Beau.

Caleb grabbed the strap of his grubby overalls. "Don't think you wanna do that, Leon."

Leon rounded on him, then over Caleb's shoulder he saw the wolves. Half in shadow, the fire caught the ripple of fur. "Yeah, maybe I don't."

"I hate to ruin your fun for the night. We'll be leaving you to your rest. I understand tomorrow will be good hunting, gentlemen." Beau sounded pleasant, but every word carried his warning. Should they pursue the wolves into the bayou, there'd be hell to pay.

"Good evening and good hunting." Beau left the fireside, crossed the clearing, and slipped into the shadows.

The men stood shoulder to shoulder, their backs to each other now as they tried to follow the disappearance of each wolf. The animals were quick and quiet. After they were gone, the menace of their leave-taking lingered, keeping the hunters alert if not sober.

"How stupid can you be?"

Beau tugged a pair of loose pants over his legs and then reached for a shirt. He rolled his eyes as his Beta continued to bitch.

"You didn't know the humans were that close when you literally hooked up with that bitch?" Cam paced around the cabin's bedroom. "She's from the Hummock Pack. They're half wild. She'd as soon fight you as fuck you."

"Enough, Cam. Tonight, we needed to fuck." He slipped his feet into well-worn moccasins. He'd needed a nameless fuck to hold memories at bay he didn't want to review.

"That's just what I wanted to hear." Serre tugged the screen door open and invited himself inside.

"Serre, not busy tonight?" Beau pulled him into a real bear hug.

Serre returned the embrace with enthusiasm. Beau grunted, "Uncle."

"So, who's the lucky lady?" Serre released Beau and offered a fist bump to Cam. "How goes it, bruh?" He stepped over to the side table that doubled as a bar.

"You know." Cam grinned and headed for the door. "He's in a mood."

Serre didn't say anything until he poured two glasses of bourbon. He turned and handed one to Beau. A sip later he took a seat on the worn but comfortable couch. "A mood, huh?"

"You, too, bear?" Beau settled into his chair. It looked out of place in the little cabin. Quinn measured him years ago when he'd taken Alpha for the pack. The Sickle Moon was no better than the hunters he'd run into earlier. Then he'd made it for Beau as a congratulatory gift. He'd called it a throne for the new king. Beau sipped the amber liquid.

"Just commenting." He eyed his friend. "I came out because I knew it was the anniversary. I never know what's going to happen." He finished his portion and put the glass down.

"I don't either Serre." He lowered his head to his hand. "We had so little time, then those bastards killed her."

"This time you let yourself get caught by a trio of drunk 'gator hunters looking for a little diversion." He sipped his drink, gaze steady on Beau. "You know you're welcome at Sanctuary. Blow off a little steam, visit family you've been avoiding..."

"If I'd been there..." Beau didn't acknowledge Serre's heavy hinting.

"They would have taken you out." Serre let the sentence stand. He knew Beau hurt with a wound that would never heal. His mate had been taken out by Daimons less than a month after they'd declared for each other.

He cleared his throat. "You looking for a Hummock bitch?"

"Damn if news doesn't travel fast." Beau stirred up a chuckle. "She was a fine woman."

"For what? Fifteen minutes that you got hung up inside?"

"Funny." Beau tipped his glass up and drained it.

"You should come to the bar. Show everyone you're still alive."

"That's the crux of the matter, isn't it?" Beau locked gazes with Serre. "Am I still alive?"

BEAU PARKED his truck in front of Serre's garage. His favorite bike met with a slick spot and slid out from under him. In addition to body work, it needed a bit of tuning up.

He got out of the truck and turned his face up to the hot New Orleans sunshine.

"Da fuck you'd do to this ride?" Serre joined him, glaring at the battered frame. He turned his flame hot blue gaze to Beau. "Dude, I'm sure you're better at this." He waved his hand at the mangled mess. "If you'd been serious, you'd be dead now."

"It slid. And it needs a tune up."

"And chrome, and paint, and a full body shop..."

"I trust you, but I can drive it to someone else." Beau shrugged. He took off the jacket that kept him warm under the canopy of trees at the house. He slung the worn leather over his shoulder.

"I think we both need a drink." Serre made quick work of the hitch, pushed it up next to the building and wiped his hands on a shop towel. It didn't do much but smear the grease.

Beau shrugged and unlocked the passenger door. "Remi cooking this early?"

"Remi cooks in his sleep."

BEAU PARKED the truck at Sanctuary. He and Serre shook hands with Dev. Business wasn't in full swing though the lunch crowd was building. "You're looking good, Beau. I heard the Hammock Pack crossed your path."

Beau's gaze sharpened on Serre. His friend stared up at the vintage sign above the door. "I guess the story has made the rounds."

"I think you'll be okay. Until she tells you she's pregnant." Dev high-fived Serre, the brothers lost to laughter.

"Ha ha." Beau pushed into the bar.

"Hey, Beau. Don't see you much anymore." Aimee caught herself and covered her mouth.

"I'm good, Aimee. What's Remi got that's good to eat?" He stepped up to her and gave her a hug. She returned it, seeing Serre arrive behind him.

"I see you drug him out of the garage. Serre, see if you can get some of that off your paws. I'll have Remi start a couple of burgers and I'll be back with drinks." She turned on her heels and walked behind the bar.

"I don't mind your hands." Beau grinned and took a seat in a booth. He watched Serre weigh the consequences of not following Aimee's dictate.

"I don't either. She's bossy." He slid into the opposite seat, although he kept his hands under the table.

Aimee set down a couple bottles, added rolled silver and extra napkins. "I didn't see you go to the men's room. You'll need these."

"Can I have a salmon burger and a side of dirty rice?" Serre fluttered his eyelids at her.

"Brat." She turned to Beau. "What would you like with your burger?"

"Fries and ketchup." He nodded. "I'll save room for dessert if you have chocolate cake."

"With chocolate ice cream?"

"You know me so well." Beau nodded.

After sips of frosty beer Serre leaned forward. "How are you doing? I was joking about the bike. And dying."

"You were out at the cabin a week ago."

"Sometimes a week is a long time." Serre shrugged.

"It has been. Spent a lot of time running the bayou driving Cam crazy." He started peeling the label off the bottle. "I let the pain fill me and then at some point it faded away." Beau lifted a shoulder. "I may have let her go."

"Damn, Beau. I'm happy for you, I think."

"Yeah. I'm not unhappy but now I need to catch up with life again."

AFTER THEY'D EATEN and Beau talked with Remi, Quinn, and Cody, he joined Serre in the garage. No stranger to a wrench, he pitched in with his bike. Afternoon drifted into dark, and the bike was a bent fender and an exhaust pipe from being finished.

"Bet my brother can rustle up a couple steaks."

Serre scrubbed his hands with orange scented soap. The concentrated odor caused Beau's eyes to water. He stepped away and dried his hands.

"I got nothing better on tap. Sounds good."

There was a line when they arrived. A warmup band was playing loud enough to encourage people to dance as they waited.

"We'll slip in the back." Serre led the way. They crossed the kitchen space and pushed through the swinging doors to the public room. "I think there's a table over there." He pointed to a space beside the stairway.

"Lead the way." Beau waved at Aimee as they passed. She nodded and he caught up with Serre, taking a seat.

The air shifted around them, and a scent stopped Beau in his tracks. Sweet goddess, the female was luscious. He stepped onto the chair seat, ignoring Serre's shocked stare. She was in the bar and close. His dark gaze stopped at every woman in search of the source of that deliciousness.

Not the blonde and her friends. The brunette had two men hovering over her. Damn it, she couldn't have crossed his path and left. He got off the chair as a fresh blast filled his lungs. The redhead. She was a head shorter than he, her body curvy, and her hair warning for lesser males. She wore a sheer shirt over a girl's wife beater. He didn't know what it was called and didn't care.

Every instinct drove him to her side. Beau didn't resist the urge.

"Hi, I'm Beau. You're new here."

"Madigan."

Beau took her hand and lifted it to his mouth. His kiss landed on softness beyond his imagination. From this close, he knew she was a wolf but couldn't place her pack. "Hi, Madigan. Would you like to join us? The table is great to see the band."

He watched her glance over his shoulder. "Um, okay." She hitched the leather strap of her bag higher on her shoulder.

Was this a sign? Had the bond joining Cassie and him broken? "What's your last name, if you don't mind my asking." He held the chair for her.

"St. Jules."

That didn't tell him much. She wasn't from this part of the state and with the little he'd heard of her accent it didn't help him any. Hell, she might not be from the state. Or the south.

"Serre, this is Madigan St. Jules. Madigan, this is my friend, Serre Peltier."

He took his seat as they exchanged greetings. Beau kept inhaling her, getting ever more drunk on her scent alone. His wolf paced and whined under his skin. If he made Madigan nervous, she didn't show it.

Beau picked up the dinner bill. Madigan and Serre insisted on keeping their drinking tabs. The band took a break. A patron filled up the juke box with quarters and recorded music from every decade began to fill the bar.

"Would you like to dance?" Beau asked Madigan. At some point Serre had left them. Madigan took his seat, so together they people watched.

"Sure." Those lips curled into a smile he wanted to taste. He led her to the wooden floor and took her in his arms. Plump breasts pressed into his ribcage. He couldn't name the fragrance that rose from her hair, but it was something citrusy that made his mouth water. He held her hips, pressing her close so that their lower bodies slid together. He didn't hide his response to holding her.

She melted in his arms. The tang of her arousal was the last straw. He didn't return them to the table, instead leading her out the front door. His truck was around the end of the parking lot. "Did you drive in?"

"No, a carriage brought me from the hotel." Her hand clutched his, her voice breathless.

"Are you sure?" He managed to halt his jog when they reached the truck.

"Can't you tell? I think I've met my so—" He cut her words off with a kiss. Not just any kiss, his lips claimed hers, his tongue demanded entrance and she gave it. He backed her into the fender of the truck, ignoring her hiss as her back met the chill metal. He lifted her thigh, parting her legs to allow him deeper access to the core of heat.

She moaned into the kiss, her hands fisted in his hair, her hips ground against him in a primal rhythm. He pulled back. "We need to go. I will not take you in a parking lot."

"My hotel is about six blocks from here." Her forehead rested against his chest. Their hearts seeking the same cadence. He sensed her wolf under her skin.

"You want to go there or go for a run?" Beau whispered his invitation. He held his breath as she considered the choices for an eternity. She lifted her head and met his gaze.

"I love to run." Her answer delivered in the same whisper.

Beau picked her up and kissed her again. His hands cupped her generous ass and her legs wrapped around his waist. He got the door open and deposited her on the seat before pulling away for a much-needed breath. "Buckle up." If he touched her, breast, hip, waist, he'd lose control.

He rounded the truck, adjusted his cock, and slid in behind the wheel. His hands itched with the need to fist her hair, as she'd done his. He wanted to hold it like a rein as her lips spread over his dick. "You're so fucking beautiful."

Madigan laughed and took his hand. "I'm not your average sized woman."

"I'm not looking at size. I'm looking at Madigan St. Jules." He managed to keep the speed down as he drove out of the city and into less populated areas.

"Where are you from?" The rush of passion waned as he focused on getting them there safely.

"I was born on the Canadian border of American parents."

"Are you on vacation?" Beau took the first turnoff to avoid his pack's home ground.

"I guess you could say that. My mother's pack is from around here somewhere. I thought, since she passed away, that maybe I could connect with her side."

"Your father?"

"He died in an accident when I was young."

"I'm terribly sorry." Beau tightened his hand around hers.

She answered his hold. "I'm okay with things. I've had time to mourn, to cry, to rant, to recover, to forgive." She looked at him and her eyes reflected the light of the dashboard. "I'm ready to live again."

Beau's throat tightened so that he couldn't speak. He nodded to show he'd heard her then pulled the truck off the packed dirt lane. He cleared his throat. "If you're ready, we're here."

She nodded and he turned off the cab lights so

they could undress in the darkness. The night sounds enveloped them as only southern insects could. An owl hooted in the distance, answered by another much closer. The gurgle of a creek added a light touch. He tossed his clothes into the driver's seat and tucked the keys under moss at the base of a tree.

She walked around the front of the truck in wolf form. He locked the truck and shifted. He pointed with his muzzle, she took the hint, and the chase was on. He gave her a few leaps before following, his mind on what she'd said.

The grieving process was the same, but different from one being to the next. He'd wallowed in his grief without moving beyond the incident. Was it just a week ago he'd allowed himself to accept Cassie's loss? He'd cleared the deck and opened himself to the world again.

His paws dug into soft ground as he leaped after Madigan. His wolf didn't have anything to add to his mental gymnastics. His thoughts arrowed to his female and the chase before him. His reward for catching her drove him into the swamp, hot on her tail.

She gave him a chase, but he caught her and shoved her off her feet. She tumbled but rose to her feet. He caught her behind her ear, her tail high, an eager whine filled the night. Beau moved behind her, his cock ready. He lined them up and thrust deep. Claimed, she gave a growl that lightened to a soft howl as he pumped. The knot locked them but not before her orgasm rolled over her, shortening his thrusts.

He shivered, his hackles rose, the silver line down his spine reflective in the moon light. He rested against her as he emptied himself in her ready body.

The night sounds that hushed as they joined, returned.

His body released her, and she rolled to her side, panting softly. He got to his feet and shook out his coat. The crack of a broken limb, proof of a footstep, brought them both to alert. She went left, he went right in a move to circle around the threat. The familiar scent tickled Beau's memory.

"Shh, Donnie. I swear that's the same mutt."

That was the last Leon said. Beau watched him take two steps, a rifle in his hand. They were determined to take out the wolves. Beau had had enough of their interruptions. He and the pack had given them fair warning to keep out of this end of the bayou. Their pelts wouldn't be fodder for bounty hunters.

As he'd captured Madigan, he took Leon by the neck. The man didn't have a chance to cry out. A muted groan and the distinct snap of bone and he released Leon. A confused cry came from his left. Damn, Madigan!

He moved downwind of the sound, cautioning himself to patience. What he wanted was to rush to her side. He stopped at the scene. Madigan stood over Donnie. He hadn't time to warn her and the scent of her blood on the air opened panic, memories, and pain.

The running steps must have been Caleb, rushing away from the danger. Both wolves turned at the loud thud, a body stumbled, a shot echoed in the trees. No more noise. Beau didn't leave her to check out the third man.

He ran his muzzle along her shoulder. The blood smelled worse than the wound hinted. His senses were on high. She touched him, nose to nose, then stepped away from the body. He watched her limp deeper into the woods. He marked the spot by peeing on a tree then took off after her.

He rushed past her, her scent lighter now in human form. He turned to find her using her cupped hands to lift fresh water from the creek to wash off blood. He shifted in mid-step and then took her into his arms.

"I forgot to warn you, but the pack ran the hunters off. I wasn't expecting them to return."

Madigan placed her fingers over his lips. She looked up into his eyes. "You're rambling. Take a breath, I'm fine. A shift and everything is healed. You know how we are."

He lifted a hand to cradle her head. She lifted her face for his kiss. He was gentle but as the excitement faded, a new form took its place. She eased from his arms and crawled away from the water's edge. Casting a come-hither look over her shoulder, she rolled to her back and parted her legs.

Beau knew exactly what he wanted. Hard and ready, he took his place. This time he gazed into her eyes. He kissed her forehead, her nose, her lips and farther down, the sweet hard nipples that topped her breasts.

Her legs wrapped around him. Her heels beat a tattoo on his ass with every thrust. Her hands ran up his chest, twisted his nipples hard enough he growled, then fisted in his hair to bring his lips back to hers.

Her orgasm claimed her, yet he didn't stop. He hitched her legs higher and dug in to thrust harder and deeper. She quivered around him, her sweet pussy tight around his shaft. Her teeth dropped and she fastened them into his pec. He growled as she marked him as hers. His body on auto, his hips a piston, his balls tightened. He grabbed a handful of that red mass and twisted her head sideways to expose her neck.

At the first pulse he bit her, striking deep and then deeper. The taste of her blood filled his senses. He pulled back and licked the wound closed. He shivered over her, his arms tired, his hips sore.

"Get down here." She pulled him onto her body. The sweetest after glow lingered between them.

"I HEAR YOU CAME ACROSS A FOUNDLING." Serre sat on the cabin's porch. He'd ridden Beau's bike back.

"I have." Beau smiled. "She's the last pureblooded Blue Hill."

"Damn, they've been gone for decades." Serre sipped the bourbon. "Wait, the girl at Sanctuary?"

"The same."

"That was only a week ago." He uncrossed his legs and leaned forward. The glass cradled in his hands. "Like ten days maybe?"

"When it's right, you know."

"Cassie?" Serre hated to bring up her name.

"I'm good. I think she's good." He refilled the glasses from the open bottle. "Madigan has heard the story and she's cool." He shrugged and then sipped. "She's beautiful, smart, sexy, funny, strong."

"I'm happy for you, Beau. You deserve happiness." He held out his glass and waited for Beau. The chime of quality glass heralded a moment of silence.

"About the hunters. Has anyone reported them?" Beau hadn't had to worry. He and Madigan had made love several more times, washed off in the creek and drank the clear fresh water before heading for the truck. She'd directed him to her hotel. A hot shower later and a soft bed claimed them for sleep.

When Beau led Cam back the next day, the hunters were gone. The rifles were found, not exactly where they fell. Cam told him the bayou claimed them and they'd never be found. 'Gators took care of most things left lying around. He'd said that with a straight face and then gaped at Beau as he'd burst into laughter that bordered on hysteria.

"You know most of these guys drifted off the grid. Didn't leave anyone of note behind. No one is asking." He sipped. "Look, man, I don't need details. I'm glad you've come back to us." He chuckled. "And brought your mate with you."

THANK YOU...

WE HOPE YOU'VE ENJOYED THIS DARK
HUNTER ANTHOLOGY.

9 781648 3928